LIE
TO HER

ALSO BY MELINDA LEIGH

BREE TAGGERT NOVELS

Cross Her Heart

See Her Die

Drown Her Sorrows

Right Behind Her

"Her Second Death" (A Prequel Short Story)

Dead Against Her

MORGAN DANE NOVELS

Say You're Sorry

Her Last Goodbye

Bones Don't Lie

What I've Done

Secrets Never Die

Save Your Breath

SCARLET FALLS NOVELS

Hour of Need

Minutes to Kill

Seconds to Live

SHE CAN SERIES

She Can Run

She Can Tell

She Can Scream

She Can Hide

"He Can Fall" (A Short Story)

She Can Kill

MIDNIGHT NOVELS

Midnight Exposure

Midnight Sacrifice

Midnight Betrayal

Midnight Obsession

THE ROGUE SERIES NOVELLAS

Gone to Her Grave (Rogue River)

Walking on Her Grave (Rogue River)

Tracks of Her Tears (Rogue Winter)

Burned by Her Devotion (Rogue Vows)

Twisted Truth (Rogue Justice)

THE WIDOW'S ISLAND NOVELLA SERIES

A Bone to Pick

Whisper of Bones

A Broken Bone

Buried Bones

The Wrong Bones

LIE
TO HER

MELINDA
LEIGH

Montlake

Published by Montlake, Seattle

www.apub.com

Amazon, the Amazon logo, and Montlake are trademarks of Amazon.com, Inc., or its affiliates.

ISBN-13: 9781542030663 (hardcover)
ISBN-13: 9781542030649 (paperback)
ISBN-13: 9781542030656 (digital)

Cover design by Shasti O'Leary Soudant
Cover images: © Stephen Mulcahey, © Olesia Saienko / Arcangel

Printed in the United States of America

First edition

For Charlie, Annie, and Tom

Chapter One

There's no line between love and hate, not even a fine one. It's a mud puddle.

Quicksand.

And you can be simultaneously mired in both.

Let me explain. You love someone. They reject you. Now you hate them. But you still can't stop loving them, even if you hate yourself for it.

A hot fucking mess, right?

I halt on the shoulder of the road. As the tires hit the gravel, the steering wheel vibrates under my hands, as if my SUV understands the significance of the moment. My heartbeat accelerates, my blood rushes, and heat blooms on my skin. I lower the window and take a deep breath, holding the cool December air in my lungs for a few seconds. I smell burning leaves and dampness. The first snow of the season is forecast for this evening. The weather won't affect my plans. Nothing will. I exhale slowly, then repeat the exercise twice more, until my pulse steadies. After weeks of preparation, the first step of my plan is finally coming to fruition. I can't—won't—lose my nerve.

Forest and fields flank the country lane. Winter has stripped the trees bare. There are three houses in sight. The blue saltbox in front of me is currently for sale, vacant and dark. It's been on the market for over a year, and clearly no one has shown any interest in buying it. The property is listed *as is*. The siding desperately needs power washing. The lawn is both overgrown and dying. Weeds strangle the shrubs, and the rusted mailbox, beaten down by corrosion and neglect, leans on its post as if too exhausted to remain upright.

My gaze shifts to the house across the street, a tiny white ranch-style home. A lamppost and a porch light both blaze. The owner left for work at four thirty, as he does every weekday afternoon. He must work nights, because he never returns until early morning. I know this because I've been watching the street, making careful notes about the residents' activities.

It's the third house that interests me, the small farmhouse on the other side of the saltbox. Spencer LaForge—the first name on my list—lives there. Lights glow inside and out.

On his dating app profiles, Spencer describes himself as a forty-seven-year-old digital marketer. His photos show a fit, attractive man with a smile full of straight white teeth and enough of a tan to make him appear outdoorsy. He claims to enjoy good conversation and a nice pinot noir. His hobbies include running, hiking, and reading. He's looking for companionship and romance.

That's not what he's going to get today.

He doesn't deserve a nice life anyway. He's a liar, a cheat, a player. But the truth wouldn't make an attractive dating profile, would it?

Superficial, middle-age douchebag seeks hot younger woman to fuck and dump wouldn't get many swipes.

Killing him might seem a little harsh, but Spencer is a liar. Not the worst one, but a liar just the same. He must pay for the way he treats people. Today, I'll cross him off my list.

I pull back onto the road, park in the driveway of the vacant house, and get out of my SUV. I take my small backpack from the rear seat and heft it over one shoulder, then hoof it across the lawns to Spencer's driveway. I stop in front of his attached garage, pull disposable gloves from my pocket, and tug them on. Then I enter Spencer's four-digit passcode into the PIN pad mounted next to the doorframe—another important detail I gleaned from watching him through my binoculars.

The overhead door rolls up. I slip inside and hurry past the black F-150. I walk past the riding lawn mower that occupies the second half of the garage. At the door that leads into the house, I press the button mounted on the wall and lower the overhead door. It closes with a metallic rattle and thud.

I draw in a long, gasoline-scented breath.

I'm in.

Despite his life of deception, Spencer is a man of routine. He uses the same passwords for everything. His dating app profile was ridiculously easy to hack. Today is Tuesday. He finished work an hour ago and is currently out for a run. He won't let a little thing poor visibility interfere with his exercise routine. He'll return soon to prepare for the date he's expecting to arrive at six o'clock. He's supposed to cook her dinner. Won't she be surprised at what she finds?

My lips pull into a grin. My face is so tight, it feels as if the skin might split open. I wish I could stay and watch her reaction. The slut deserves what she gets, although none of this is her fault. I'm sure Spencer plans to treat her the same way he treats all women. She's just another one of his victims.

Most people are willing to take their lumps and move on. Not me. I hold a grudge, nursing it like a newborn.

Focus!

I make my way through the mudroom into the kitchen. Spencer didn't spare any expense on the renovation, with professional-grade appliances, granite counters, and a high-end slate floor. French doors open onto a covered patio. The teak outdoor table is set, complete with a vase of flowers, two plates, and two wineglasses. A neat pyramid of split logs, kindling, and tinder fill a sunken firepit. Graham crackers, chocolate, and marshmallows are lined up on a small table.

S'mores.

The only desserts Spencer will be having are his just ones.

I turn back to the great room. I've been in the house before. I needed to get familiar with the layout. A good plan minimizes potential surprises. I hurry for the stairs and jog to the second-floor landing. Down a short hall, I stick my head in the extra bedroom. Excitement ripples up my arms as goose bumps as I scan Spencer's collection. There are things you just don't expect to find in the average home.

Don't get ahead of yourself. Stay in the moment. The plan must proceed one step at a time.

Turning back, I return to the kitchen. I spot two thick steaks marinating on the counter. Filets. Romantic setting, good wine, a hearty meal. He's pulling out all the stops. Clearly, he's banking on sex. After all, this is their third date. In Spencer's very limited mindset, he deserves sex tonight.

The bastard.

How many women has he used and discarded?

Anger heats the back of my neck.

I check the time on my watch. Spencer will be back soon. I need to get to my hiding location. My hand strays to my jacket pocket, where my tools weigh heavily. I have no desire for a fight. For my plan to work, Spencer must comply. Once he's restrained, the rest of the plan will play out smoothly.

Easy as pie, as my grandmother used to say.

But first I must obtain control. A sudden burst of nerves assaults me. My skin grows prickly and itchy. My stomach rolls over. Doubt tempts me to abandon my plan. But I can't. I promised myself I would get even. I'd better get my shit together. Tonight is only the beginning.

Users will be punished.

I head for a small closet that faces the kitchen and great room. The door is louvered, so I'll be able to see. Perfect. I push aside a ski jacket and step in, closing the door behind me.

The minutes tick by. My heart skips, and I'm suddenly aware of the sound of my breathing. Is it loud, or is it echoing in my ears because of my adrenaline rush? A tune plays silently in my head, a damned earworm for sure.

Every breath you take.

I concentrate on controlling my lungs. I can't have Spencer hearing me. Can't have him ruining what I've so carefully planned.

I hear the motor of the garage door opener engage. A minute later, the door rattles closed.

Spencer is home.

CHAPTER TWO

Breathing heavily, Spencer LaForge jogged up his driveway and let himself in through the garage door using his PIN pad. In the kitchen, he glanced at the clock on the microwave. Less than an hour until his date was due to arrive. He could hardly wait. He grabbed a bottle of mineral water from the fridge, twisted off the cap, and drank deeply.

Opening the dating app on his phone, he stared at her picture again. Avery was hot with a capital *H*, with long legs and boobs to die for. In person, she looked like a model. He wanted to wrap that long hair around his hand and hold on tight. The photos didn't do her justice.

Water bottle in hand, he sauntered up to the granite island and turned the filets in the marinade. They'd be ready for the grill by the time he finished his shower. He glanced through the glass doors at the romantic scene he'd set.

A snow flurry drifted in the air, and Spencer smiled.

Cue the snow.

An outdoor dinner with a roaring fire and snow flurries was about as romantic as it could get.

He sipped his drink. He needed to be adequately hydrated, he thought with a grin. He'd fueled up with a lunch of raw oysters on the half shell. The night was going to be spectacular. He'd primed Avery with two romantic evenings and a fuckton of flattery. On their second date, she'd practically melted. She was a sure thing.

Now for his shower. He turned toward the stairwell. A *click* stopped him. He looked down the hall. Empty. He stood still, listening hard. The noise had sounded like it had come from inside.

Nah. Couldn't be. He lived alone. No one had the code to his door or a key to his house except his biweekly cleaning woman, and she wasn't due until the following day. Had an animal followed him into the garage and gotten trapped? He headed for the hallway to investigate.

At the entrance to the hall, the closet door sprang open, and a figure leaped out.

Startled, Spencer had no time to assess the intruder. He pulled back an arm to deliver a punch. Something crackled. A burning pain seared Spencer's hip and shot through his body. His muscles stiffened, and then his nerves seemed to short out. He pitched forward, his limbs limp and useless, and fell over like a bird electrocuted on a live wire. He wanted to throw out an arm to catch himself, but he had no control over his body. He crumpled to the floor. Pain knocked through his elbow and shoulder. He lay on his back, his muscles still not responding.

"Hello, Spencer," the intruder said.

Spencer wanted to speak, but his jaws were clamped tight, and his lips wouldn't work.

"Are you all right? You don't look well at all."

Spencer blinked hard, but the figure remained featureless. He tried to roll over to his hands and knees, but his muscles were still on strike. He managed to get two words through his gritted teeth. "Help me." A plea.

The intruder rolled Spencer onto his side, tied his hands behind his back, and bound his ankles. Spencer wanted to struggle, but he couldn't control his arms. By the time his muscles started to obey his commands, it was too late. He was fully restrained.

Two hands grabbed him by the ankles. The intruder dragged him out the french doors. Spencer thumped over the door tracks. The patio pavers burned against the side of his face. Nausea stirred and swirled in his belly. But the fresh air helped clear his head, at least for a few seconds. A flake of snow drifted across his vision.

"It's snowing." The voice sounded impressed but also condescending. "You've outdone yourself tonight. This would have been the perfect date."

Spencer gained control of his tongue and managed to spit out a weak, "Fuck you."

"Fuck me? No, I think you're the one who's fucked." The intruder jammed a small device at him. It crackled as it made contact with his skin, and the flash of electricity was like liquid fire roaring through his nervous system.

As he convulsed on the ground, his body useless, his brain screamed, *Stun gun!*

The figure leaned over him. Spencer's eyes were not cooperating. Outside sounds echoed as if he were in a tunnel. But his own heartbeat raced in his ears. That he heard loud and clear.

The intruder struck at him again. Another wave of current rushed through him. Aftershock or fresh shock? He looked up at the dark sky. A snowflake landed on his face. "Please," he rasped.

A shadow loomed over him. "Shut up." The voice faded. Blackness swirled at the edges of Spencer's vision. He squeezed his eyelids tightly closed. When he reopened them, nothing had changed. It wasn't a dream. It was a nightmare—except Spencer was wide awake.

A hand slapped his cheek. "Stay with me. I want you to know what's happening. I want you to experience every single second of terror and pain. I want you to suffer. You're a user, Spencer. You need to pay. You've never suffered any consequences for your actions before, have you? Guess what? Today is full of firsts—mostly for me. For you, it will be full of lasts."

Even if he wanted to, Spencer couldn't respond. He was helpless, and deep inside him, he knew this was the day he was going to die.

CHAPTER THREE

Sheriff Bree Taggert adjusted the latch on the stall door with a screwdriver. The barn was cold, and her breath fogged in the early December evening air.

Her sixteen-year-old nephew, Luke, raked the dirt floor, leveling the surface. The stall hadn't been used in years, and horses had the uncanny ability to hurt themselves. When he finished with the rake, Luke used his pocketknife to cut the twine wrapped around a bale of straw.

"There's no guarantee that I'll find the right horse at the sale tomorrow." Bree tested the door. The latch worked smoothly. She shoved the screwdriver into the pocket of her jacket and helped her nephew spread the straw.

"You *have* to find Uncle Adam a horse." Eight-year-old Kayla stood in the aisle, holding a lead rope attached to her sturdy little horse, Pumpkin. "His birthday is Sunday! He needs to be surprised."

Since Adam had specifically asked for a rescue horse, Bree doubted surprise was on the table. But she hoped he'd be pleased.

"I'll do my best." Bree had inherited a farm and three horses when her younger sister was murdered. She had also been granted guardianship of her niece and nephew. It hadn't even been a year since she'd moved from Philadelphia to upstate New York, but Bree felt like she'd become a whole new person. She'd shed her old life and left it behind like a snakeskin. She didn't miss it at all.

"How old will Uncle Adam be?" Kayla asked.

"Twenty-nine," Bree answered. She couldn't believe this would be her baby brother's last year in his twenties. Sometimes, it seemed barely any time had passed since he was an infant. Since she'd held him on a bitter winter night as they and their sister hid under the porch of their farmhouse while their father murdered their mother.

"Wow. That's old," Kayla said.

Bree laughed. "It is."

"Can we name the new horse?" Kayla dropped the rope, picked up a soft brush, and began brushing dried mud from Pumpkin's legs. Pumpkin, who never exerted energy unless it was absolutely necessary, cocked one hind leg and shifted instantly into nap mode. His head and eyelids sagged.

"Don't you think Uncle Adam should name his own horse?" Bree emerged from the stall, brushing straw dust from her jeans. From her napping spot next to the tack room door, Ladybug, the rescue dog, opened one eye. Satisfied her people were still there, she resumed sleeping.

"I guess," Kayla grumbled.

But Bree knew the little girl would have dozens of suggestions for her uncle.

Luke's horse, Riot, kicked his stall door.

"OK, Riot." Luke laughed. "I know what time it is." He headed for the feed room.

Kayla picked dirt out of Pumpkin's hooves, then put the pony-size Haflinger in his stall and planted a kiss on his nose. The scene was adorable, and Bree's heart swelled with warm fuzzies, a feeling she hadn't known existed until she started parenting. Her eyes misted—another new reaction—and she didn't understand why she was tearing up when she was happy.

Except that Christmas was coming—the first one without their mother—her sister, Erin. If it weren't for the kids, Bree wouldn't even bother to celebrate. The festivities would only make her grief come roaring back. But that felt cowardly, and the kids deserved better. Bree had to show them by example that they could keep Erin in their hearts and simultaneously move forward.

If only she had some idea of how to do that.

Bree stopped in front of Cowboy's stall and rubbed the paint gelding's head. The sweet-natured horse had belonged to her sister. His company made Bree feel closer to Erin, and that soothed her. Impatient, Riot nickered over his half door. Bree stepped sideways so she could scratch both horses' foreheads at the same time. As always, spending time with the kids and horses brought her a peace she hadn't known existed. Sometimes she was so content with her new life, she felt guilty. Erin should be the one enjoying an evening with her kids. But that was not to be.

Bittersweet. Everything in life was bittersweet.

"Well, we'll be ready if you get lucky." Luke emerged from the feed room, carrying three containers. He dumped grain while Kayla tossed hay over doors and Bree topped off water buckets.

A few minutes later, Bree checked the stall door latches before leading the way out of the barn. Never wanting to be left behind, Ladybug got up from her napping spot and hurried to keep up. Bree turned off the lights, closed the barn door, and headed toward the back porch. A damp wind cut through her jacket, and she shivered.

"It's snowing!" Kayla turned her face to the sky and opened her mouth, trying to catch a flurry on her tongue. Only a handful of flakes drifted through the night sky, but Kayla was an optimist. "Can we have hot cocoa?"

"Of course." Bree opened the back door. The dog ran through the opening.

Bree and the kids shed their jackets and dirty boots at the back door and washed their hands. She checked the time and turned to Kayla. "If you get your shower and put on your pajamas, we can watch a movie."

"Yay! I'll hurry." The little girl raced for the stairs. She was a slip of a thing, but her feet thundered up the wooden steps, loud as hoofbeats.

Luke started the popcorn while Bree went upstairs and changed into flannel pajama bottoms and thick socks. Her black tomcat, Vader, uncurled himself from his sleeping ball and sauntered across the bed for an ear rub. When she left the bedroom, the cat followed her to the kitchen. Vader bumped Bree's leg and gave her a demanding meow.

"OK." She spooned cat food onto a plate, carried it to an empty patch of counter, and set it next to his water bowl. Vader followed, and purred while he ate. Yes. Feeding the cat on the counter was gross. But Bree had no options because the dog would eat anything she could reach. Also, the cat refused to share a water bowl with the dog. There were some aspects of Bree's new life that were simply ridiculous.

The microwave dinged, and Luke poured the popcorn into a bowl.

Kayla ran into the room in pink fleece pajamas. "Can I carry the popcorn?"

Bree eyed the dog, who was eyeing the bowl. Ladybug looked innocent, but she'd never met a morsel of food she didn't love. Also, the pudgy pointer mix was much faster than she looked.

Bree redirected Kayla. "Can you get the napkins?"

"OK." Kayla rushed to the pantry.

Bree loaded the mugs and popcorn onto a tray. "Movie choices?"

Kayla shouted, "*Frozen!*"

"Again?" Luke rolled his eyes. "You've watched that movie a hundred times. How about *Iron Man*?"

"Too scary." Kayla followed her brother into the family room.

Bree set the tray on the coffee table. "How about a movie neither of you have seen?" She picked up the remote and began to surf through the options. Her phone vibrated in her pocket. She pulled it out and read the screen. DISPATCH.

Regret washed over her like cold rain. She didn't want to answer the call but knew dispatch would not reach out to her when she was off duty unless it was serious. "I have to grab this call." She got up and went to the kitchen before pressing "Answer." "Sheriff Taggert."

"Sheriff, we have a reported 12-77," the dispatcher said.

Bree peered through the doorway at the two kids.

Shit.

The dispatcher gave an address on the opposite side of Randolph County.

Bree placed the address on a mental map. "ETA twenty minutes."

After sliding the phone back into her pocket, she returned to the family room.

Luke scanned her face, his own expression neutral. "You have to go."

"Yes," Bree said. "I'm sorry."

Disappointment crashed over Kayla's face. "But we were going to watch a movie."

"I know, honey. I'm sorry." Guilt filled Bree.

"It's OK." Kayla sniffed. "You're important. People need you," she said in a small, heartbreaking voice.

This kid . . .

Luke gave his sister a playful poke in the shoulder. "We can watch *Frozen.*"

"Yay!" Kayla snatched the remote from the table.

"Thank you," Bree mouthed at Luke. Her eyes went misty again at the scene. When she'd moved in last January, he'd been a teenage boy, but he was fast becoming a man—one who made her proud every day.

She ran upstairs and changed into her uniform. She jogged back down a few minutes later, shoving her gun into its holster on her hip. As she passed through the room, she kissed both kids. "I love you. Dana will be home from her date in a couple of hours."

Bree's best friend and former detective partner had retired and now lived with them as a sort-of nanny. Bree didn't like to leave the kids alone. Her cop brain only generated worst-case scenarios, but Luke was mature enough to babysit.

Before she could issue any further instructions, Luke held up one hand in a *stop* gesture. "I know. Set the alarm. Get Kayla to bed by eight thirty. Do my homework."

"You got it." She smiled and headed for the door. She donned boots and a jacket and went outside. After the warmth of the house—and her flannel pj's—the yard felt cold and sad.

She slid behind the wheel of her official SUV, turned on her lights and siren, and roared down the street. She checked in with dispatch for details and updates, then reached for her phone to call Matt Flynn, her criminal investigator—and boyfriend, for lack of a better term. She was going to need him.

12-77 was radio code for homicide.

Chapter Four

Bree came to an abrupt stop and stared.

She wasn't easy to shock. Before she became the sheriff of Randolph County, she worked for the Philadelphia PD, first as a patrol officer, then as a detective. Her last assignment had been in homicide.

Next to her, Matt muttered, "Fuck," under his breath. Bree glanced at him. He propped both hands on his hips. As a civilian consultant, he wore a tan jacket bearing the sheriff's department logo, tactical cargo pants, and work boots. Snowflakes dotted his closely cropped reddish-brown hair and short beard.

"Yeah." Chief Deputy Todd Harvey stood at her other side. "Fuck."

Bree had no better response.

Their three flashlight beams brightened a patio made of gray stone pavers. A sunken firepit had been built into one of the outside corners. The body of a man was sprawled between the french doors and the firepit. Something shiny and opaque covered his face. No, it was wrapped around his whole head.

Bree leaned closer. "Is that plastic food wrap?"

"I believe it is," Todd answered.

A resounding *fuck* echoed in Bree's brain.

Todd continued. "Avery Ledger called 911 at 6:07 p.m. to report finding the dead body of Spencer LaForge. Mr. LaForge is the homeowner."

Using the few details she'd provided, dispatch had labeled the call as a 12-77, a possible homicide. Legally, *homicide* was a broad term defined as the killing of one person by another. That killing could be legal, as in self-defense, or illegal, as in murder and manslaughter.

Bree eyed the victim's hands, bound behind his back.

No question. This was definitely murder.

Matt gestured to the zip ties around the victim's wrists and ankles. "Zip ties will dig into the skin if you try to get out of them. I don't see any deep cuts. The victim was either surprised and/or quickly overpowered and restrained."

Bree stepped back to view the scene in its entirety. She eyed the tipped-over, broken glass vase and scattered flowers on the pavers. A bottle of wine stood upright on the table. The chairs were still neatly tucked under the table. "An extensive struggle would have left a bigger mess. They didn't even knock over the bottle of wine." She pictured an efficient, fast, well-planned attack. "He isn't a small man, and he looks to be in good physical condition. He should have put up a fight."

"There could have been more than one intruder," Todd suggested.

"That's possible." Bree scanned the grass but saw no path of crushed blades that would indicate a body had been dragged. A bloodless kill meant no obvious trail of blood to follow. The victim wore running clothes: black track pants and a zip-up jacket with neon stripes on the sleeves. One sneaker was missing. Bree spotted it on the patio near the door. "The sneaker by the door suggests he was dragged from the house or kicked it off at some point during the murder."

Her gaze returned to the plastic-shrouded head. Had he been conscious? Had his lungs burned from lack of oxygen? Had he known what was happening?

A urine stain darkened the front of his pants. His bladder could have voided after death as normal—or in his last moments as he panicked. He would have blacked out in a couple of minutes, but those could have felt like very long minutes.

Unease swirled sickly through her gut. No matter how many murder scenes she'd worked, the sense of wrongness never failed to flatten her. How could one human do such terrible things to another?

"Could this victim be someone other than the homeowner?" Bree asked. "We can't see his face." And they'd have to wait for the medical examiner to remove the plastic wrap, which could contain trace evidence, fingerprints, and/or touch DNA.

"The woman who found him recognized his tattoo. She says it's a full sleeve." Todd pointed to the edge of Spencer's jacket sleeve, which was pushed up, revealing three inches of intricate ink above the zip tie. Todd scrolled on his phone, then tilted it so Bree could see the screen. "Here's his driver's license photo and info."

At six feet tall, Spencer LaForge had been a fit one hundred seventy pounds. He was clean-shaven, and his dark hair was short and cut in a precise style.

"OK. So, it's probably him." She blinked, shifting her gaze to her chief deputy. "Did you clear the property?"

"Yes, ma'am." Todd turned his shoulders and pointed behind him, at a set of french doors. "We gained entry through the patio doors, which were unlocked. There was no one inside."

Large windows spanned the back of the restored farmhouse. Lights blazed inside, providing a clear view of the open floor plan interior. Bree could see into a large, modern kitchen and family room. There was too much glass to call the house a fishbowl. It was a frigging aquarium.

Todd said, "It was clear he was dead, so I thought it best not to remove the plastic."

"Good call." Bree pointed her flashlight at the body. The visible skin of the hands and neck looked gray in the artificial light.

Saving a life was always the number one goal, but if that wasn't possible, preserving the evidence was the next priority. Once evidence was moved, there was no putting it back.

Todd exhaled. "I notified the medical examiner's office and called for a forensics team."

"We'll need additional deputies too," Bree added, turning her attention to her chief deputy. Back in September, he'd been kidnapped, beaten, and nearly killed in an investigation. He'd recovered and even resumed both his work and his triathlon training, but he'd lost weight from his already-lean six-foot frame. Bree was concerned about his emotional well-being. This would be his first murder investigation since his trauma. Though he'd been cleared for duty by a psychiatrist, she would keep a close eye on him.

Todd nodded. "On the way."

"Call in everyone you can get. Get an ETA from the ME. If she's going to be long, set up a tarp or tent over the body. Prioritize searching outdoor areas." Bree eyed the sky. Flurries drifted in the damp wind. The big, wet flakes melted as they landed, but the temperature was dropping. Normally, she preferred daylight to search outdoor crime scenes, but tonight, they couldn't wait. "We need to find evidence before it's covered in snow. We'll need a generator and portable lights."

"Already requested," Todd said.

"Good." Bree was impressed with the improvement of his investigation skills since she'd taken office.

The distant wail of a siren signaled the approach of additional responders. She heard voices and vehicle doors being slammed. Bree exhaled, the tightness of her lungs indicating she'd been restricting her breath. "Sounds like reinforcements are here. Matt, you take over out here. Todd, take me to the 911 caller, then get that ETA from the medical examiner."

With a fresh corpse, the sooner the ME arrived, the more accurate her assessment of time of death would be.

As Bree followed Todd from the backyard around the side of the house toward the street, she heard Matt check in with a deputy setting up barriers and stringing up crime scene tape. When she reached the front of the house, she saw a red Prius in the driveway and two more patrol vehicles parked on the street. The road was a dead end, with only two other houses in sight.

"Did you knock on the neighbors' doors?" Bree asked.

"Yes, ma'am." Todd pointed to the house next door, which sported a for-sale sign and a fair amount of neglect. "That one looks vacant." He indicated the house across the street. "No one answered there, but the place looks occupied."

He led Bree to the second patrol car. A woman was huddled in the back seat.

A deputy stood next to the vehicle. "She was shivering. I put her in the car and turned on the heat."

Peering into the vehicle, Bree recognized a dark sheriff's department blanket wrapped around the woman's shoulders.

Todd opened the rear door. "Ms. Ledger?"

The woman looked up. Tears spilled from red-rimmed eyes and streaked down her face. "You can call me Avery." Her voice was small and trembly.

"Could you step out of the vehicle, please?" Todd asked. "The sheriff would like to speak with you."

"Of course." She climbed out, wobbling on her high heels. She was in her midtwenties, and she'd put effort into her appearance that night. Tight jeans, thigh-high boots, and a cute puffy jacket flattered her young figure. But crying had taken its toll. Her hair was tangled. Long strands stuck to her tear-dampened face, mascara ringed her eyes, and her lipstick was smeared. Though she was wearing a jacket, she kept the blanket around her shoulders, clutching the edges together in front of her chest.

Todd introduced Bree, then bowed out.

Bree pulled a pen and notebook from her jacket pocket. "I understand you found Mr. LaForge?"

Avery nodded and pressed a hand over her mouth. Swallowing hard, she closed her eyes, visibly composing herself. She opened her eyes. "Yes," came out in a shaky whisper.

Bree gave her a few seconds to elaborate, but Avery just blinked, like a raccoon caught in the beam of a flashlight. Bree prompted, "What brought you here?"

Avery regarded the ground, her eyes unfocused, like she was seeing something other than the asphalt. "We had a date. He was going to make me dinner. He didn't answer the door. I went around back because he'd said he was going to grill steaks. I thought he might be outside. But he was . . . He was . . ." Her voice broke. "He was dead," she sobbed.

"I'm sorry that happened to you," Bree said. Interviewing witnesses required a delicate balance between empathizing and extracting information. She felt terrible making shocked people recount their trauma, but the early hours of an investigation were critical. She wanted to catch the killer before he inflicted suffering on anyone else. She gave the woman a few seconds to compose herself, then asked, "What time did you get here?"

Avery wiped her face with two shaking hands. "Around six."

"Where were you before that?"

"Work," Avery said. "I left the office at five and stopped home to change before driving out here."

"How well did you know Spencer?" Bree asked.

Avery sighed. "This was only going to be our third date, but we've been messaging a lot."

"How did you meet?"

"On the dating app TechLove.com," Avery said.

"I assume that's a dating app for people who work in tech?"

Avery nodded. "I'm a social media content creator with Get Fit Apparel. Spencer is—was—a digital marketer, but he's self-employed."

"Have you met any of Spencer's friends, family, or coworkers?"

"No." Avery sniffed. "I've only known him about two weeks. On our first date, we were supposed to just meet for coffee. I don't like to commit to anything more than that. There are too many creeps out there. But Spencer and I seemed to connect right away, so we ended up walking around town after the coffee. It was a nice day, so we got ice cream and sat on a bench at the park. We talked for hours. The next weekend, we had dinner together." She hiccuped. "I thought I might have found The One." She bawled out the last word. Her breath hitched, and she pressed her fingertips to her closed eyes.

After Avery lowered her hands, Bree asked, "Did he mention family nearby?"

"His parents are dead, but he has a brother here in Grey's Hollow. His name is Jasper." Avery pressed a knuckle to her lips. "They were really close. Jasper named his oldest boy after Spencer. He's going to be devastated."

Bree motioned toward the farmhouse. "Had you ever been to Spencer's house before tonight?"

Avery shook her head. "No, and he hadn't been to mine either."

"When was the last time you communicated with him?"

"He called me last night to confirm our date and tell me to wear something warm. He wanted to light his firepit and watch the snow. I thought it was a really romantic idea. That's the last time I spoke with him." Avery swiped the back of her hand across her face.

"Thank you for your help. We may need to ask you additional questions." With no reason to doubt her story, Bree collected Avery's contact information and summoned a deputy. "See that she gets home safely."

"Yes, ma'am," the deputy said.

Bree found Todd standing behind the open trunk of his patrol vehicle, cell phone held between his chin and shoulder. As she approached, he lowered his phone and shoved it into the clip on his duty belt. "I called in four more uniforms to help search the crime scene."

Bree brushed a snowflake from her sleeve. The flurries were thickening. "We have no time to waste."

CHAPTER FIVE

An hour later, Matt scanned the rear of the property. A generator hummed, and portable lights blazed across the yard, brightening it like a football stadium. Spread out every ten feet or so, deputies walked in a line across the yard. At the end of that line, Matt pointed his flashlight at the ground. Flurries drifted through the cold air. Despite the falling temps, the ground had not yet frozen. The snowflakes melted as they landed, and his boots squished in a thin layer of mud.

The cold-bloodedness of the murder set off all his instincts. Matt had plenty of experience working crime scenes. He'd worked as both an investigator and a K-9 handler for the sheriff's department until a shooting—and the previous corrupt sheriff—had ended his career as a deputy. But the details of this killing made all the hairs on the back of his neck not only stand up but wave a flag as well. Only a psychopath could wind plastic wrap around a man's head and watch him suffocate. Matt wanted this sick bastard in a cell before anyone else appeared in his crosshairs.

He moved slowly, carefully scanning his section of the ground for evidence. In the area next to Spencer's driveway, Matt's beam fell on a footprint. Had the killer walked around the house? Maybe casing the place? Matt squatted and examined the print closer. The grass was too thick to see much more than vague impressions. No tread was visible, and he doubted they'd even be able to determine the size of the shoe. Still, the prints needed to be documented.

He called out to the closest deputy. "We need to block off this area."

Another deputy jogged over with stakes and crime scene tape. They cordoned off the footstep impression.

Matt didn't find anything else of interest. At the overhead garage door, he shined his flashlight through the high window. A pickup truck and lawn mower sat side by side.

Matt went looking for Bree. He found her on the back patio, examining the doorknob. Her duty belt and bulky sheriff's jacket camouflaged a lean, athletic body. She was shining her flashlight on the patio door handle, no doubt looking for scratch marks or other indication that the lock had been picked or the door forcibly opened.

Snow dusted the shoulders of her jacket. A canopy had been erected over the body to protect it from the precipitation. The medical examiner had not yet arrived, so the body remained *in situ*. Deputies and forensics techs moved around the sprawled victim, photographing and sketching the scene, setting up evidence markers. It felt clinical, almost obscene, to work around the corpse as if it weren't there.

"Any sign of forced entry?" Matt asked.

"No." She straightened and clicked off the light. "And the other doors and windows are secure. Spencer didn't have a security system. He didn't even have a doorbell camera."

"Spencer is dressed for a run. Maybe he left the back door unlocked." Matt knew plenty of people who lived out in the country didn't bother locking their doors, particularly in the daytime. He told her about the footprint. "There's no tread to cast."

"Damn." Bree shook her head. "Ready to take the search inside?"

"Let's do it."

They donned shoe covers and gloves before they went inside. The kitchen was sleek and modern. The adjoining living room took clutter-free to new heights. A leather couch faced a fireplace with a TV mounted above it. Every surface shone.

"No photos. No knickknacks. No fingerprints or smudges." Matt's gaze swept the bare space. "Except for the dinner prep, it doesn't look like anyone lives here."

"When I lived in my apartment in Philly, I hardly ever made a mess that needed to be cleaned up. I ate over the sink."

"That's sad." Matt had watched her change since she'd moved to Grey's Hollow. The Bree of the past had been alone, even in a roomful of people. But to help the kids process their mother's death, Bree had been forced to give up her aloof loner ways. Matt was profoundly grateful.

She lifted a shoulder. "It didn't seem so at the time, but now that I'm used to general chaos, I think a little mess is homey."

"I'm a bachelor too, but my house looks lived in."

"You have a big dog."

Surveying the operating-room sterility of Spencer LaForge's house, Matt was grateful for the clumps of dog fur and drool trails on his own tile.

Bree took a photo of a steak marinating in a dish on the counter. "Avery said Spencer had planned to grill steaks for them for dinner."

A laptop sat on the kitchen island. Matt lifted the lid with one gloved finger and touched the space bar. The computer woke. The screen brightened to show a dating site called Cool Beans. The tagline at the top of the screen described it as a low-key app for no-pressure dating.

Bree peered over his shoulder. "Avery said she met him through a different site."

"Plenty of online daters use multiple apps."

Bree frowned. "Avery thought he might be The One for her. If Spencer was actively seeking more dates, maybe he didn't share that sentiment."

"The app logged him out, so I can't see his account." Matt closed the laptop, then scanned the delicate wineglasses and general tidiness of the space. "No sign of a struggle in here."

"And we'd know if anything was out of place. This guy was particular about his space." Bree pointed to a drawer she'd just opened.

Acrylic organizers separated pencils from pens from paper clips. Writing implements all pointed in the same direction. She moved to another drawer. "That's weird. This one is empty."

Matt opened cabinets. "Half his cabinets are empty too. He has the basics, but not the amount of equipment I would expect with this fancy kitchen setup."

"Maybe the renovation is recent."

"Or he ran out of money."

Bree opened the fridge. "His condiments are lined up by bottle height with all the labels facing the same direction."

"That's beyond neat."

"After living on a farm with two kids, a big dog, and a cat, I find this level of organization disturbing."

They walked through the rest of the first floor, finding nothing that looked out of place.

"Let's try the upstairs." Bree led the way to the second floor.

The first bedroom was a home office. Matt checked the desk drawers. "Not much in here. Plans for his kitchen renovation, receipts. A few bills. Aha. Here's a collection notice." He riffled through a neat stack of papers in a drawer. "And another one."

Bree opened the closet. "There's a fire safe in here. He might keep his important records in that. We'll have to get someone to open it."

Matt ducked into the next room. "This is strange." Glass tanks in varying sizes lined shelves. The tanks were outfitted like mini habitats with branches, water bowls, and heat lamps for the reptiles that occupied them.

Bree followed him in. "Turtles, lizards . . . what is that?" She pointed to a tank on the end.

"A snake."

Bree sighed and shot him a *Really?* look. "What kind? I've never seen anything like it."

He leaned in to get a better view. About three or so feet long and slender, the snake was mostly white with scattered red scales. He pulled out his phone. "Google says it's a Palmetto corn snake. It seems corn snakes are friendly, easy to care for, and popular as pets. This one is rare because of its color."

Bree's face did not approve.

"It's harmless and kind of cute," Matt said.

Bree scanned the tanks below it. "There are five of them."

"This could be a hobby *or* a side business," Matt suggested.

She stopped in front of an empty space on the middle shelf. "What do you think of these empty spaces? Looks like three tanks were removed."

"He could have sold some animals." Matt leaned closer. "But the surface is very dusty, and the rest of the house is spotless. Feels like he would have dusted the shelf if he had the time."

"Maybe he's been busy with work." Bree opened the closet. "Gross."

"What?" Matt walked to her and peered over her shoulder. The closet was fitted with industrial shelves lined with containers of turtle pellets, live crickets, and mealworms.

A small chest freezer squatted on the other side of the closet. "Not sure I want to open this." She lifted the lid, then quickly let it drop. "Ugh."

"What?"

She raised the lid again and turned her head to read a label. "Pinkies." She grimaced. "Baby mice." Her gaze shifted. "There are larger mice and rats too."

"Snake food."

"Yeah." Bree shivered. "Not a fan."

Matt shrugged. "Personally, I prefer furry animals, but lots of people keep snakes as pets. Most of them are completely harmless, even beneficial."

Bree waved a hand. "I know they keep the rodent population in check. I wouldn't want to hurt one. But I also don't want to hug one."

Matt surveyed the space. "Since it appears three habitats are missing, the most likely conclusion is that the animals were either stolen, sold, or died. But we should keep an eye out, just in case."

Bree stopped cold. Searching the floor, she made a noise he couldn't quite identify, but she didn't sound happy. They stepped into the primary bedroom.

"Someone will have to care for Spencer's animals," Matt said.

"I'll call animal control." Bree turned right. "I'll take the bathroom."

Matt crossed the pale gray carpet to stand by the bed. A wallet sat on the nightstand, next to an iPad. He took a picture, then picked up the wallet and thumbed through it. "Cash and credit cards are still in his wallet."

Bree poked her head out of the bathroom and frowned. "I found a two-year-old bottle of Vicodin in the medicine chest. More than twenty pills are left."

"So it's unlikely he was a drug addict. And this wasn't a burglary gone wrong unless the stolen items were rare reptiles." Matt closed the wallet. Cash, drugs, and electronics were the most commonly stolen household items.

"Gunshots or blunt force trauma say burglary gone wrong. Plastic wrap around the head feels personal." Bree ducked back into the bathroom.

Matt turned to the closet. Clothing was organized by type, with color subgrouping. He checked labels and pockets. There were no dry-cleaning bags shoved onto shelves, not a single stray dirty sock. Shoes were lined up in a neat, polished row on the floor.

"Find anything?" Bree asked from the doorway.

"Every pocket is empty." Matt straightened the hanger of the suit pants he'd been searching. "Spencer liked designer labels."

"He used pricey personal grooming products too," Bree said. Her phone buzzed. She tilted the phone, still attached to her belt, to view the screen. "The ME is here."

Matt followed her out the front door. In addition to the medical examiner's van, several news crews had also arrived. A deputy was barring them from the property, so they were setting up to deliver sound bites from the road. Bree made a sharp turn, clearly avoiding the media, and they walked along the side of the house to the rear yard. When they reached the back patio, Todd joined them at the edge of the pavers.

The medical examiner, Dr. Serena Jones, was a tall African American woman. She was all business, from her unflinching gaze to her ground-eating stride. On the cases Matt had worked over the past months, she'd proven to be an excellent ME. Thorough, compassionate, dedicated. She stood a few feet from the body, scanning the scene. She wore rubber boots, a parka, and a knit hat over her close-cropped hair. She exchanged a pair of leather gloves for surgical ones. While she sized up the crime scene, her assistant took pictures. He moved in a spiral pattern around the body, photographing the victim and scene from all angles and distances.

"Killer did a thorough job of it." Dr. Jones leaned closer to the victim's head. "That's a lot of plastic wrap. I'm going to wait to remove the plastic until I get him to the morgue. Don't want to lose any evidence."

Bree nodded in agreement.

Dr. Jones tilted her head, assessing the victim's hands. "I don't see defensive wounds, but I'll have to confirm that on autopsy."

The ME pressed the skin on the back of the victim's hand and moved a finger. "He looks relatively fresh. Rigor hasn't set in yet." Rigor mortis, the postmortem stiffening of muscles, typically began about two hours after death, though the cold could slow the process. "Hard to judge lividity with a fully dressed body, but I doubt he's been dead more than two hours. Body temp should give us a decent approximation of time of death."

In general, a dead body lost approximately 1.5 degrees of heat after death in a process called algor mortis. But using body temp to determine the postmortem interval, or PMI, was complicated by factors such as ambient temperature, the body's state of dress, and how lean the corpse was. Once a dead body reached ambient temperature, algor mortis was no longer useful in determining time of death.

Once her assistant stepped back, Dr. Jones pulled a scalpel from her kit. Squatting next to the body, she began to raise the hem of the jacket and underlying T-shirt. Liver temperature was the most accurate way to measure core body temp. "Look here." She pointed to a pair of small red marks on the victim's hip. "Burns from a stun gun."

"Now we know how he was overpowered," Bree said.

"Was it definitely a stun gun and not a Taser?" Matt asked.

"Yes." The ME pointed to the burns. "There are no punctures from barbs."

A Taser fired a projectile that attached to the target, while a stun gun was a close-range weapon that required the user to physically hold the device in place to deliver the shock. A Taser could be used from ten feet away. A stun gun was up close and personal.

The ME continued. "There are multiple strikes here at the hip. There's a nerve center at the hip. Hitting him here maximizes the effectiveness of the stun gun."

Matt leaned over to see the marks more clearly. "So, the killer or killers knew what they were doing."

"Great." Bree's voice rang with sarcasm. "Just what we needed, an experienced killer who likes to get close to his victim."

Chapter Six

Several hours later, Bree drove toward Jasper LaForge's address, dreading the news she needed to deliver. In the passenger seat of her official SUV, Matt leaned sideways to access the dashboard computer. They'd dropped off his Suburban at the sheriff's station.

A death notification was one of the worst duties she had to perform. But it needed to be done that night, before Spencer was identified by the press or on social media. No one should accidentally find out about a deceased loved one. It was bad enough to find the police on your doorstep late at night.

"What do we know about the brother?" Bree asked. The purpose of their visit was to deliver the death notification, but they were also investigating a murder, a dual process that required a delicate balance of compassion and intrusion.

"He's fifty-seven. He's lived at his current address for eleven years." Matt tapped on the keyboard. "I don't see any legal issues other than a couple of speeding tickets. He has a motorcycle license in addition to a regular auto license."

The GPS announced their arrival. Most of the homes on the block were neat. But not this one. Not much light managed to penetrate the filthy glass of the front porch lamp, but even in the dimness of a half moon, Bree could see mold spreading over the siding and weedy vines crawling through cracks in the driveway. Darkness and neglect gave the house a menacing air. It was the sort of house neighborhood kids dared each other to tag.

Bree studied the run-down property. "Are we sure this is the right address? It doesn't look much like Spencer's place."

Matt checked the screen of the dashboard computer. "This is it."

They got out and walked toward the small, one-story house. The rusting carcass of an ancient sedan perched on cinder blocks in the side yard. There was no garage, but a tarp-covered motorcycle occupied the carport. Blinds covering the front window were closed tight.

Next to her, Matt pressed the doorbell. No chimes echoed inside. The house remained quiet. He rapped his knuckles on the door next to the peephole.

She'd left Todd at the scene, assisting forensics and requesting the appropriate warrants for Spencer LaForge's cell phone, financial, and other personal records, including his dating app profiles and history. The ME had taken away the body, but the forensics techs in Tyvek coveralls were still crawling over the house and patio, dusting and swabbing surfaces and bagging and tagging evidence.

The door opened. A big bald man in his late fifties stood in the opening. Spencer had been a clean-cut, sharp dresser. This man was tall, with a shaved head and an unkempt gray beard. He wore dirty jeans, a sweatshirt with the sleeves cut off, and huge biker shitkickers. He looked nothing like the victim. Could they have the wrong address?

"We're looking for Jasper LaForge." Bree's nerve endings prickled. She tried to look past the man and into the house. The interior was dark.

Bree was suddenly very aware of the weight of her weapon on her hip. Next to her, Matt tensed. He didn't carry a gun—he'd been shot in the hand years before and had never recovered his accuracy with a handgun—but his hand-to-hand was first-rate.

"What do you want with him?" The man scanned her uniform.

If this was Jasper, his reaction was weird.

Also suspicious.

Bree's belly cramped, but this wasn't the first time she'd delivered a death notification to someone who didn't trust the police. "I'm afraid we have some bad news. Are you Jasper?"

The man's eyes narrowed to wary slits. "Why do you want to know?"

Fabric rustled inside the house. He wasn't alone.

Bree introduced herself and Matt. "May we come inside?"

Jasper crossed his arms. "Do you have a warrant?"

"No," she said.

"Then you can say whatever it is right here." Jasper stepped toward her.

She moved backward to make room for him on the small stoop. Before his motorcycle boot hit the concrete, a gunshot sounded from inside the house. A bullet whizzed through the open doorway. Bree dropped into the flower bed, her heart jackhammering. Matt jumped off the stoop.

Jasper crouched, covering his head with his arms, and shouted into the house, "What the fuck is wrong with you?"

He shifted to duck back into the house, but Matt launched himself through the air and tackled Jasper to the dormant grass. They hit the earth and rolled. Matt landed on top, of course. He cuffed Jasper and patted him down. Lying flat on the front lawn, Matt and Jasper were protected by the concrete stoop. The shooter didn't have a clear shot at them, but they couldn't make it to the SUV without passing through the shooter's potential line of fire. They were pinned.

On her knees in the dirt, Bree drew her weapon and used her lapel mic to call dispatch and request backup, though her department was small and most of her on-duty deputies were across town at the crime scene. Unless a state trooper happened to be nearby, she and Matt were on their own.

But the shooter didn't know that.

She called out, "This is the sheriff. Drop your weapons and come out with your hands on your head!"

"Fuck you!" someone replied.

Matt lifted Jasper's face off the ground. "How many people are inside?"

"One," Jasper hissed as Matt dropped his head and his cheek hit the grass. "One fucking moron."

A second shot rang out. The bullet hit the stoop next to Bree, kicking up bits of concrete.

Stupidity got people killed.

"Knock it off, Ricky!" Jasper yelled.

"Where is he?" Bree aimed into the darkness.

"I don't fucking know," Jasper answered.

Bree's finger curled around the trigger. She was trained to stop a threat, but she didn't want to shoot blindly into the dark, with no visible target. She needed to deescalate the situation, not make it worse.

But how?

She spotted rocks in the flower bed. She curled her fingers around one the size of a golf ball. She lobbed it toward the corner of the house. It struck the siding with a loud crack. She tossed a second rock and struck the house closer. Then she yelled to no one, "Go around back!" She threw another stone right through the window, breaking the glass.

A yelp sounded inside the house.

Bree turned back to the open doorway and shouted, "You're surrounded. This is your last chance. Drop your weapon and come out of the house with your hands on your head."

Something moved in the dark. Bree held her gun steady and listened. A faint scratching sound came from the house. As her eyes adjusted to the darkness, she saw a shape moving inside.

"Don't shoot me," came the desperate-sounding plea. "I'm coming out."

Bree kept her weapon trained on the doorway. A shadow appeared.

"Let me see your hands!" she yelled.

"They're up. They're fucking up." The figure stepped over the threshold, his hands raised as high as he could get them.

33

"Where's your weapon?" Bree scanned his clothing for suspicious gun-size bulges.

"Inside! On the floor," Ricky cried. "Don't shoot." He stepped into the dim light of the porch lamp. Blood bloomed on the sleeve of his gray hoodie.

"Why are you bleeding?" she asked.

"A piece of glass from the window hit me," Ricky sniveled.

Bree was on him in a second, taking control. She spun him around, shoved his face into the doorjamb, and cuffed his hands behind his back. She lifted the hem of his shirt, looking for weapons in the waistband of his low-riding jeans. "Anything sharp in your pockets? Is anything going to stick me?"

"No," he cried. "You're hurting me."

Bree turned out his pockets. She found keys, cash, and two small packets of white powder. "What's this?"

Ricky didn't answer.

"You know I'll get it tested," Bree said.

"It's just a little H."

Heroin.

"I need a doctor," Ricky whined.

"You'll get one." Bree pressed her lapel mic and called for an ambulance.

"You can't arrest me." True disbelief rang in his voice. "I didn't shoot anybody."

"You opened fire at law enforcement officers." Bree turned him around to face her. Her heart clenched. He was just a kid. A high schooler, maybe fifteen or sixteen years old.

"I didn't mean to shoot. I got scared. I freaked out." Panic lifted the pitch in the boy's voice.

He's about the same age as Luke.

Bree felt sick. If the situation had gone sideways, she could have shot a kid. She'd thought of an alternative at the last moment, but if her diversion hadn't worked . . .

Yes, the situation was Ricky's fault, but when she looked at him, her mind's eye saw Luke's face. Her throat tightened.

"Everything OK?" Matt stood over Jasper, who was sitting on his ass on the lawn, his legs outstretched, his hands cuffed behind his back.

"I'm bleeding," Ricky complained.

Bree took a deep breath, buried her emotions, and refocused on the job at hand. She widened the rip in Ricky's sleeve to check the boy's injury. A thin stream of blood ran down his arm. The wound was definitely not life-threatening. The skin below the wound revealed Ricky's real problems. Red welts and scars ran down his pale inner arm. Track marks. His wound was superficial, but he was an addict.

"I'm gonna pass out," Ricky cried.

Bree assured him, "You might need a few stitches, but you will not bleed to death. You will be fine."

"I'm not fine. I'm gonna barf." Ricky retched. Vomit hit the concrete and splashed onto Bree's shoes.

"Sit." Bree guided Ricky onto the step. "Put your head between your knees."

The kid obeyed, the arrogance and overwhelming dumbassery apparently scared out of him. Tears and snot streamed down his face. "It hurts."

But it could have been so much worse. Bree could have shot and potentially even killed him. The realization swam like mud through her gut until *she* wanted to puke. This wasn't the first time she'd been involved in a shooting, but the other incidents had been with adults. They'd made the choices that brought them into her sights. This felt different. For all Ricky's faults, he was just a kid, and she couldn't see him the same way.

Ricky lifted his chin. "My dad's gonna sue."

Bree had no doubt he would. She'd resolved the situation without anyone getting seriously hurt, but the truth didn't always matter. "Are you related to Jasper?"

Ricky shook his head.

"Did you come here to buy heroin?" she asked the teen.

"I don't sell drugs!" Jasper yelled from the grass. He sounded indignant, as if the question were offensive.

"Are you sure there's no one else inside the house?" Matt asked him again.

Jasper hesitated, then said, "Yeah."

Bree didn't like the way he'd paused, but she couldn't clear the house until backup arrived.

A siren wailed in the distance.

Ricky's posture stiffened. "I'm not saying anything else without a lawyer."

Great. Now he uses his brain.

Bree suppressed an eye roll. "I need your parents' contact information."

Ricky balked. "I don't have to tell you anything."

Bree rubbed an ache in her temple. "You know I have to call them."

Ricky grumbled but gave her his father's phone number.

She glanced at Jasper, to the bleeding teenage shooter, to the vomit spatter, which she now noticed had splattered her pants as well as her shoes.

She almost said, *Could this night get any worse,* but stopped herself.

Because it could always get worse.

Two deputies arrived. Lights swirled from the tops of their patrol cars. Bree instructed them to lock the prisoners in their vehicles. She stopped at her SUV and retrieved her AR-15 for Matt. He couldn't aim a handgun, but he could shoot a long gun just fine.

Working as a team, she and Matt entered through the front door. Ten steps into the house, a foul odor hit the back of her throat. The smell was unmistakable. "Decomp."

"Yes." Matt coughed.

Something—or someone—was dead.

The front door opened directly into a living room. The black vinyl couch was peeling and ripped. Several piles of cash and a game controller occupied the coffee table. The only other furniture was a huge, new-looking recliner that faced a big-screen TV mounted on the wall. A video game console sat beneath the TV.

A pistol lay on the floor.

Bree gestured to it. "That could be the one Ricky used to shoot at us. He said he left it on the floor."

They moved quickly through the rooms. In the hall closet, they found a sawed-off shotgun under legal limits. Once the rooms were cleared, they'd wait for the warrant to come in before conducting a detailed search. Bree didn't want any recovered evidence to be thrown out of court.

The kitchen was worn but surprisingly clean. The primary bedroom contained a king-size bed, one nightstand, and another big TV. The second bedroom held a desk and computer. They checked closets and peered into any spaces large enough to conceal a person. But they found no one.

A short hallway led to the laundry room and another door.

Bree had seen narrow windows in the foundation. "Basement?"

With a nod, Matt stopped beside the door. Their eyes met. She silently counted to three, exaggerating the words with her lips. On three, Matt opened the door. The smell that rushed out pushed them back a step.

Belly roiling, Bree covered her mouth and nose with her lapel. "Something is definitely dead down there."

Matt's face pursed in disgust. He pulled out his flashlight and shined it down a set of stairs. They could hear movement in the darkness. Bree reached past him and flipped a wall switch. Light illuminated a narrow set of wooden steps.

Bree sized up the stairwell. Stairwells were the worst—which was why they were called *fatal funnels* in training. If someone was hiding down there waiting to ambush them . . .

To control her heartbeat and minimize the onslaught of adrenaline, Bree took a few deep breaths—then regretted it. She gagged as the smell of rotting flesh filled her sinuses and mouth.

Matt's face tightened, and his skin had paled. He was breathing shallowly.

"Let's get this over with." Bree kept her shoulder to the wall and started down. She moved slowly but steadily, making sure she could see each slice of the room before any potential armed suspect could see her. The basement had been roughly finished. Sheet vinyl covered the concrete floor, and the cinder blocks had been painted a pale shade of blue. Three walls had been fitted out with metal shelving units. Rows upon rows of glass tanks lined the shelves.

The movement she'd heard from upstairs had been slithering.

Snakes occupied the tanks.

Next to her, Matt muttered, "Fuck."

"Seems to be the best word to sum up our entire night," Bree agreed.

"There must be fifty of them."

Bree began counting. "More than fifty." Her gaze locked on a tank that contained a rotting snake carcass. "At least seventy-five. Plus, a few dead ones."

"That explains the smell."

"Bright side," Bree said. "Dead snakes are better than dead people."

"You make a good point."

A thin rattling sound drew her toward a tank. With her gun raised, she approached. The snake inside was thick-bodied and reddish brown in color. A diamond pattern flowed down its back. The animal lifted its triangular-shaped head, stared at Bree, and hissed. The tip of its tail quivered, sounding like a small maraca.

See? Her night could get worse.

Matt drew in a sharp breath. "That's a rattlesnake."

CHAPTER SEVEN

Matt watched the ambulance containing Ricky and a deputy pull away. Another deputy had taken Jasper to the sheriff's station.

Bree approached, cell phone in hand. "Warrant's in. Ready to search the house?"

She'd obtained an emergency search warrant for Jasper's house. Shots fired at law enforcement gave her a compelling reason for a late-night phone call to a judge.

"I guess." Matt didn't mind snakes, at least the ones that weren't venomous. "Handling rattlesnakes feels like it's above our pay grade."

"No kidding. We're not handling anything in the basement." Bree started toward the house. "We have a guy who handles snakes at animal control, but he doesn't have the capacity for the sheer number of animals we're dealing with. I called the zoo. They're sending over a team of specialists. When they get here, we'll revisit the snake pit."

Matt followed Bree into the house. They started in the living room, donning gloves. Bree started lifting couch cushions. "Found a Glock."

Matt opened a drawer in the coffee table. "I've got a bag of weed."

"How much?"

He held it up. "Enough for a couple of joints."

"Personal use." She sounded disappointed.

After the furniture had been searched, he checked the corners and sides of the carpets, looking for a loose edge. Criminals were known to keep secret hidey-holes. But the wall-to-wall was nailed down tight. They looked inside heat vents and appliances. He even opened a plumbing access panel but found nothing behind the wall but insulation and dust.

In the home office, he pulled out desk drawers to look behind and under them, as well as riffle through the contents.

"We haven't come across any heroin or drug dealer paraphernalia." Bree scanned the room.

Drug dealing required equipment like scales and baggies.

"No," Matt agreed. "Jasper didn't seem high either. Maybe he was telling the truth when he said he didn't sell drugs."

"Stranger things have happened," Bree said.

Matt removed a spiral binder, opened it on the blotter, and skimmed pages. "Seems Jasper breeds snakes and keeps detailed records."

"Maybe it's a family business."

Jasper's house was small, and he lived Spartanly. The search didn't take long. Not only did they not find any drugs, but they found nothing to link him to his brother. There wasn't even a photograph of Spencer anywhere.

Activity drew Matt's attention to the front window. A minivan with the zoo's emblem on the side had arrived. Three people dressed in khaki jackets appeared at the door. They carried plastic containers with air holes and several long-handled hooks.

Bree motioned for them to come inside. The lead keeper introduced herself. She wore cargo pants and heavy boots.

"I'm Sheriff Taggert," Bree said. "This is Investigator Flynn."

Matt nodded. "There are some decomposing animals down there."

Bree handed Matt an N95 respirator mask at the top of the steps. No one wanted to inhale decomp if they didn't have to. He adjusted the straps around his head. The zookeepers had brought their own. They filed into the basement.

"The homeowner kept breeding records," Matt said. "We'll send copies."

"Thanks." A keeper gestured around the room. "We've got this," he said, as if he wanted them to go away and let him work.

"We'll leave you to it, and thank you." Bree inclined her head toward the stairs.

Matt followed. "Are we running away?"

"You betcha." Bree hurried upstairs and through the house to the front door. "I'll assign a deputy to inventory everything the keepers take with them."

Matt's beard prevented a good seal with his mask, and the smell of rotting snakes had found its way inside. Outside, he ripped off the N95. The night air hit his grateful lungs. "I'm glad to be out of that stink."

Bree peeled off her mask and sniffed her jacket. "I'm going to need to bribe my dry cleaner. She hates me."

"Can't blame her." Matt followed her to her vehicle to wait. "We stink."

Thirty minutes later, the zoo people emerged.

The lead keeper approached. "Sheriff, we cataloged seventy-seven snakes, eleven different species, including pythons, rattlesnakes, and several endangered Asian vipers." The keeper paused. "And six alligators."

Matt lifted his brows. "What?"

"Baby alligators. About this big." The keeper spread her hands in the air to indicate the gators were about a foot long. "Some of the animals appear to be in rough shape. It's common in these situations. Illegal breeders buy, sell, and trade constantly. All it takes is one diseased snake to infect a whole collection."

"Will they recover?" Bree sounded concerned.

The keeper lifted a shoulder. "I don't know. The last time we had a haul this big, half the snakes were infected with a virus. Most of them died." She exhaled, anger vibrating in her breath. "Mites are also very common. Alligators are hardier, which is why they are living dinosaurs. The care of exotic species is complicated."

"And Jasper wasn't up to the task." Bree's brows drew into a flat line.

Anger heated Matt's chest. Some of the snakes might be potentially deadly, but neglecting any animals in one's care was inexcusable. "Considering that he left dead animals to rot in their tanks, I'd say he didn't try very hard."

The keeper nodded but looked sad. "We'll do our best to save as many as possible."

"Thank you," Bree said. "It's illegal to possess either constrictors or venomous snakes in New York without a special permit, which Jasper does not have. I'll bring up every charge I can think of. Snakes are living creatures that deserve to be treated with the same level of compassion and care as any other animal."

Matt's work with his sister's dog rescue told him Jasper would not be adequately punished for his callousness. It was hard enough to charge people with cruelty toward cute and furry animals. Jasper would probably walk away with a fine. But he also knew Bree would do her best to nail his ass on the weapons charges.

"Thank you, Sheriff." The keeper inclined her head. "We'll get these snakes out of here tonight, and I'll send you a full report after they've been evaluated by our veterinarian. We'll need to run tests. It'll take time to process this many samples."

The two other keepers had retrieved additional plastic containers.

Matt pointed to a hook. "What is that for?"

"Moving the snakes into transport containers without touching them," the keeper said.

"You're opening the tanks?" Bree asked, one brow raised.

"Yes." The keeper laughed. "You don't want the glass to break on a rattler's enclosure while you're driving down the interstate."

"I guess not." Matt swallowed, thinking of a loose rattler slithering under the car seats. *Snakes in a van?*

"Don't worry," said the keeper. "This is what we do."

The three keepers returned to the house.

"Why does anyone want venomous snakes or alligators as pets?" Bree asked.

"People are weird." Matt froze, a light bulb exploding in his mind. He turned to Bree. "We have possible missing reptiles at Spencer's house. His brother keeps snakes."

The wind kicked up. A few hairs escaped Bree's ponytail and whipped across her face. "Maybe they bought snakes from the same person. Maybe Spencer bought snakes from Jasper."

Matt zipped his jacket. "Maybe Jasper stole Spencer's snakes."

"Only one way to find out. Let's go talk to Jasper." Bree issued instructions to the remaining deputy, then slid behind the wheel of her SUV.

In the passenger seat, Matt rubbed his hands together. The bullet scar on his palm ached from the cold. He flexed his fingers to ease the stiffness.

Bree drove to the sheriff's station and parked in the fenced lot behind the building. They entered through the rear door, and she headed to her office. Starving, Matt beelined for the break room. He considered another cup of coffee, but it looked—and smelled—like tar, and his stomach was already brimming with acid. Instead, he crossed to the vending machine and chose a snack-size bag of almonds. He went to Bree's office and peered inside. Elbows on the desk, she was rubbing her temple with one hand, her phone pressed to the opposite ear. He waited for her to finish her call.

She put down the phone and waved him in. "That was the deputy with Ricky at the ER."

"How is he?" Matt popped an almond into his mouth and offered the bag to Bree.

She opened her hand, and he poured a few nuts into her palm. "Ricky's full name is Richard Sanderling. The wound was superficial.

They gave him a tetanus booster, stitched him up, and sent him over to juvie. Ricky told the deputy that he went to Jasper's to buy a rattlesnake. He said they were"—Bree used air quotes—"cool."

"Jasper was right about one thing. Ricky is an idiot."

"Jasper has no room to criticize. He has a basement full of dangerous reptiles," Bree pointed out. "This is not Ricky's first visit to juvie. He's been picked up for narcotics possession, shoplifting, petty theft . . ." Stealing was common among addicts. They needed money to buy their drugs and could rarely hold a job. "The only thing longer than his arrest record are the track marks on his arms."

"School?" Matt asked.

"I doubt it." Bree sighed. "The deputy called his father, who came down to the hospital. Ricky's mother left three years ago. She had an Oxy addiction. Ricky's drug use began by stealing her pills. No one knows where she is. Mr. Sanderling says he doesn't know what to do with Ricky. He's repeatedly brought guns and drugs home. He can't be trusted around his brothers. The youngest is only six."

"So, a rattlesnake is a perfect choice of pet." Matt blew out a disgusted breath.

"Then Ricky and his dad had a blowout argument in the ER, which ended with Mr. Sanderling telling Ricky not to come home." Bree scrubbed both hands down her exhausted face. "The only good news is that Mr. Sanderling expressed no interest in suing the sheriff's department."

"Can you write off your own kid?" Matt couldn't imagine, but then he also couldn't imagine having a teenager who was completely out of control and constantly endangering his younger siblings.

"I don't know the whole story, so I won't judge the dad yet. But I will reserve the option to judge him later. Maybe he's done all he can and is simply out of options except to protect his younger kids." Bree moved toward the door. "Thankfully, Ricky is only fifteen." In New

York State, he couldn't be processed as an adult until he turned sixteen. "He'll be processed as a juvenile. They're trying to find a spot in rehab."

"That's the best possible outcome," Matt said. "When can we talk to him?"

"Probably tomorrow. He has to get through intake at the juvenile detention center today."

Bree's administrative assistant, Marge, poked her head into the room. Her hair was a halo of dyed brown curls. "Jasper LaForge's attorney is here." Somewhere around sixty years old, Marge was a wonder of efficiency and common sense. Today, she'd layered a turtleneck under her cardigan, and she'd traded her sensible shoes for sensible boots.

Bree pushed up from her desk with both hands. She grabbed a notepad and jotted down a few notes. "Let's see if we can get some answers."

CHAPTER EIGHT

"How do you want to handle him?" Matt finished his almonds and tossed the bag into the trash can. He was still hungry, but his snack would have to suffice for the moment.

"I didn't get a good feel for Jasper at his house," Bree said.

"Yeah. He seemed . . ." Matt reached for the right word. "Indifferent?"

"That's a nice way of saying he didn't give a fuck about anything, and that attitude will make questioning him a challenge." Bree grabbed a water bottle from her desk. "Let's see how it goes. If he responds better to you, go ahead and take the lead."

He glanced sideways at her. "You know you've become a very good sheriff."

She laughed. "Because I'm learning to delegate? You know I still *want* to do everything myself. It's just impossible if I also want to raise two kids. And you're an excellent interviewer."

"Because you know how to let people do their jobs without your own ego getting in the way. That's a rare quality. Among politicians, you're practically a unicorn."

Sheriff was an elected position, so technically, Bree was both a politician *and* a law enforcement officer, though he knew politics drove her crazy.

Color flushed her cheeks, and she opened her mouth. He could tell by her expression that she wanted to protest his compliment. Then she nodded and said, "Thank you. Now, let's get to work."

Questioning suspects was a skill. You had to be willing to play whatever role encouraged the subject to talk. Sometimes, you had to lie to get the job done. You had to side with abhorrent opinions. Matt had once agreed with a man when he said women needed a punch in the face now and then. The process could feel a little slimy. But getting information or a confession was worth the temporary discomfort. There was no law against lying to a suspect. Cops did it all the time.

But first, they needed to know what motivated Jasper, and so far, they hadn't found anything.

They headed down the hall toward the interrogation room, where a deputy was babysitting a handcuffed Jasper. On the way in, Matt activated the video camera that would record the session. Jasper's lawyer sat next to his client. He wore an off-the-rack suit, but his gaze was hard and sharp. Matt judged him as street smart rather than fancy. He had no time for bullshit and would be willing to scrap in the dirt.

Bree eased into a chair, facing Jasper over the table. Matt sat next to her, across from the lawyer. To better read body language, he preferred to sit next to the subject, without a barrier between them. But the lawyer had taken the spot next to his client.

After tossing her notepad on the table, Bree removed Jasper's handcuffs. Then she read the names of all present, gave the date, and read Jasper his Miranda rights. Jasper signed the acknowledgment without fuss.

Bree sat down and stared at Jasper. "This would have been easier at your house."

"No shit." Jasper sounded disgusted. "Ricky is a fucking moron. I told him to sit down and shut up, and everything would be fine, but no. He panicked."

"How did he get your gun?" She folded her hands on her notes. They didn't know if the gun belonged to Jasper or Ricky, but sometimes a bluff paid off.

Jasper was too smart to fall into her trap and answered without missing a beat. "What gun?" Fake innocence and mild amusement lit his eyes, as if he were enjoying the interview process.

Or even playing with them.

"We found several illegal weapons in your house." Bree recited the list.

"I have no idea what you're talking about." Jasper blinked at the question. Matt could see the lie plainly enough, but Jasper had no guilt, no remorse. He didn't even seem nervous. Ownership of the handgun Ricky had used was questionable, but Matt was 99 percent sure the other weapons found in the house belonged to Jasper.

"You're in deep trouble, Jasper." Bree fixed her gaze on his face. "We found guns, cash, and a basement full of illegal reptiles."

Jasper held eye contact.

The attorney said, "My client will not comment on the charges against him." He glanced at Jasper. "You are under no obligation to answer any questions."

Jasper nodded. "I know."

Matt changed tactics. "Don't you even want to know why we came to your house?"

Jasper's head bobbed. "Yes."

Matt continued. "Your brother, Spencer LaForge, was found dead at his home this evening."

"Spencer is dead?" Jasper's mouth hung open. "You're not shitting me?"

"He's dead," Bree assured him.

Jasper looked from Bree to Matt and back again. Confusion flashed in his eyes. As a reaction to learning of his brother's death, it seemed weak, but at least they'd provoked an emotion.

Considering the circumstances, Matt's next statement felt ridiculous, but he said it anyway. "We're sorry for your loss."

"I can't believe it." Jasper leaned back, as if distancing himself from the conversation.

"When was the last time you talked to your brother?" Bree asked.

"I don't know." Jasper blinked hard. "We weren't close."

Matt picked a soft question, one that didn't feel important. He needed to get Jasper talking. "Are your parents still living?"

"No." Jasper's mouth flattened, and his eyes went hard. "Spencer didn't even show up at Dad's funeral last year. He was embarrassed by his family. He didn't want to be reminded of where he came from."

Gee, wonder why? Matt swallowed the sarcastic response. They needed information. They needed Jasper to cooperate. With most subjects, coaxing was more effective than hostility. But at least Jasper apparently did care about his brother's estrangement from the family.

He was angry. How could Matt poke at that sensitive subject?

Bree sat back, her posture deceptively casual. "When did you see him last?"

Jasper lifted both hands, and the effort to return to his relaxed posture looked forced. "Before last month, I hadn't seen him in years."

"What happened last month?" Bree asked.

Jasper leaned sideways and whispered something in his attorney's ear.

The attorney held up a hand. "My client isn't going to answer that question."

"How many times did you see him last month?" Bree asked.

Jasper cocked his head and contemplated her question for a few seconds. "Once."

"Phone calls? Texts?" Bree asked.

Jasper exhaled hard through his nose. "We had a couple of phone calls before and after."

Matt leaned forward. "Did Spencer call you or did you call him?"

"He called me," Jasper said.

"About reptiles or guns?" Matt guessed.

"Nope." The lawyer shook his head. "We're not going there."

But Jasper didn't flinch. His lie came out as smooth as satin. "He just wanted to catch up."

Matt's guess was reptiles, since they hadn't found any guns at Spencer's house.

Bree made a note. "Prior to that, when did you communicate with him last?"

"I called him on his birthday back in July. He didn't answer. I left a message. He didn't call back." Jasper scratched his chest. "Did he fall or something? I can't imagine he had a heart attack. He's always running and shit."

"No." Matt watched his eyes. "Your brother was murdered."

Jasper didn't respond for several seconds, then he blinked. "What?"

"He was murdered," Bree repeated.

"How?" Jasper's shock seemed genuine.

With the investigation still in its infant stage, Matt didn't want to give out any information yet. Jasper's attorney would want to draw on any incident that might help Jasper's case. The attorney would contact the press if he felt that would benefit his client's defense. Matt stuck with a vague, "The medical examiner hasn't officially declared a cause of death at this time."

Anger flashed in Jasper's eyes. "But you saw him. Was he shot?"

"No," Bree said. "He wasn't shot."

Jasper's brows dropped. "Then how was he killed?"

"He suffocated." Matt left out the details in case they needed to differentiate false leads or confessions from real ones.

Jasper's brows shot up. For one brief second, he actually looked horrified and speechless.

While Jasper's emotions were engaged, Matt dived in. "Where were you between four thirty and five thirty p.m. yesterday evening?"

The ME had narrowed down the time of death to a one-hour window.

Seemingly surprised, Jasper touched his own chest. "Me?"

"You don't have to answer that question," the attorney interrupted.

Jasper ignored him. "I was home. Why?"

"Can anyone verify that?" Matt asked.

"Stop talking." The attorney put his hand on Jasper's forearm.

Jasper stiffened. "You aren't going to pin Spencer's murder on me. I didn't kill that little prick."

The lawyer looked bored. "They have zero evidence. They're fishing, and you don't have to answer any of these questions."

"If you didn't kill Spencer"—Matt shifted forward—"help us find who did."

Jasper didn't break eye contact. "How?"

"Do you know of anything dangerous your brother could have been into?" Matt asked.

Jasper scratched the back of his neck. "I don't know what he's been doing recently, but Spencer liked to spend money. He liked fancy clothes and shiny shoes. When he was younger, he was always running some kind of scam."

"What kind of scam?"

Jasper turned up a palm. "Little side gigs, like telling old people their computer is compromised, then charging them to fix it."

"But there was no problem," Bree said.

"Exactly." Jasper tapped a finger on the table for emphasis. "Or if there was, Spencer caused it."

"Was his business profitable?" Matt asked.

"What business?" Jasper swept a hand over his sweaty, stubbled head. "Last time I saw Spencer, he was the assistant manager at Electronics Depot."

"Wait." Bree lifted a hand. "He's not a digital marketer?"

Jasper lifted an indifferent shoulder. "Not that I know of."

"Did he know about your reptile business?" Matt asked.

"Don't answer that," the lawyer interrupted.

Bree jumped in. "Did your brother breed reptiles?"

"Don't answer that," the lawyer said.

"Why do you like snakes?" Matt asked.

Jasper scratched his arm. "Our old man always had reptiles. We grew up with them, and we both like them. It's probably the only thing we have in common."

Bree flattened a hand on the table. "So, you didn't sell or give him any rare species?"

The lawyer leaned closer to his client. "Don't answer that."

Jasper clamped his molars together. He was smart enough to listen to his lawyer.

Instead of a direct question, Matt circled around. "What kind of reptiles did your brother like?"

But Jasper didn't fall for it. He crossed his arms and kept quiet.

"Did Spencer keep any venomous snakes?" Matt asked.

Jasper dropped his hands to the table. "Venomous snakes aren't evil or even aggressive. You just have to know how to handle them."

Matt deserved a medal for not rolling his eyes or yelling *bullshit*. Exotic—and deadly—animals should be cared for by professionals. But he wanted to keep Jasper talking, so he agreed. "Lots of animals can be dangerous if you don't know how to handle them."

"Right?" Jasper rapped his knuckles on the table.

"Did Spencer have any other pets?" Bree asked.

"Hell no," Jasper protested. "A dog or cat would mess up his fancy house. Spencer could never tolerate fur balls or muddy footprints. Plus, he's too in love with himself. Not much left over for other creatures. He liked snakes because they're clean and low maintenance. They don't get attached."

"Do you know anyone who is close to your brother?" Matt asked.

"Nope," Jasper said. "Spencer never had friends."

"Never?" Bree's voice rang with skepticism.

"Nope. Not even as a kid." Jasper's brows knit, as if he were recalling a memory. "He could fake it around other people, but he never got close to anybody that I saw."

"Fake what?" Bree pressed.

"Caring? Connection. I don't know the terms, but Spencer really didn't give a fuck about anyone but himself." Jasper's voice left no room for doubt.

Matt tried another approach. "Were you close as kids?"

"Not really." Jasper shook his head. "We're ten years apart, and neither one of us is the warm-and-fuzzy type."

"How about girlfriends?" Bree tapped her pen on the table.

"He dated, but Spencer wasn't a one-woman man," Jasper said. "He kept them around long enough to get some sex, but not long enough for them to develop any attachment."

Silence hovered for a couple of seconds. Then the lawyer shifted forward. "My client has answered all of your questions. You have nothing to link him to his brother's death."

Bree sat back. "We're charging him with illegal weapons possession. The sawed-off shotgun is under the legal limit. Also, your client doesn't have a permit for the handgun."

The lawyer referred to his notes. "You can't prove it's his handgun. The kid could have brought it with him. In fact, maybe the kid brought all of the weapons."

Bree's gaze never left the lawyer's. "Nice try, but we'll prove it."

"You'll need to," the lawyer said, his voice matter of fact rather than cocky. His gaze moved from Matt to Bree and back again, studying them. No, he was sizing them up.

Definitely shifty.

"The kid didn't bring seventy-seven snakes with him," Matt added. "Including illegal constrictors and rattlesnakes."

"Don't forget the endangered species," Bree said. "And all the equipment in that basement."

"We're done here." The lawyer didn't blink. "Jasper, don't say anything else."

And that was that.

The lawyer left. Bree handcuffed Jasper and handed him over to a deputy to be transported to the jail and processed.

Matt stood and stretched. "The lawyer is right about our lack of evidence to tie Jasper to his brother's murder, other than the shared interest in snakes."

"The phone calls will show on his cell provider records."

"He volunteered that information. He didn't try to hide them." Matt thought Jasper was pretty damned smart. "And there's no way to prove the subject of the phone calls was anything other than what he stated."

Bree collected her notes. "We have him on a weapons violation for the sawed-off and not having a license, illegal possession of wildlife, and illegal possession of venomous reptiles. If Ricky's statement holds, we can add illegal sale of wildlife. Considering the dead animals, we'll try to make animal-cruelty charges stick too."

"We can try for reckless endangerment as well."

Bree agreed with a nod. "I was hoping we'd be able to hold on to him for a day or so, but that slick lawyer will have him bailed out tomorrow. He has no priors. You know the drill." They left the interview room. Stopping in the break room, she took two bottles of water from the fridge and handed one to Matt. Twisting off the cap, she took a deep swallow, her expression thoughtful. "He seemed surprised about his brother's murder—and disturbed about the method. Could that have been an act?"

They headed to Bree's office. Matt followed her example and drank some water. His eyes felt dry and gritty. "I wouldn't rule him out. Some of his reactions seemed genuine, but at other times, he was clearly toying with us. Plus, he sells venomous snakes to minors, so I doubt ethics are an issue for him."

"No kidding." Behind her desk, Bree rapped a palm on her desktop. "Who sells a rattlesnake to a kid?"

"A psychopath."

"Exactly. There are few lines a man like Jasper won't cross," Bree exclaimed. "We'll have to wait for more evidence. On that note, Todd applied for warrants before he went home to grab a couple hours of sleep."

Matt checked the time on his phone. Nearly four a.m. "Something we should both do."

The first hours of an investigation were critical, but a catnap could keep them functioning better than no rest at all.

Bree nodded. "You're right." She shut down her computer, then they walked out of the station together. Their vehicles were parked side by side in the employee lot behind the building.

"Coming over?" Matt paused, one hand on the door of his Suburban.

"Yes. If that's OK."

"Of course it is."

She'd taken to sleeping over when work kept her out late. She didn't like to wake the kids or Dana by coming home in the middle of the night. Matt understood her struggle to balance work and family, but he wished she'd stay over occasionally when they weren't preoccupied with a murder.

"You have a standing invitation," he said. "You don't need to ask." He searched her eyes. "In fact, I'd love to have a weekend alone with you. Maybe we could go somewhere?"

"I'd love that." But her smile was apologetic. "But I can't even think about leaving the kids right now."

"Maybe we can revisit the idea after this case."

"It's not just the case." Pain slid across her face. "This will be their first Christmas without their mother. I don't know how they're going to cope."

Guilt stabbed Matt in the heart. "I'm sorry. I should have thought of that. Of course you can't leave them right now."

Her eyes warmed. "You know I would love to take a trip with you." She touched her own chest. "There's nothing personally that's holding me back." She touched his forearm. "I'm committed to you—to us."

He smiled. "Back atcha."

But as he drove toward home, he wondered if there would ever be enough of her to go around. Between her job and the kids, there wasn't much time left for a relationship.

CHAPTER NINE

"You need a name," I say to one of the serpents in my living room.

The dirt-colored body is coiled in its water bowl in the corner of the aquarium. When I think about a snake, I envision a slender, lithe animal, but this one is short and thick, only about four feet long from its primitive-looking rattle to the blunt, wedge-shaped head.

The snakes had hissed and rattled as I moved their aquariums to my SUV and drove home. I check the latches on the top of each tank. No one wants an agitated rattlesnake loose in the house. The lids are secure. But I don't kid myself. I did plenty of research before I embarked on this step of my plan. The glass between us creates an illusion of control, but these animals are angry and dangerous.

Like me. Maybe that's why I identify with them—why I had to have them the moment I first saw them. I, too, am poised to strike.

Snakes sense vibrations. I did my best to minimize their stress, but riding in the back of my SUV must have been sensory overload for such creatures. The other two have gone quiet, but not this one. I can feel its animosity with every flick of its tongue. Or perhaps I'm projecting my own hostility.

Dawn is hours away. I watch the serpent with a macabre fascination. Even motionless, it exudes power and confidence, as if aware of its deadly capabilities.

I would love to have its self-assurance, its lack of complication. The snake doesn't worry about its purpose or understand the constructs of past and future. It can't comprehend regret. It lives in the moment. It exists.

It simply *is*.

And there is something magnificent in its single-mindedness.

I wish I could harness its coldness, but my rage feels hot. The snake feels no emotions. I feel too many.

"I know it's not a politically correct term, but considering what I've done—and what I'm still planning—I shouldn't be concerned with social boundaries. You are my spirit animal, and you're going to be part of my signature."

The animal stirs. The head rises, slowly, intently. The tongue flicks out; the head turns a few degrees. Another tongue flick, as the snake pulls my scent into its mouth over and over, processing the smells of its new environment—of me.

"You're a bit smaller than the other two. I'm going to guess you're female." The smile spreads across my face like the Grinch. Who is the most famous female killer? "I'm going to call you Lizzie. Those two can be Ted and Jack."

Now I need to learn their triggers. My voice didn't do it.

I wave my arm and jump up and down a few times. The floorboards shudder under me. The lid on the tank shakes. It—Lizzie—seems to coil more tightly, as if preparing to strike. I sense her tension. The tip of the snake's tail shivers in response. A soft rattle emanates from the tank. The other two are a few feet away, but they also begin to show signs of agitation, restless movements and tongue flicks. Another's tail rattles.

"Yes," I croon. "That's it."

The rattling sound both thrills and scares me. I can't imagine the terror of being close to one without the benefit of its secure enclosure.

Snakes strike when they feel threatened. The natural response to being trapped with a venomous snake is to panic. Sudden movements scare the snake. My plan is going to work nicely.

I'm almost giddy as I imagine it. "Won't they be surprised?"

But for now, I'll concentrate on the most important detail: my next target.

I read my list to the snakes and hold up each person's profile picture, turning the image to the animals so they can see my prospective victims' faces. "Who do you think should die next?"

CHAPTER TEN

Bree opened her eyes to darkness, but her internal clock told her she needed to get up. She liked to be home before the kids woke for school. She tried to roll over, but her movement was impeded by a huge dog head resting on her ankles. Matt's German shepherd, Brody, was wedged in between their bodies. She flexed her toes. Pins and needles shot up her calves. She slid her feet out from under his head, making a ridiculous attempt not to wake the dog.

"He'll move," Matt said in her ear.

"I hate to disturb him."

Matt chuckled. "It's not like he has to get up and go to work. He's going to sleep approximately twenty hours today."

Bree laughed. "As a retired hero should."

Brody had been Matt's K-9 partner. He'd been shot in the same friendly-fire incident that had ended Matt's career as a deputy.

"I'll make coffee." Matt kissed her neck, then slid out of bed. His movement triggered a motion-sensing nightlight, which cast a semicircle of light on the floor. Wearing only a pair of boxers, he cut a fine figure even in the dimness.

Watching him, Bree smiled. He made her happy in ways she hadn't known were possible ten months ago. She slid out of bed and padded to the bathroom in one of Matt's T-shirts, which was warm enough when she was under a comforter with his heat-producing body. A minute later, she hurried back to bed, shivering.

Brody army-crawled up the bed and stretched out alongside Bree, his body pressed against her from her ribs to her toes. The dog produced as much heat as his owner. She stroked his shoulder, then scratched behind an ear. "Who's a good boy?" she crooned.

The dog's tail thumped on the mattress.

A childhood mauling had left Bree terrified of dogs for most of her life. Ten months ago, she hadn't imagined spooning with one.

Yet here she was. And that phrase described so much of her current life.

Matt carried two mugs of coffee into the bedroom. He set one on her nightstand, then rounded the bed and climbed back onto the mattress. "Hey, Brody, how about a little room here?"

The dog ignored him. Matt tugged a section of the comforter out from under the dog and tossed it over his bare legs. Then he leaned back against the headboard and sipped his coffee.

Bree wiggled to a sitting position, tucked a pillow behind her back, and reached for her cup. "Your dog sure understands passive resistance."

"He taught himself to play dead."

Bree ruffled Brody's ears. "He's a smart boy."

"The smartest," Matt agreed, stroking his dog's head.

"Do you think he's missing Greta?" Bree asked. Matt had fostered a young German shepherd for his sister's canine rescue group. He'd recognized Greta as a potential K-9 working dog. Bree's department hadn't had a K-9 unit since Brody had retired. The rescue had helped raise the money for Greta's equipment and training. She and her handler were currently at the academy.

"Maybe a little, but her energy was wearing on him." Matt laughed. "What's on the agenda for this morning?"

Bree took a long, deep swallow of coffee, hoping the caffeine made a speedy entry into her bloodstream. Three hours of sleep were not enough. "Stop home and see the kids off to school. I want to drive by the crime scene to get a look at the yard in the daylight and see if the across-the-street neighbor is home. After that, we should review progress and plans with Todd."

"Do we know when the autopsy will take place?"

Bree reached for her phone and checked her email. She opened one from the ME. "Dr. Jones has it scheduled for eleven thirty."

"Sounds like a busy morning."

She sighed. The day already seemed like chaos, and it hadn't yet begun. "It does." She set her phone back on the nightstand and drained her coffee.

Matt peered into her mug. "Damn. Impressive."

"Necessary." She stretched. "I need to wake up."

Matt set his coffee aside and checked his own cell phone. "You're ahead of schedule this morning."

"We could get in a really fast mile or two. I could use the cardio." Bree hadn't run in a few days.

"I can think of another way to raise your heart rate." He turned, leaned over her, and kissed her softly on the mouth. His lips trailed down her jaw, over her neck, and lingered on her pulse point.

Heat zoomed through Bree's limbs. She wrapped her arms around his broad shoulders. "I have fifteen minutes."

He lifted his head and grinned. "I'd prefer an hour or so, but I can work with a tighter deadline."

Already more awake, she kissed him back and repeated firmly, "I have fifteen minutes."

"Twenty," he countered, sliding a hand under the covers.

Bree groaned. "Deal."

His voice went husky. "I know how to push all the important buttons."

You certainly do. Bree arched into his touch.

The next twenty minutes were totally worth rushing through her subsequent shower. Bree tugged on a sweatshirt as she breezed through the kitchen.

Matt wore jeans and a T-shirt. Despite the chill, he was barefoot. And Bree wished she had another twenty minutes. She glanced at her phone screen.

"Your hair is still wet." He scooped kibble into a bowl. Brody sat patiently.

"Someone used up my blow-dry time."

"That was me." He smiled broadly. "Hold on." He set down the bowl and ducked into the laundry room. He came out carrying a knit hat, which he tugged over Bree's still-damp hair. "It's cold."

"Thanks." She leaned against him for a goodbye kiss. "I'll meet you at the station."

"You got it."

It was still dark as Bree hurried to her vehicle. Barking erupted from the kennels as she breezed past. Matt's sister, Cady, waved from the doorway. After his initial retirement from the sheriff's department, Matt had used his settlement to buy the house and build the kennels to house K-9s in training, but his sister had filled them with rescue dogs before he could get his business off the ground. Now he was focused on finding homeless dogs like Greta to train for law enforcement.

Blasting the heat, she drove home nursing a stupid smile. As she turned into the driveway, she was surprised to see her brother's junker SUV. She parked next to it and jogged to the kitchen door. Inside, Ladybug slammed into her legs, almost taking her out at the knees. Bree steadied herself with a hand on the wall and stopped everything to pet the dog. The dog's tail nub wagged in a frantic circle. "How can you be this excited to see me every single day?"

"She loves you." Adam sat at the kitchen table inhaling a cappuccino. Paint splattered his sweatshirt and jeans. He looked like he hadn't combed his shaggy hair in a few weeks.

"I love that you're here, but it's early. Is something wrong?" Bree hung up her coat and tossed her keys on the counter.

Dana crouched in front of the oven, staring through the tiny window. "Morning."

Bree echoed the greeting.

Vader immediately jumped onto the counter. The cat made eye contact with Bree, then deliberately sent her keys flying off the edge. Bree picked up the keys, stowed them on a higher shelf, and gave the quirky feline an ear scratch. He was an asshat, but he was her asshat.

Adam shrugged. "I worked all night. The new painting isn't cooperating. I thought I'd come over, bum breakfast, and clear my head."

"The kids will be thrilled." Dana pulled a baking sheet out of the oven.

Bree stopped to toe off her boots. "What is that smell?"

Dana set the baking sheet on the stovetop. "Blueberry lemon scones. Sit." She motioned to the table. "I'll bring you a cappuccino."

Adam sipped his coffee and sighed in contentment. "She's in a baking mood. Don't fight it."

"I never do." Bree gave him a one-armed hug. She turned to Dana. "Please make it a double. Maybe a triple."

Dana worked the fancy-ass coffee machine she'd brought with her from Philadelphia. Then she dusted cocoa powder over the foamy mixture and brought it to the table. "This should jump-start your heart."

Adam gave Bree a side-eye. "You're in a good mood for someone involved in a murder investigation."

"I am." Bree pushed back the creep of guilt. She deserved a life—a realization she still struggled with when a big case landed in her jurisdiction.

Adam smiled. "I'm happy for you. I'm glad you and Matt found each other, though I am just a little jealous."

"Same." Dana drizzled glaze over the scones. "These are supposed to cool before you eat them, but I'm not waiting."

Bree's mouth watered. "What about that guy you dated last week?"

Dana shook her head. "The lawyer? Zero chemistry." She brought the plate of scones to the table. "I haven't really been attracted to any of them. At this point, I wonder if it's them or me."

"Dating apps seem backward to me." Bree broke a scone in half, releasing steam. "You're supposed to date someone because you're attracted to them, not date them and then see if they're hot."

"That would be optimal, but if I wait to meet someone organically in this town, I'll be alone at ninety." Dana sipped from her mug. "Don't get me wrong. I love living upstate. Life is slower. The air is cleaner. I don't hear traffic and sirens 24/7. But the dating pool in Grey's Hollow is barely a puddle."

"No kidding." Adam shoved half a scone into his mouth. His eyes closed for a second. "These are amazing."

Dana sighed. "Maybe I need to fully accept that love at first sight doesn't exist."

Bree didn't believe in love at first sight, but lust at first sight? That was real. Matt had made her blood hum the first time she'd met him. Bree shot her brother a look. "When did you start dating?"

"I've always dated." Adam shook back his wavy hair. "It's not like I've been a monk my whole life. It's just that things have been crazy this year. My social life got put on hold."

But he never mentioned dating to Bree. Nor did he talk about friends. She'd assumed he was an introvert. But then, before January, they'd barely known each other. They'd been separated after their parents' deaths. Since they'd reconnected, their lives had definitely been upended. But they clearly needed to talk more.

Kayla slumped into the kitchen, still in her pajamas, her eyes bleary. She was not a morning person. She gave Adam a sleepy smile, pulled a chair close to his, and rested her head on his shoulder. "Hi. Why are you here so early?"

He kissed the top of her head. "I came to have breakfast with you."

Dana set a glass of milk in front of Kayla. "What do you want for breakfast?"

"Can I have scrambled eggs?" Kayla asked.

"Of course." Dana whipped them up in a few minutes.

Luke walked in, fully dressed. He plopped into a chair, ate a plate of eggs and two scones in what seemed like four bites, then drained a glass of orange juice.

"I have to get ready for work." Bree finished her scone and picked up her cappuccino to take upstairs with her. Dana must have loaded it with espresso, because Bree's brain was clearing. She changed her uniform, pinned her still-damp hair into a quick bun, and said her goodbyes.

Then she picked up Matt at the station before heading to the crime scene. They slid out of her SUV at the base of Spencer's driveway.

Their breath fogged in the cold morning air. They'd gotten lucky overnight—the snow had never accumulated beyond a patchy layer on the grass. But the temperature had dropped, leaving the ground frozen.

Bree's phone vibrated. She glanced at the screen. Nick West, a local reporter, was calling. She had no time to answer his questions right now, so she ignored the call. A minute later, her phone beeped with a new voice mail, which she also ignored.

Matt pointed to the house across the street. A black Honda Accord sat in the driveway. "Looks like the neighbor's home."

Bree started across the road. "Let's talk to them." She didn't want to miss the opportunity. The crime scene would still be there in twenty minutes. Who knew if the neighbor would?

They climbed the steps of the front stoop. Footsteps approached. A man who looked to be around forty opened the door in scrubs. He took in their uniforms with tired eyes. "What happened? I saw the crime scene tape at Spencer's house."

Bree introduced herself and Matt.

"I'm Dean Unger," the man said. "Did Spencer get robbed or something?"

Bree shook her head. "Unfortunately, Mr. LaForge is dead. His body was discovered yesterday evening."

Dean's mouth opened, then closed. He gave his head a small shake. "Shit. He's dead? Really?"

"Yes," Bree said.

Dean rocked backward, as if the news had been a blow. "How'd he die? I always saw him out running. He seemed healthy."

"He was murdered," Bree said bluntly, watching for his reaction.

Dean's posture snapped straight. "Whoa. How?"

Bree skirted the question. "The medical examiner hasn't declared a cause of death yet."

Dean didn't move for a couple of seconds, as if processing the information. "Wow. I don't know what to say. I deal with death every day, even shootings, but I've never known anyone personally who was murdered. It doesn't seem real. You know?"

"I assure you that it's real," Bree clarified.

Dean shook his head.

"We'd like to ask you a few questions," Matt said. "May we come in?"

"Yeah. Sure. Sorry." With a quick shake of his upper body, as if rousing himself, Dean motioned them inside. "Come back to the kitchen. I was just making breakfast before I go to sleep. It was a long night."

Bree and Matt stepped into the house and followed Dean down a hallway into the 1990s. The pickled oak kitchen cabinets, Formica counters, and faded blue-and-pink wallpaper were original, not retro. But beyond the dated kitchen was a wall of sliding glass doors and tall windows that overlooked a rolling meadow and a large pond. Thick woods framed the view.

An open carton of eggs sat next to pieces of eggshell piled on a paper towel. Four eggs had been broken into a large mixing bowl.

"Nice view," Matt said.

Dean moved behind the kitchen island and seasoned his eggs with salt and pepper. "Thanks. The view is why I bought the house. I wish I had time to renovate."

"How long have you lived here?" Bree asked.

"Two years." Dean picked up a whisk and whipped his eggs with an experienced hand. "Can I get you anything? Tea?"

"No, thank you," Bree said. "We won't keep you long."

"Do you work nights?" Matt asked.

"Yes." Dean poured the eggs into a frying pan. The mixture sizzled. "I'm a physician's assistant at the hospital."

"What time did you go to work yesterday?" Bree perched on the edge of a stool.

Dean moved his eggs around with a spatula. "I left here at four thirty. Same as always. Got home around seven this morning. We had a patient code . . ." Deep lines bracketed his frown as he remembered what had clearly been a disturbing incident. "Anyway, I usually work a twelve-hour shift. I was late getting home."

Bree folded her hands on the counter. "Have you seen any unusual activity at Spencer's house?"

Dean lowered the flame under the pan. "I saw police cars this morning, but before that, everything seemed normal."

Matt leaned a hip on the counter. "What about strange cars on the street?"

"Not that I've noticed." Dean slid two slices of bread into the toaster. "We don't get much traffic here."

"How well did you know Spencer LaForge?" Bree asked.

Dean returned to the stove, scraped the eggs from the bottom of the pan, then adjusted the burner. "Well enough to wave at him when I'm getting my mail or bringing in the garbage can."

"Did you know his family or friends?" Matt asked.

"No." Dean turned off the heat, lifted the frying pan, and dumped the scrambled eggs onto a plate. "We were not buddies. We didn't barbecue, drink beer, or watch football together. I moved here because I wanted solitude. I spend twelve hours a day with people. When I get home, I'm done peopling."

"I get that," Matt said.

Bree tried to remember the last time she'd been alone, not counting trips to the bathroom, and couldn't. Now that she thought about it, the dog even followed her into the bathroom, and sometimes Kayla talked to her from the other side of the door.

She spotted an unopened package on the counter. "When was that delivered?"

Dean glanced at it on his way to the toaster. "I assume it came yesterday after I left for work. It was at the front door when I got home this morning." He tossed his toast onto his plate.

Matt took a photo of the shipping label. "In case the delivery driver saw something."

"Have at it." Dean went to the fridge and took out a bottle of hot sauce and single-serve containers of guacamole. He shook hot sauce on his eggs and spread the guac on his toast.

"Thanks for your help." Bree left a business card on the counter. "We might be in touch if we have any more questions. Until then, we'll let you get to your breakfast."

"Thanks." Dean took a fork from a drawer. "I'm beat. Should I be concerned, Sheriff? Without Spencer, my nearest neighbor is . . . Actually, I don't even know the distance."

"At this moment, we have no reason to believe there's any threat to the community." Bree's instincts told her that Spencer's murder had been personal, but instincts weren't evidence—and they could be wrong. "You don't have an alarm?"

"No," Dean said.

"It might be worth considering," Bree said. "Be sure to lock your doors."

"I will." Dean frowned at his breakfast, as if he were no longer hungry.

Bree couldn't blame him. "Call if you have any concerns."

"OK." Dean pushed his plate aside, and his gaze drifted to the expanse of glass that spanned the rear of the house.

Great view.

So open.

But also vulnerable.

"We can see ourselves out." Matt led the way back to the front door. They went outside.

"It's a good alibi."

"Yes." Matt glanced back at Dean's place. "I didn't get any deceptive vibes from him at all, but I'll call the hospital to confirm his story."

Bree scanned the woods that loomed behind the house. The beautiful view came with a price. Isolation.

Matt tracked the package online. "We're in luck. The package was delivered at 5:20 p.m. I'm going to call the distribution center and see if we can talk to the driver." He lifted his phone to his ear and talked his way to a supervisor. A few minutes later, he lowered it.

"The driver is finishing his morning run now. He's due back at the distribution center in about twenty minutes to load up for his second route. If we hurry, we can catch him."

Chapter Eleven

In the passenger seat of the sheriff's SUV, Matt checked the driver's motor vehicle records on the dashboard computer while Bree drove toward the distribution center.

"The driver's name is Kent Barone. He's been with the delivery service for eight years." Matt scanned Kent's motor vehicle records. "He has a couple of speeding tickets, but that's all I see."

She turned into the parking lot of a huge warehouse near the entry ramp for the interstate.

"Park at the office. The supervisor is calling Barone in to talk to us while his truck is being reloaded."

Bree drove past the loading bays full of delivery vans and parked in front of the office. They went inside. The supervisor met them in the lobby and escorted them down a fluorescent hallway. "Kent's waiting for you in the break room." He jerked a thumb at the doorway.

"We won't keep him long," Bree said.

Matt led the way into a typical break room. A single refrigerator stood in the corner. Microwave ovens were lined up on the counter. Plastic chairs clustered around a few small round tables.

A tall, thin African American man in a gray uniform sat at a table. He stood as they entered, and they crossed the scuffed linoleum floor.

"Mr. Barone?" Bree asked, stopping in front of him.

"Yeah. You can call me Kent," he said.

"I'm Sheriff Taggert." Bree gestured to Matt. "And this is Criminal Investigator Flynn."

Bree took the chair across from Kent and waited for him to sit. Matt pulled another chair up to the table next to Kent.

Kent's gaze darted back and forth between Matt and Bree. "Is something wrong?"

"No," Bree assured him. "We just need to ask you a few questions about your route from yesterday evening."

"Why?" Kent asked.

Ignoring his question, Bree read off Dean Unger's street address. "You delivered a package to this house yesterday evening?"

Kent nodded. "Yeah."

"Do you deliver to that street often?" Bree asked.

Clearly uncomfortable, Kent shifted in his chair. "A couple times a week. What the hell is going on?"

"Did you notice anything unusual yesterday evening?"

"What do you mean by *unusual*?" Kent's voice rose. "I dropped the package and left. I'm on a tight schedule, especially this time of year. Business is already up for the holidays. It's like folks are already in a rush this year. Why do you want to know? Tell me what's going on," he demanded.

Bree and Matt exchanged a look. They wanted information without bias, but Kent was too worried.

"A man was killed at the house across the street," Matt said.

Kent paled. "Killed?"

"Yes," Bree said.

Kent stood abruptly, sending his chair sliding backward with a high-pitched scrape. "I didn't have anything to do with that."

"We didn't suggest that you did." Matt kept his voice calm.

Kent lifted his chin. "You are not pinning this on me."

"Of course not." Bree looked puzzled. "I assure you, you're not under suspicion."

Kent's mouth turned down in a doubtful frown.

Matt decided to stop dancing around Kent's attitude. "You're clearly upset. Can I ask why?"

"I was pulled over two weeks ago by locals for no reason." Kent spit out the words. "They pulled me from my vehicle and made me do every sobriety test they could think of. They tried to provoke me into doing something stupid. Thankfully, I am not stupid."

"Did they give you a Breathalyzer?" Bree asked.

Kent shook his head. "Nope. They knew I wasn't drunk. It was pure harassment."

Bree's brows lowered. "Were they sheriff's deputies?"

"No." Kent's jaw tightened. "And I won't say which department they were with. I don't want to start any trouble. But now you know why I'm so touchy."

"I'm sorry you experienced that, Kent." Bree's voice softened. "I assure you, we only want your help."

Matt scanned their positions. He'd wanted a clear view of Kent's body language, but he'd inadvertently boxed him in. Matt understood that he was a very large, sometimes intimidating person. Usually, that worked to his advantage, but occasionally, his stature got in the way.

Like now.

He leaned back to give Kent some room. If the man had been recently harassed by police, Matt invading his personal space wouldn't convince him to cooperate.

Kent pulled out his chair and sat back down, leaving more distance between himself and Matt. Then he gave Matt and Bree each a long look, as if making a decision. "I did see something different on that street."

Matt and Bree waited, not rushing him.

Kent licked his lips. "There's a house for sale across the street from the delivery address. I've never seen anyone there. But yesterday, I saw a vehicle in the driveway." He shrugged.

"Can you describe the vehicle?" Bree asked.

Kent closed his eyes. "It was white."

"Sedan, SUV . . . ?" Matt prompted.

Kent's eyes opened. "It was bigger than a sedan. Maybe an SUV or minivan?" Was that a statement or a question?

"You're not sure?" Bree confirmed.

"No." He looked thoughtful for a few seconds. "Sorry. I didn't pay better attention. I noticed it as I was driving away. I didn't stop to get a better look. I just noted it as odd and kept going." He brightened. "I'm pretty sure it was white, though."

Pretty sure . . .

"That's OK," Matt assured him. "We appreciate the information."

Bree drew a business card from her pocket and set it on the table. "If you remember anything else, please call me."

He took the card and nodded. "I have to get back to work."

"Thank you for your help." Bree held out her hand.

Kent shook it, then took Matt's. Kent gave him a wary eye, but he also accepted the handshake.

Back in the SUV, Bree gave the steering wheel a light punch. "I really hate asshole cops."

Matt shrugged. "There will always be assholes in every walk of life. It's part of the human condition, unfortunately."

"I know, but sometimes, that garbage behavior makes our job even harder."

Matt pulled out his phone. "On the bright side, you gave Kent a positive experience—and we got an important piece of information."

Bree started the engine. "Let's check with the realty company and see if anyone was scheduled to be at the vacant house yesterday."

"Already on it." Matt made the call. He had their answer in a few minutes. Lowering the phone to his lap, he said, "There were no showings scheduled for that house yesterday. In fact, no one has been to that address for any reason for months. The property has generated no interest."

"Let's go back and expand the scene to include the house next door." Bree turned back toward the crime scene.

She parked at Spencer's house, and they walked up the driveway of the vacant house.

"I found a footprint impression in the grass over there." Matt pointed to the area staked out with crime scene tape about thirty feet away.

"Here's a partial tread." Bree squatted at the edge of the driveway. "It looks like the vehicle parked crookedly, with the outer edge of the tire in the mud here."

Matt crouched beside her. "It's only a small slice of tread." Juries loved forensic evidence that reminded them of an episode of *CSI*, but in the real world, criminal investigations weren't as sexy.

"Not enough for a tread comparison." Bree straightened.

Matt stood. "But now we know where the killer parked."

CHAPTER TWELVE

Bree leaned a hip on the conference room table, blew across the surface of her steaming coffee, and studied the murder board. Todd sat at the table, his laptop open in front of him. Matt paced the narrow space behind the chairs. Folders and papers lay in stacks on the long table.

The victim's driver's license photo smiled back at Bree. Spencer had been a good-looking man, but there was something about him that put her off. She glanced at the next picture, Spencer with his face shrouded in plastic wrap. She imagined his last moments, and cold horror sliced through her. She shook off her revulsion and studied the picture. "Why so many layers of plastic wrap? A few would have been sufficient, but the killer kept wrapping until Spencer's features were unrecognizable."

"It wasn't to conceal his identity," Matt said. "Or they would have moved the body, not left it at the victim's own house. Sometimes killers cover their victim's faces if they don't want to be reminded of who they killed, but I'm feeling the opposite here, as if the killer's intention was to obliterate Spencer as a person."

Bree could imagine the killer winding the plastic around Spencer's head, over and over, filled to the brim with determination—and rage.

"The overkill could have been driven by emotion," she added. "Anger, resentment, jealousy . . ." She took a deep sip of coffee, and the liquid burned her tongue, but she welcomed the heat sliding down her throat. "Which brings us to the women in Spencer's life. We know he was active on dating sites. Let's start with Avery Ledger. She found him. What do we know about her?"

While she waited for Todd to pull up the information, Bree pinned Avery's photo to the board with a magnet.

Todd turned to his laptop. "Her background check is clean. She's had some minor acting roles, but her main employer is Get Fit Apparel, where she works as a social media content creator. The company maintains office space in Scarlet Falls. Her commute is about ten minutes." He scrolled. "As far as the timeline goes, she said she left work at five. I called the office. No one could confirm the exact time she left, but the manager said it was probably around then."

"Spencer was dead by five thirty. How long would it take Avery to drive to his place?"

"Maybe another ten minutes," Todd answered.

"That only gives her another ten minutes to incapacitate and kill Spencer." Bree picked up a dry erase marker and wrote out Avery's timeline.

"What if she went straight to Spencer's house from work?" Matt suggested.

Bree rolled the timeline around in her head. "The scene didn't feel rushed. Let's see if we can get some kind of physical confirmation of the time she left her office—as well as a photo to see if she changed clothes, et cetera. A few minutes either way could make a difference in the timeline. The company probably has parking lot or video surveillance cameras."

"I'll send a deputy," Todd said.

Bree filled him in on the package-delivery development. "I wish he gave us a better description than *SUV or minivan, probably white*, but that's all he would commit to."

"Better than being overly sure of himself and incorrect," Todd said.

"This is true," Bree agreed. Nothing was worse than bad information that sent the investigation in the wrong direction.

"Too bad the tire tread was insufficient."

Rarely did one piece of obscure forensic evidence break a case. Most police work was boring drudgery: interviewing witnesses, comparing statements for discrepancies, writing and reading reports, studying photos, logging every small piece of evidence in hopes it all pointed to the same suspect. Investigations were largely built on meticulous paperwork and painstaking attention to detail.

Matt spun on his heel. "Avery Ledger drives a Prius, and she would have no need to park next door. She was supposed to be at Spencer's house."

Bree tapped on Avery's photo. "Who is to say she did it alone? Maybe she had help."

"It's possible." Matt paused, his head cocked. "The murder would have been an easier job for two people, that's for sure."

Bree turned away from Avery's photo. "Do we have Spencer's phone or financial records yet?"

"No," Todd said. "But the warrants were signed first thing this morning. They've been forwarded. Records should start coming in later today."

Some companies were more cooperative than others. Banks, as highly regulated institutions, tended to be hard-asses about dotting i's and crossing t's.

Matt leaned over the table and opened a manila folder. "The techs opened Spencer's fire safe. He kept physical copies of his tax returns inside. There is no business listed. His only income came from his job at Electronics Depot." He shifted papers. "Looking at the invoices from his kitchen reno, unless he had some sort of windfall, I expect to see some deep debts on his financials."

"His brother did say Spencer lived above his means." Bree drank from her mug.

Matt stopped and rubbed his beard. "His tax returns verified he's worked at Electronics Depot for years. There's no self-employment income listed."

"So, he's not a digital marketer." Bree set down her cup.

"He lied about other things as well." Todd tapped on his keyboard. "Spencer used two dating apps, TechLove and Cool Beans. Both companies are cooperating fully. We have full access to his accounts."

Most people didn't read the terms of service before they clicked the little box at the bottom of their screen, but many smartphone apps included a disclaimer that the company could share personal information with law enforcement.

"I'm still digging into the data," Todd said. "So far, I've found nine women he dated in the past thirty days."

"Busy guy," Matt said.

"How much detail do the apps provide?" Bree asked.

Todd checked his notes. "Messages are saved for thirty days, unless the user deletes them. After thirty days, messages are purged."

"Did he date any of the women repeatedly?" Matt asked. "One bad date doesn't seem like enough to generate the kind of rage that wraps layer upon layer of plastic on a man's face."

Todd tapped his computer keyboard. "Six of Spencer's dates didn't make it beyond the initial coffee meet. According to in-app messages, three of the women refused a second date. Spencer broke it off with the other three. He actually told one woman she wasn't as attractive in person as in her dating app photos. He accused her of photo editing the pictures."

"Wow." Matt's brows lifted. "That seems harsh."

"Yeah." Todd blew out a hard breath.

"He didn't text with these women using his cell number?" Bree asked.

Todd shook his head. "He was very regimented in his approach. He didn't give any of the women his cell number until a third date was agreed upon. Three women made it to that magical third date, and in-app messaging ceased. Their conversations likely moved off the app to the cell provider at that point."

Matt said, "Then his phone records will likely pick up where the app messages leave off, but most cell providers don't keep actual texts very long."

"We'll have the time and date of his texts, just not the content." Bree held up one hand, fingers crossed. "We can hope for more data."

"An interesting note on the in-app messaging I've reviewed so far," Todd said. "Not only did Spencer lie about everything, it seems he tailored his imaginary background to what he thought they wanted to hear."

"Example?" Bree asked.

The chair legs squeaked as Todd rocked back and stretched his neck. "In their first conversations, Avery talked about her niece. Spencer responded with a story about his brother's kids, but we know Jasper doesn't have any children. Another woman told stories about her dog. Spencer responded with his own story about the golden retriever he lost to cancer last year. He told her he was so heartbroken that he couldn't bring himself to get another dog yet."

"Didn't Jasper say Spencer was too much of a neat freak for pets that shed?" Matt asked.

"He did." Bree nodded.

"Basically, he lied to all of the women he dated." Todd shifted forward again. "He created the persona he thought they'd like."

"How would you keep all the lies straight?" Matt's question sounded rhetorical. "Seems like a lot of work."

"Right?" Bree agreed. "I'd never be able to keep track."

Todd shrugged. "Since it appears he didn't go out with any one woman more than five or six times, it didn't matter. He wasn't looking for a long-term relationship."

"Jealousy is a potential motive," Bree said.

"So is anger and revenge," Matt added.

Bree frowned. "What do we know about the three women?"

"We already discussed Avery Ledger." Todd scrolled on his computer. "Monica Linfield is a model-slash-actress, and Farah Rock is a technical writer. They're both attractive—and local. I'll print their photos." He clicked the touchpad. The printer in the corner chugged and spit out two images.

Matt retrieved them and put them on the board next to Avery Ledger's photo. "It seems Spencer has a very specific type."

All three women were in their midtwenties, slender, with long dark hair.

"Is Spencer's brother, Jasper, still on our suspect list?" Todd asked.

"For now, yes," Bree answered. "But we have no evidence to link him to the scene—or to his brother."

Todd pointed to his laptop screen. "We have his computer and his cell phone. The techs are working on getting access to those today."

"The autopsy is scheduled for eleven thirty." Bree checked the time on her phone. It was nearly eleven o'clock. "Matt and I will attend. Todd, dig into the backgrounds of the three women Spencer recently dated at least three times. See if you can rule any of them out." Her gaze slid to the murder board. "We have more than enough motivation. Now we need evidence."

CHAPTER THIRTEEN

By eleven thirty, Matt stood in the autopsy suite and stared through his face shield at the body on the stainless-steel table. Next to him, Bree crossed her arms and did the same. The ME had started the autopsy ahead of schedule. In front of them, Spencer LaForge's naked body lay exposed, except for the plastic wrap that still covered his head. His full-sleeve tattoo was unimpressive, a hodgepodge of unrelated, mediocre ink. Overhead lights glared down mercilessly, exposing every dark secret. Nothing could hide.

It wasn't the gore factor that made an autopsy hard for him to watch. It was the cold, sterile surroundings. He knew the victim was no longer present in a sentient way, but the clinical treatment of their body still made him a little heartsick. Every dead body was also a spouse, sibling, or child. He worked hard to never forget that.

But there was only one way to determine how someone died. Dr. Jones treated every victim with respect, yet she still had to dissect their body.

"You haven't missed too much. We're still on the external exam." Dr. Jones waved a hand over the corpse. The body would have been painstakingly photographed and searched for trace evidence before it was undressed. Then the entire process was repeated after the clothing was removed. The clothing would be sent to the crime lab for further analysis. "The victim is male and in good physical condition. I found no sign of sexual assault on external examination." She drew a circle in the air over the hip area. "As we discussed at the scene, these burn marks indicate the use of a stun gun to incapacitate the victim."

Matt counted. "He was zapped three times."

Bree said, "Which explains why the ligature marks are so faint."

"He didn't do much struggling." Dr. Jones pointed to the victim's left elbow. "There are bruises and abrasions on the left side of the body, likely from falling and hitting a hard and rough surface after being stunned." She indicated a scrape on the underside of the victim's jaw.

"Like the paver patio?" Matt asked.

"Yes." Dr. Jones picked up a pair of scissors. "I'm going to cut the plastic and remove the layers intact, as this will be the best way to preserve both the method of wrapping and any trace evidence in the layers."

She snipped the plastic wrap from bottom to top and carefully separated the edges. Silence fell over the autopsy suite. The victim was definitely Spencer. Matt had seen his driver's license photo. A piece of duct tape covered Spencer's mouth, but that wasn't the biggest shock.

The word *liar* had been carved into Spencer's forehead.

Matt swallowed, his mouth dry.

Bree cleared her throat. "Did the mutilation occur before or after death?"

Dr. Jones examined the inside of the plastic wrap. "Before. There's blood here, so probably before."

If the wounds had occurred after death, they would not have bled much. Once the heart stopped beating, blood no longer circulated but began to pool in the lowest parts of the body.

"The edges of the wounds are clean, so they were carved by a sharp blade." Dr. Jones continued to peer at the plastic wrap. "See this moisture? It's a by-product of respiration."

Bree shifted her weight. "So, the plastic was definitely put on while he was alive and breathing."

"Yes," Dr. Jones agreed. "Its presence supports asphyxia due to suffocation as the cause of death. Smothering is also confirmed by presence of cyanosis." Lack of oxygen tinted the skin blue. "And petechial hemorrhages on the eyelids." She pointed to red dots that appeared when blood vessels in the skin ruptured due to intense pressure. They were common in deaths by strangulation, hanging, or smothering. After the morgue assistant took photographs, Dr. Jones peeled off the duct tape. "I see more petechial hemorrhages in the mouth. What's this?" She picked up a magnifying glass and leaned closer to the plastic wrap. "Looks like some kind of animal fur." Using tweezers, she plucked the item from the plastic, then moved to a microscope on the other side of the room. Holding the end of the tweezers under the lens, she said, "Don't hold me to this. We'll need to send this for DNA analysis, but cat fur tends to be finer than dog fur or human hair. This looks like fur from a long-haired black cat."

Dr. Jones bagged the hair, then reached for a scalpel and approached the victim's side. The next step was for her to make the Y-incision and begin the internal examination.

Matt inched away from the table. Bree caught his eye and nodded toward the exit. Seemed they were of the same mind. He'd watch the entire autopsy if he felt it would help him solve the case, but autopsies were gross, and the investigation was short on time.

"Thank you, Doctor," Bree said.

"I'll call you if I find anything else interesting." Dr. Jones pressed the tip of the scalpel to the victim's collarbone.

Matt turned toward the exit. He pushed through to the antechamber with Bree right behind him. The saw started up with a high-pitched whine as the autopsy suite doors swung shut behind them.

"The cat fur could have come from anywhere." Bree stripped off her face shield and mask. "It's impossible to have pets without the fur getting everywhere. I find Ladybug and Vader fur in the weirdest places. It's worse than Kayla's glitter."

Matt tossed his used gown into the labeled bin. "Brody's undercoat almost seems magnetic. I keep a lint roller in my glove compartment."

"And one in my desk." Bree stopped, her head cocked. "Fur from a long-haired black cat goes on the list."

"We can hope forensics pulls more evidence from the plastic wrap." Matt stopped at a sink to scrub his hands, even though he hadn't touched a single thing in the autopsy suite.

"I doubt there'll be prints." Bree did the same. "Everyone knows to wear gloves nowadays."

"True." Matt dried his hands. "We can hope for a human hair."

"What do you think about the word on his forehead?" Bree asked.

"I think it confirms the possibility that his murder was personal and suggests we're on the right track by investigating the women he dated."

"I agree." Bree checked her phone. "I need to get to the horse auction. We don't really have the time, but I promised the kids. I won't let them down."

Matt checked his watch. "We'll consider it our lunch hour."

Bree snorted. "As if we ever actually take a lunch hour."

"Todd is still working the investigation. You're delegating now, remember. That means you get to share the load. We'll have time to interview Monica Linfield and Farah Rock afterward."

They reached the SUV and Bree opened her vehicle door. "I know the work is being done, and Todd is more than capable."

"But?"

"I still have control issues."

"At least you know your faults." Matt shook his head, and they climbed into the SUV. "You know you can't keep Todd busy with phones and paperwork forever."

"He was in charge of the crime scene."

Matt gave her a look. "You know what I mean."

"You're right." Bree huffed. "But last time he got more actively involved in an investigation, he was kidnapped and almost killed."

"Yep," Matt agreed. "But he needs to get back out there before he starts to doubt himself. There's a horseback-riding analogy . . ."

"Ugh. Am I damaging his self-confidence?"

"Not yet," Matt said. "But if you keep him under wraps, he could interpret that as you losing faith in him, which would be a serious blow to his confidence. Has he given you any reason to doubt his ability to do his job?"

"No." Bree blew out a long breath. "Have you seen any signs that he isn't up to the task?"

"No. He seems OK. Eager to get back to it."

She pulled out her cell phone and called Todd. "Matt and I are tied up with something. Would you interview Spencer's manager and coworkers at Electronics Depot? He's been there for years. See if he made any enemies or anyone there noticed unusual behavior recently."

"Really?" Todd sounded almost excited.

"Yes."

"I'm on it." Enthusiasm rang in Todd's voice as he signed off.

Bree pocketed her phone. Stress lines bracketed her mouth. "That was hard."

"It was the right thing to do. Todd needs to get back into the field."

"I know, but I don't want anything bad to happen to him. We've already been shot at on this case."

"Todd's a cop. You can't shield him from what he wants to be," Matt said. "Besides, statistically patrol is more dangerous than working investigations."

"I know."

Domestic disturbances and traffic stops were the worst.

Bree's phone buzzed. She glanced at the screen. "Nick West. Again."

"You have to deal with the press," Matt warned.

"I know. I'll do a press conference later today, after we have a little more information." Because if she didn't release enough details, the media would speculate and dig. No good ever came of that.

CHAPTER FOURTEEN

Trying to suppress her worry about her chief deputy, Bree started the engine. Matt was correct. This was her issue, not Todd's.

"Are we stopping for the horse trailer?" Matt asked from the passenger seat.

"We are. I'm being optimistic today."

"Nice."

She drove home, where they hooked the horse trailer to the farm truck. Matt drove the big pickup, and Bree followed in her official SUV because she needed to be prepared to respond to an emergency if necessary.

They parked in the dirt lot at the auction. The sun shone from a dazzling blue winter sky. Bree grabbed a halter and lead rope from the trailer and slung them over her shoulder.

Matt gave the ground a dubious glance. "Let's be quick. If this mud thaws, the trailer is going to get stuck."

Bree quickened her pace. They left the sunny parking area for the large auction barn. Inside felt colder than outside. They walked between rows of pens. Steam rose from animals' backs. Some milled around, stamping nervous feet. Others stood with heads hanging. An occasional thin whinny pierced the freezing air.

"So many horses." Matt stepped around a pile of manure. "I want to take them all home."

"I know it." Bree focused ahead, bypassing a corral containing seven mules and another full of yearlings. A gorgeous chestnut quarter horse caught her eye. But he shied away, his eyes wide and white-rimmed, as she approached him. She backed away. "I don't need fancy. I need sound and sensible."

Not only was Adam an occasional rider at best, but Bree didn't have the skill or time to train a youngster properly. Plus, she had to consider Kayla, who ran through the barn and pasture like a wild child. A well-mannered, mature horse would fit into their lifestyle.

Ahead, a half dozen horses crowded together in the corner of a pen. Resting her elbows on the top wooden slat, she assessed the animals. "I like the looks of the Standardbred. Number three sixty-five." She referred to the number on the horse's hip sticker. Bree slipped into the pen and easily moved the Standardbred aside. His dark brown coat was shaggy and caked with mud. His gaze was soft as Bree slipped the halter over his head. He cooperated like a gentleman, lowering his head a few inches so she could easily fasten the buckle. She rubbed the crest of his neck, and he leaned into her touch.

Matt opened the gate, and she led the brown horse into the aisle. Four of the animals stood back, but a huge black draft horse crowded the gate, trying to squeeze his enormous body through before Matt closed the latch. Matt halted him with a hand on his nose. The draft horse pressed his chest against the slats. The boards groaned.

"Easy, big boy. Your pal will be back in a few." Matt gave his big head a scratch.

While Matt held the lead rope, Bree examined the Standardbred gelding.

"I'm no expert, but he looks younger than I first thought." She ran her hand along his side. Under the mud, his ribs protruded a bit more than they should have, but he wasn't in terrible condition. "Some weight and a good grooming would help."

"He's quiet," Matt said.

"He does have nice manners." She felt along the horse's spine. He didn't react. She bent a knee and asked Matt to give her a leg up.

"Sure." He lifted her by the shin and boosted her onto the horse's back as if she weighed nothing.

Even in the busy stockyard barn with only a halter and lead rope, the brown horse trotted up and down the aisle, turning and stopping politely when asked. She didn't detect a limp in his gait as she brought him back to Matt.

Bree slid to the ground. "Erin was the more experienced horsewoman. I wish she was here." She rubbed at the sudden pressure behind her heart.

Most of the time, she felt as if she'd come to terms with her sister's death, but grief still ambushed her at random moments, and she occasionally felt guilty, as if her own joy had come at the expense of her sister's life. Her new life with the kids—with Matt—held a richness she hadn't even known possible.

Matt rested a hand on her shoulder. His touch brought her back to the present. "Your sister would want you to be happy, and she'd be thrilled about what you're doing today."

"How do you always know what I'm thinking?"

"We're in tune." His smile sent warmth radiating through her.

"We are." Feeling all sorts of content, she turned back to the horse. "It's nice that Adam wants to continue the family tradition of rescuing unwanted horses."

"It's all he wants for his birthday," she said.

Her relationship with her brother had also deepened since she'd moved back to her hometown. They'd both made the effort, and they were becoming a family in more than just name.

She checked a sheet posted on the side of the pen. "Number three sixty-five, Amish buggy horse, broke to ride and drive. Seventeen years old. That's all it says." She slid the paper back into the hanging folder.

"I like him."

"Me too," Bree agreed. "Amish buggy horses have high mileage, but they're accustomed to traffic and noise, so they're generally easygoing. He seems sound."

She ran her hands up and down the horse's legs. He had some lumps and bumps, to be expected for a horse with a lot of blacktop under his hooves. She lifted his feet and examined his hooves. "Needs trimming but his feet are in decent shape." After years of being a working beast, living on Bree's farm and going on an occasional easy trail ride would be a nice retirement for this handsome boy.

"Are you going to bid on him?" Matt patted the horse's neck. Dust billowed.

"I am." Bree hated to put him back in the pen, but he went willingly. "It feels right."

The draft horse nickered as the two horses greeted one another.

"What about his buddy?" Matt pointed to the draft horse.

Bree consulted the sheet again. "Percheron, also broke to ride and drive. Fourteen years old."

"That's a lot of horse."

"Yes." Bree forced herself to look away. She couldn't rescue them all. But damn, his sad nicker renewed the ache in her chest—in the same place that housed her grief for Erin. What would she do with a draft horse? He was enormous, standing close to eighteen hands high.

"He has a gash on his rear leg," Matt said.

Bree turned back and craned her head to assess the Percheron's wound. Blood dripped above his hock. "That looks fresh. He was probably kicked."

Matt's voice went tight. "Lameness won't improve his chances of scoring a decent home. He'll probably get picked up by the kill buyer."

Bree sighed. "Probably."

"Can you ride a horse like that?"

"Definitely. Percherons were warhorses. They needed big, strong horses to carry knights and heavy armor."

"If I were interested in a horse of my own, what kind would you recommend for me?" Matt asked, his eyes on the Percheron.

Bree shoved her cold hands into her jacket pockets and surveyed the pen. The Percheron was nudging the Standardbred with a giant nose. A true beast of burden, he had probably done the heavy moving on the farm. She would bet he'd pulled everything from plows to tree stumps.

She turned back to Matt. He was a big-boned six foot three. With his reddish-brown hair and trimmed beard, he often reminded Bree of a Hollywood Viking, but today maybe a medieval knight would make a better comparison. He was certainly capable of swinging a broadsword or battle-ax.

She glanced between Matt and the giant horse and smiled. "A big one."

Matt grinned back. "Can we check him out?"

"Let's do it."

The Percheron followed Matt out of the pen, as eager as a puppy. Luckily, he was wearing a halter, because the one Bree had brought wasn't big enough for his ginormous head. One by one, Bree lifted his dinner-plate-size feet. He stood quietly as she ran her hands over his body and legs, looking for sore spots. Like his pal, he was a little underweight but not drastically. The gash worried her. "He's favoring that leg. I can't really assess his soundness."

Matt ran a hand across collar marks at the base of the muscular neck. "He's worked hard."

"He has."

"Interest in that one, Sheriff?" a shaky voice asked.

Bree turned to see a wiry old man in a heavy canvas coat and work boots approaching. He looked like he'd walked out of a Louis L'Amour novel.

"Maybe." She pointed at the Standardbred. "We're also thinking about that gelding. Do you know anything about either of them?"

"I do." The old man held out a hand. "I'm Stanley Dutt. I work here."

Bree gave his arthritic hand a gentle shake and introduced Matt.

"They came from the Abrams farm. Old Josiah died about a month ago. His son doesn't want to take over the farm, so he's selling everything." Dutt shook his head. "Anyway, those are two nice animals. They have a bit of wear on them, but they're both still willing to work. The Standardbred was a solid buggy horse." He reached forward and gave the Percheron a nose rub. "This big guy looks intimidating, but Josiah's grandkids used to run under his belly and pile on him bareback, not that I'm advocating such behavior. Just saying the horse isn't spooky or shy. He can't get enough attention."

"Thanks for the information." Bree turned back to the horse. Now was the time to test the old man's story. "Boost me up."

"OK." Matt gave her a leg up.

Bree felt like a child on the broadback. In deference to the horse's leg injury, she simply walked him a few paces down the aisle. She neck-reined with the lead rope and turned him around like a bus in a tight parking lot. She brought him back to Matt. "He acts like a gentleman."

"Of course he does." Dutt pulled a can of chewing tobacco from his back pocket and stuck a pinch between his cheek and gum.

"Good thing." Matt grinned. "He must weigh close to two thousand pounds."

"You really want him?" Bree asked.

"I do." Matt put the Percheron back in the pen. "Can I board him at your place?"

"Of course. You're there almost every day anyway."

His grin widened. "I am."

"Then let's go buy some horses."

"I'm glad." Dutt spit in the dirt. "I was worried for them." He turned away. "Good luck to you."

"Do you know their names?" Bree called to him.

"They deserve new names for their new lives, don't cha think?" he answered over his shoulder.

Bree picked up the Standardbred at a reasonable price. But the kill buyer was very interested in the Percheron, and Matt had to bid over the going price per pound. Still, a short time later, they completed the paperwork and walked the two horses through the parking lot.

"I only prepped to bring one horse home." She offered both horses a drink from the single bucket. "They'll have to share the hay net."

"They'll be fine." Matt relocated the net to the trailer's divider so the animals could share their snack. "It's a short drive."

The animals both loaded with no hesitation. Though the Percheron had to duck his head a little, he did so willingly.

Matt slid behind the wheel of the farm pickup truck. "This is nice."

"It is." She stepped back, allowing him to close the vehicle door.

He lowered the window. "I know we've only been together for a short time, but everything about this"—Matt waved in the general direction of the trailer hitched behind the truck—"feels right."

Like they were building something together—something that still had plenty of room to grow. The feeling filled Bree with warmth, like standing in a patch of sun on a clear winter day.

She stepped up on the running board and kissed him through the open window. "I agree."

Matt kissed her back. "Let's take our new babies home and get them settled in."

"The kids are going to be so excited." And Bree was looking forward to sharing their joy. Nothing gave her pleasure like seeing them happy. "Maybe some animals in need of TLC will help the kids get through Christmas."

"That's going to be hard for all of you, the first without Erin."

"It will." Bree glanced back at the trailer. Could she make it easier, or was rebounding grief a part of the healing process they needed to work through? She wished for the former but suspected she'd have to accept the latter. "Kayla will want to name them both."

Matt laughed and jerked a thumb over his shoulder. "That big boy doesn't look like a Pumpkin," he said, referring to Kayla's own little horse. "Or a Disney character."

"Ha! Good luck with that." She couldn't wait to watch Matt field hundreds of name suggestions from an enthusiastic and persistent eight-year-old.

Bree returned to her own vehicle and followed the horse trailer out of the lot. A half hour later, they parked at the farm. Contentment bloomed inside her. Who would have thought she would enjoy such domesticity?

She jumped from the SUV and opened the barn doors. Pumpkin, Riot, and Cowboy stood at the pasture gate, curious about the newcomers. "Give me a few minutes to prep another stall."

She raked the dirt, spread fresh straw, and filled a water bucket. Back outside, she spotted Dana and the kids emerging from the house. School had been a half day for some administrative reason. Bree couldn't keep track. Dana sported a bright blue hat over her short and shaggy blonde-and-gray hair. Luke wore a grin as wide as his face. Kayla bolted from the porch steps with an excited squeal.

Luke caught his little sister by the hood. "Easy. They're new. Let's not spook them."

"OK." Kayla slowed to a deliberate walk.

Dana shoved her hands deep into the pockets of her down parka. "Did you get one?"

"We got two." Matt lowered the ramp at the rear of the trailer, then opened the side door. He backed the Standardbred down the ramp. "This guy is for Adam."

Dana reached out to give his neck a pat. "He's sweet."

"I love him!" Kayla clamped her hands under her chin, prayer-style.

Bree took the brown horse's lead rope. The kids came over to pet him. The horse dropped his head and sniffed their pockets. She suspected his former owner's grandkids had brought him treats.

Matt backed the Percheron out of the trailer.

"Holy hell—cow," corrected Dana. "He's a tank."

"He's my tank." Matt rubbed behind the draft horse's ear. When he stopped, the Percheron gave him a gentle nudge, as if asking for more pets.

"You got a horse too?" Luke asked. "He's cool."

"Is he really yours, Matt?" Kayla bounced over.

The Percheron didn't even blink at her exuberance. Instead, he lowered his head so she could pet his nose, then he snorted and blew snotty hay all over Kayla's clothes. As a farm kid, she barely blinked at the mess on her jacket. Kayla rested a small hand between his nostrils. Her mouth opened in a nearly reverent O. "He's beau-ti-ful." She drew out the word. "What's his name?"

"I don't know yet," Matt said.

"He looks like Mulan's horse, Khan, or Angus from *Brave*." Kayla was an expert on Disney animals. "But he could be the Beast too."

"Beast." Luke laughed. "I like it."

"He's too big to name after a cartoon," Matt protested.

"Wow." Dana circled the horse, giving him a wide berth. "He's huge."

"He's been pretty docile so far," Matt said.

Dana inched closer and held out a tentative hand. As a born-and-bred city girl, she hadn't had much exposure to horses until she'd moved to Bree's farm. She would pat noses and hand out carrots, but Bree had not been able to tempt her friend to learn to ride yet.

The Percheron arched his neck, and Bree swore the horse batted his eyelashes at Dana.

"You are a charmer." Dana stepped forward and stroked his neck.

Bree turned to Luke. "I have to go back to work after I get them settled. The vet is coming to stitch the Percheron's leg in about an hour. Can you handle it?"

"Sure." Luke had inherited his mother's horsemanship. He took the lead rope from Matt. "I'd better hose off his leg for now."

"Good thinking." Bree led the Standardbred into the barn, settled him in his new stall, and gave him some hay.

A few minutes later, Luke brought the draft horse inside and put him away.

Kayla followed them in. "Should we call Uncle Adam and tell him? He's going to be so excited."

Bree tossed a flake of hay over the big horse's stall door. She looked at the enthusiastic little girl. "I thought you wanted to surprise him?"

"I do. But I want to tell him right now too." Kayla bounced on her toes.

Bree pulled out her phone and dialed her brother's number on speaker. The call rang three times before Adam's recorded voice asked her to leave a message. "Adam, it's Bree. Call Luke when you get this message." She pressed "End." "There. You two can decide what to tell him when he calls back." Because her brother could be forgetful and spacey when he was working, she also sent him a text with the same message.

"I can't decide!" Kayla bounced again, her face scrunched in happy conflict.

Bree grinned. The decision would be a good distraction for Kayla, better than thinking about celebrating the upcoming holiday without her mom—or even worse, the anniversary of Erin's death, which was also approaching fast.

"You can go, Aunt Bree." Luke latched the door. "I've got this."

"I know you do." In the midst of a seemingly endless growth spurt, he was several inches taller than her. She rested her head on his shoulder. "I just wish I could hang out and share the moment with you guys."

"What you do is important," Luke said. "We'll hang out later."

"Thanks for helping." Bree's eyes misted. Damn. Why did that happen so often? And for no reason other than she was proud or happy.

"It's what family does, right?"

"Right," Bree agreed, even though she felt like she was still learning what families were supposed to do. Until then, she was totally winging it.

CHAPTER FIFTEEN

On the way to Scarlet Falls, Matt watched the scenery flash past the passenger vehicle window. The literal enormity of what he'd done dawned on him. "I can't believe I bought a horse."

"Me either." Bree grinned at him from behind the wheel. "And that's a *lot* of horse."

Matt suffered a quick jolt of unease, then shoved it back.

"Don't look so worried." Bree glanced at him. "His leg will probably heal just fine. But what's the worst that can happen? He's lame, and you are the proud owner of a two-thousand-pound dog? You love big dogs."

"I do." Matt laughed. "And you have a point."

"You rescued him because he stole your heart. You didn't buy him as a show-jumping prospect."

"You're right." Matt shoved aside his buyer's remorse. The horse wasn't a new car he'd bought on impulse. He was a living, breathing creature who needed a safe place to land, which Matt would give him regardless of his potential as a riding horse.

The GPS announced their arrival, and Bree turned into Monica Linfield's condo complex.

Matt surveyed the rows of luxury vehicles. The small town neighbored Grey's Hollow. Though Scarlet Falls had its own police department, as part of Randolph County, it was also included in Bree's jurisdiction.

Bree pointed to an SUV. "There's her Audi Q5."

"A white one," Matt noted.

Empty parking spaces were marked with numbers that clearly corresponded with the actual units. Bree pulled her SUV into a row marked GUEST PARKING. They stepped out of the vehicle and walked past the cluster mailbox. Units were arranged in a U-shape around a rectangle of well-manicured green space.

Matt knocked on Monica's front door. Bree stood on the other side of the stoop, so they flanked the door. The previous day's shooting was fresh on his mind.

The door opened, and a tall, slender brunette blinked at them. Monica Linfield's driver's license photo did not do her justice. Matt considered Bree to be the most beautiful woman in the world. But he couldn't fail to recognize this model was gorgeous in an artsy way, with long, shiny hair and a lean, bony face highlighted with dramatic makeup. Black yoga pants and a slim white sweater draped her long-legged frame. She was stunning, but there was something about her that was also . . . too poised? No, too *posed*. Her stance seemed as unnatural as the deep red of her lips and the thick sweep of her fake eyelashes.

She scanned their uniforms, then her eyebrows dipped in a concerned V. "Can I help you?"

"I'm Sheriff Taggert." Bree gestured toward Matt. "And this is Criminal Investigator Flynn."

"Ma'am." Matt nodded.

Bree turned back to the woman. "Are you Monica Linfield?"

Her eyes widened and her posture tensed in alarm. "Yes. What's wrong?"

Police on the doorstep rarely meant good news.

Bree didn't keep her waiting. "Do you know Spencer LaForge?"

She nodded, and her shoulders curled forward.

Bree continued. "We'd like to ask you a few questions about him."

Her eyes brightened with moisture, as if she were going to cry. She blinked hard. She clearly wasn't over Spencer. She hugged her own waist with both arms. "Why?"

Matt felt eyes on him and turned his head. A neighbor watched from the mailboxes. As he met her gaze, the older woman quickly averted her eyes, shoved her key into the slot, and retrieved her mail. Matt faced Monica again.

Bree hesitated. Clearly, she did not want to tell Monica about Spencer's death while they stood on the doorstep.

"Can we come inside?" Matt asked in a gentle voice.

"OK." Though Monica sounded reluctant, she opened the door wider and moved back to give them room.

Bree and Matt stepped across the threshold into a sleek, modern space that looked weirdly perfect, more like a photo shoot than a living room.

Monica closed the door. "Please sit down."

She crossed the room, her steps gliding, as if she were walking the runway instead of pale gray wall-to-wall. She stopped in front of a white leather couch. Elegantly folding her long limbs, she sank onto the cushion, pulled a throw pillow onto her lap, and hugged it.

Bree sat next to her. Matt eased into a pencil-legged chair, almost surprised it held his weight. Those skinny legs must be titanium.

Bree rested her folded hands on her knees. "Have you seen the news, ma'am?"

"No." Monica shook her head. "I was in a bathing-suit shoot all day yesterday. The wind machine kept malfunctioning. When they got it running, it would only function on high. The director yelled for hours. I thought his head was going to explode. What a disaster." She touched her temple, as if the memory gave her a headache. "I got home late, went straight to bed, and slept in this morning. I have to work again tomorrow, and I needed the rest."

"Spencer LaForge died yesterday evening," Bree said. Her words sounded more like a death notification than questioning a witness.

"Spencer is dead?" Shock turned Monica's expression blank for a few seconds as she seemed to process the news. Then she burst into tears.

Without a word, Matt picked up a box of tissues from an end table and handed it to her.

She accepted the box and sobbed, "Thank you," in a breaking voice.

"We're sorry for your loss," Matt said.

Monica and Spencer had dated only a few times, but the news of his death had upset her. Yet there was something about her emotions that didn't feel entirely genuine. Tears poured from her eyes, but her face remained strangely devoid of expression. Monica was a model, but maybe she was a decent actress too. Her shock could be fake. Something about her felt off. Usually, Matt was better at reading people's emotions.

"I'm sorry." Her breaths hitched. She plucked a tissue from the box and dried her eyes. Composing herself with a deep, shaky inhalation, she brushed a strand of long hair off her face. "What happened to him?"

"He was killed." Bree stuck with vague.

"Killed?" Monica's voice squeaked. "In a car accident or something?"

"No, ma'am." Bree paused, as if deciding how much information to give her. "He was murdered."

"Murdered?" Monica sobbed.

She cried into a tissue for a few seconds, then shuddered and lifted her head. Somehow, crying didn't make her eyes red or puffy. Her skin was still flawless. She managed to look both devastated *and* camera-ready.

She pulled an elastic band off her wrist, gathered her long hair, and arranged it in a bun on top of her head. Long tendrils framed her face. "He broke off our relationship last week." More tears threatened to spill over. Her eyes went bright, sparking with anger before shifting back into sadness.

"Did he say why?" Bree asked.

She shook her head hard. "Not really. He said some stuff about our chemistry not feeling strong enough." Her face tightened, and her next words sounded bitter. "But our chemistry was good enough to sleep with me."

Bree made a noncommittal yet empathetic noise. "How many dates did you have with him?"

Instead of answering, Monica started sobbing again. Was she trying to evade the question? Again, her response didn't feel entirely authentic, and Matt couldn't identify why.

Bree waited for Monica to compose herself, then repeated the question. "How many times did you go out with Spencer?"

"Five." Monica sniffed. "But to me, it felt like more. Then, after our fifth date, he sent me a text saying we were through. He wasn't *feeling it*. Can you believe that? He broke up with me in a damned text." She looked to Matt.

"That was rude," he said, commiserating. Then took a poke at her anger. "Did that make you mad?"

"I would have been furious," Bree agreed.

"Of course I was mad," Monica snapped. Then she pressed a knuckle to her mouth. "I was angry and sad and depressed." She swiped a tear off her cheek. "I've never been dumped before."

Now that Matt could believe.

"I can't believe he's dead," Monica said.

Bree jumped in. "Did you go to his house?"

Monica nodded at her. "Twice."

"Did you see his snakes?" Matt asked.

She frowned, her eyes narrowing. Her words were clipped, as if she were offended. "I hope that isn't an inappropriate euphemism."

"No, ma'am," Matt said with no trace of humor. He held eye contact. "Spencer had a reptile collection, including snakes."

"Oh." Monica shuddered. "I didn't see one, and he never mentioned having any weird collection."

"You said you were on a shoot all day yesterday. What time did you finish?" Bree kept her voice casual, but the question was key.

Monica wasn't fooled. Her tears shut off like she'd tightened a spigot. "Are you asking me for an alibi?"

"It would be great if you had one." Bree lifted a shoulder. "The more people I can rule out quickly, the better. When and where was the shoot?"

"We worked from eight in the morning until nine last night." Monica gave them the address of a studio in an office park.

"You were there all day?" Bree asked.

Monica nodded. Matt pulled his phone from his pocket, opened the note app, and typed in the address. "Can you give us a name or two, people who could corroborate your hours?"

"Sure." Monica picked up her phone from the coffee table and read off two names and phone numbers. "They're both models who worked the shoot with me."

"Thank you." Matt noted the names and numbers, then dropped his cell phone back into his pocket. "Did Spencer ever mention getting a threat or having an altercation?"

Monica lowered her phone to her lap. "No, but I'm not sure how honest he really was with me. The breakup felt . . . insincere. One week he was falling in love with me. After we slept together twice, he was over me. Frankly, I felt used."

Bree wrapped up the interview, and they returned to her vehicle. She slid behind the wheel. "Real or fake tears?"

"Both." In the passenger seat, Matt fastened his seat belt. "She was mad and sad about the breakup. The tears over his death didn't feel as authentic."

"That was my impression too." Bree glanced over. "I'm not a good judge of tears, though."

Matt shrugged. "While I was growing up, the house was full of Cady's friends. When they were teenagers, someone was always crying. In my limited experience, real tears tend to be messy. Ms. Linfield didn't smudge her lipstick or mascara."

"Good observation." Bree pulled away from the curb. "We need to verify her alibi anyway. Can you plug the address of that film studio into the GPS? I want to drive by."

When they reached the studio, Matt went inside and spoke with a cameraman, but it wasn't the same crew who had worked the previous day. He stopped at the receptionist's desk, where the young woman checked the studio schedule and confirmed the hours of the shoot. She also obtained the surveillance videos for the previous day and emailed them to Matt.

When he returned to the car, Bree was writing in a spiral notepad. "Both of Monica's model friends confirm her alibi."

"But they're her friends, so that doesn't mean all that much," Matt said. "I have the surveillance video from the studio."

"Forward it to Todd. He can have a deputy review it."

The evidence was mounting. Hopefully, they would accumulate enough to separate the truth from the lies.

CHAPTER SIXTEEN

Todd hovered over a stack of paperwork. His stomach grumbled. He'd missed lunch. He considered running through a drive-through but resisted. He was in training for an IRONMAN competition and tried to avoid fast food. Instead of giving in to temptation, he texted Cady.

HAVE TIME FOR A LATE LUNCH?

YES, she responded. YOUR PLACE?

He typed, PERFECT.

He'd been dating Matt's sister for a few months. After the trauma of being kidnapped, Todd had learned that taking a small chunk of time for a normal activity, even in the middle of an important investigation, could help him maintain balance, manage his stress, and curtail burnout.

He used to roll his eyes at the term *self-care*, but no more. He would actively try to not work 24/7 in the future. Everyone needed to breathe.

He drove home. Cady had a key and was already inside when he arrived. His yellow lab, Goldie, met him at the door. At seven months, she was a long-legged, good-natured chewing machine. Todd had adopted her after a friend had died on the last major case—the one when Todd had been kidnapped.

Goldie jumped on his leg but sat when asked, though her butt bounced on the floor. Todd toed off his boots and set them in the closet next to Cady's. Seeing their shoes lined up together made his house feel more like a home.

"I already walked her." Cady stood at the stove, wielding a spatula. She wore jeans, a sweatshirt, and thick socks. Her face was bare, and her long strawberry blonde hair was pulled back into a ponytail. "I know you're short on time, so I thought I'd start lunch."

Todd swept aside her ponytail and kissed the back of her neck. "What are we having?"

She leaned back against him. "Grilled cheese sandwiches and tomato soup." She flipped the sandwiches, then gave the saucepan of soup a stir.

They brought the food to the table and sat for a quiet lunch. Goldie slept with her head on Todd's foot. Cady talked about the progress she was making with her current crop of rescue dogs. Todd, needing a mental break, just listened.

As if she knew he needed the time, she talked for ten minutes before asking, "How is your case?"

"It's OK."

She gave him the assessing look he'd grown accustomed to, the one that double-checked that he wasn't answering on reflex.

"Really," he said. "I'm paying attention, which is why I'm taking this break."

"Good." She picked up the crust of her sandwich and dunked it in her soup.

When lunch was over, Cady waved him toward the door. "I'll take the dog out again before I leave. Let me know if you need me to pick her up later. I can always take her to my place for the night. It's good for her to socialize with my crew." Cady had four dogs of her own.

"Thanks." Todd kissed her on the mouth.

"I promised I would help with her when I talked you into adopting her."

"You did." A smile tugged at the corners of his mouth. An early marriage and divorce had left him lackluster on dating. Then Cady had come along, for which he was ever grateful. "I'll call you later."

The comfort food and her company cleared his head better than if he'd taken a long nap. With his belly and heart full, he drove to Electronics Depot. The freezing wind cut into his face as he crossed the parking lot. His nerves jangled as much as his duty belt. Interviewing a store manager should be routine for him, but this was the first time since he'd been kidnapped that the sheriff had assigned him an investigative task out of the office. He hoped she hadn't lost faith in him. Bree said it wasn't his fault, but he still felt stupid about letting himself get ambushed.

He wasn't nervous about his safety. It was the interview itself that worried him. Talking to the manager of an electronics store was a low-risk endeavor. But he was out of practice, and he did not want to fuck up the case.

He stepped through the sliding doors into the big-box store. After the cold wind in the parking lot, the warmth burned his cheeks. He made his way to the register and asked to see the manager.

The clerk spoke into a phone at the register, then waved toward the back corner of the store. "She's in the office. Go on back."

Todd weaved his way through the aisles to a doorway that led to a narrow corridor. He passed a set of restrooms and an EMPLOYEES ONLY sign.

The manager leaned out of her office. "Officer?" She motioned with her hand for him to join her. "Please, come in. Have a seat."

Todd walked in. The restroom might be larger than the small, cramped office. The manager sat on a tiny wheeled chair behind the desk. To her right, a row of monitors showed live black-and-white images of the store's interior.

A single plastic chair faced the desk. The metal feet scraped obnoxiously on the commercial tile as he dragged the chair backward and sat. Even with the chair pushed all the way to the wall, his knees touched the desk.

"Sorry for the tight space." The manager was a fiftysomething woman with short blonde hair. "I'm Brandy Malone. How can I help you?"

"Chief Deputy Harvey." Todd touched his own chest. "I have some questions about Spencer LaForge. He worked here, correct?"

"Yes." Brandy looked troubled. "What do you mean, *worked*?" She emphasized the past tense.

"I'm sorry to inform you that Spencer died last evening."

"No." She shifted back in her chair as if the news were a physical blow. "He didn't show up for work this morning . . ." Her voice trailed off, and regret dragged the corners of her mouth down. "I called him, but he didn't answer. I assumed he'd had a personal emergency. I never imagined . . ." Her eyes lost focus, as if she were thinking instead of seeing him. She digested the news for about thirty seconds, then shook off her shock and made solid eye contact. "How did he die?"

"He was murdered," Todd said simply. The family had been notified, and the sheriff was going to give a press conference in a couple of hours anyway.

Brandy just stared, speechless for a few seconds. "I don't know what to say. I've never known anyone who was murdered before."

"It's distressing."

She leaned forward again, resting her forearms on the desk and reengaging with him. "What can I do?"

"The only thing you can do for Spencer now is help us catch whoever killed him," Todd said.

Brandy's head bobbed in an enthusiastic nod. "Of course."

Todd began. "How long did Spencer work here?"

"Six years," she said without needing to look up his personal information. "He's been with the store longer than I have."

"Did he start out as the assistant manager?"

"No." Brandy looked down at her keyboard. Her blonde bangs dropped into her eyes. She brushed them away with a fingertip as she tapped on the keys. She lifted her face to read the monitor. "He worked as an associate for two years, then was promoted to assistant manager just before I started here."

"Was he a good employee?" Todd asked.

Brandy gave him a weak nod. "He was generally punctual, and we didn't have any customer complaints about him. He never stole anything."

That bar felt low, but Todd knew little about running a retail store. "But?"

"But he wasn't what you would call a go-getter, if you know what I mean."

Todd did, but he didn't want to assume her definition matched his. So he waited for her to explain. He'd learned from watching Bree and Matt conduct interviews that people disliked silence and tended to fill it. They often gave up more—or different—information than when asked a direct question.

"I don't mean to say he wasn't a good employee. His reviews are all just fine." Guilt softened her features. "He did his job, but he never went the extra distance. He wasn't personable. He didn't relate to customers. He didn't connect with coworkers. Spencer came and left with almost zero social interaction, not even a *how are you?*" She looked puzzled. "I could never quite figure him out, but retail is a tough industry. Employee turnover is expensive. So, I was content to keep him as one of the assistant managers, but I didn't consider him promotable. His job performance was . . . average."

"Have you noticed any strange behavior lately?" Todd asked.

"No. He seemed normal all day yesterday."

"What time did he leave work?"

"Four o'clock," she said. "He was just as punctual about clocking out as in."

"Did Spencer express any concerns for his safety in his personal life recently?"

Her lips flattened. "Not exactly."

Todd waited.

"A week or two ago, this woman came into the store." She hesitated, clearly looking for the right words. "She was wearing sunglasses and a hat pulled low on her face. One of the staff immediately flagged her as a potential shoplifter and notified me and security. Sometimes thieves try to shield their facial features from the security cameras." She took a breath. "But she wasn't a shoplifter. The security guard and I watched her on the monitor. She was acting very shifty. Hiding at the end of aisles, peering around displays. But we didn't see her try to steal anything."

Todd sensed the story wasn't over.

Brandy seemed to mull over her next words. "Finally, by following her on the cameras, we determined she was following Spencer. I called him into the office, and the security guard went out to intercept her."

"Do you remember her name?"

She looked at the ceiling and scrunched her face. "Farah something. The name stuck with me because it's not common, and I'm old enough to remember Farrah Fawcett." She turned back to her computer and clicked the mouse. "I filled out an incident report. Let me look." Her eyes moved as she scanned the monitor. "Here. Her name is Farah Rock."

"What happened after security intervened?" Todd asked.

"Spencer came out of the office and confronted her, and she went ballistic. Yelling about him lying to her and using her. She said, 'I'll get even with you. No one treats me like that.'"

"Wow."

"Yeah." Brandy lifted both eyebrows. "She stopped ranting when I told security to call the police."

"Did you?"

Brandy looked regretful. "No. She immediately apologized, but it didn't feel like she really meant it. She left the store without resisting, and Spencer said he didn't want to make an issue out of it. He was mortified. It was the first time I'd ever seen him show real emotion. We filled out an incident report and let it go." She met Todd's gaze. "Maybe I should have made a bigger deal out of it, but at the time, I thought I was doing the right thing."

"I don't know what else you could have done," Todd said. "Spencer could have filed for a restraining order. She didn't physically attack him or anyone else?"

"No, she yelled, and then she cried. Once she calmed down, she cooperated with the security guard, giving him her name and ID, et cetera."

"Do you have a copy of the security video?"

"I do." Brandy's mouth split in a satisfied smile. "I kept a copy with the report in case she ever came back to the store, which I expressly asked her not to do."

"You banned her?"

"Not exactly." Brandy huffed. "Technically, she didn't commit a crime or attempt to commit a crime. Coming to the store and looking for an employee isn't illegal. This is private property. The store could ban her, but I'm not sure corporate would have backed me up if she complained."

"That's sad."

"That's business." She lifted both hands off the keyboard in a *whatever* gesture. "Anyway, I hoped the embarrassment and stern lecture would be enough to keep her away."

"Did she come back?"

"Not that I know of," Brandy said.

"Could I speak to Spencer's coworkers?" Todd asked.

"Yes." Brandy stood. "You can use my office. Should I send them in one by one?"

"That would be good. Thanks."

Todd spoke with five store employees. None gave any more information than Brandy. Before he left, Brandy emailed him a copy of both the incident report and the security video of the confrontation.

He left the store with more energy and confidence than he'd had going in. In his vehicle, he used his computer to write up a quick set of interview notes before he forgot any details. Then he dialed the sheriff's number.

Bree needed to know Farah Rock had stalked Spencer before she interviewed her.

Chapter Seventeen

"Nice job, Todd." Bree ended her call with her chief deputy and turned to Matt, who sat in the passenger seat of the SUV. "Well, that's some interesting news. Todd is sending me an email. Would you open it?"

He took her phone and accessed the email. Skimming it, he summarized Todd's interview with Spencer's boss.

Excitement whirled in Bree's belly. She loved the feeling of an investigation developing, shifting the small pieces around until the puzzle began to take shape.

"Good thing we're headed to Farah Rock's place," Matt said.

The GPS chimed in, telling Bree to prepare for a turn. Farah lived outside the town limits. Bree followed the audible direction, taking a narrow country lane that cut through the forest. Twenty minutes later, she turned into a gravel driveway that led through the woods. The driveway ended in a large clearing occupied by a rustic cabin and matching barn. In most of the county, the dusting of snow had melted early that morning, but in the thick woods, white patches remained wherever the sun's rays couldn't penetrate.

Matt gestured toward a white Toyota Highlander parked next to a little blue Subaru that was registered to Farah.

"I see that." Bree snapped a photo, making sure to capture the license plate.

Gravel and ice crystals crunched under their feet as they walked to the front door and knocked. No one answered. A muffled thud sounded behind the house. Bree and Matt walked around the cabin to the rear yard.

"That sounded like it came from the barn." Bree started across the clearing. The double doors weren't completely closed. She peered through the gap, with Matt looking over her shoulder. The inside of the barn had been renovated into a home gym. Dividers had been removed to make the interior one large open space. An interlocking rubber puzzle-piece mat covered the floor. Dumbbells, a balance ball, and resistance bands filled one corner. Another corner was utilized for storage of sporting equipment. A kayak hung on the wall, and what appeared to be camping equipment occupied ventilated metal shelves. A mountain bike hung on a rack.

But the rest of the space had been converted into a homemade climbing wall. Plastic handholds dotted the two-story walls. Under what had once been the hayloft, more handholds had been affixed to the ceiling. A woman clung like a spider about ten feet above the floor. Bree recognized Farah from her driver's license photo. She wore a snug long-sleeve shirt, black tights, and pointy-looking climbing shoes. Her hair was bound in a ponytail.

A space heater in the middle of the room was inadequate for the size of the space and did little to chase out the chill. Still, sweat dripped from Farah's forehead. She reached for a grip, pushed off the wall with her legs, and swung her second hand to a new hold like a competitor on *American Ninja Warrior*.

Bree knocked loudly on the door. Farah looked over, releasing one hand and dangling upside down from the remaining hand and two toe grips. Bree flinched, expecting her to fall on her head. Farah slowly released her toes and unfurled her body to hang straight down. The movement was controlled and deliberate. Bree could manage a yoga headstand, but Farah's core strength was impressive. Farah landed lightly on the mat. She brushed her hands on her thighs, leaving white streaks on the black fabric. Her nails were short, but Bree was surprised to see bright red polish. Rock climbing and nail polish didn't seem to go together.

Superficially, she resembled Avery and Monica—tallish and thin, with long dark hair—but Farah was less polished, more outdoorsy and rugged than the other women.

"Can I help you?" she asked in a *you must have the wrong address* tone.

"Farah Rock?" After she nodded, Bree introduced herself and Matt. "We'd like to ask you a few questions about Spencer LaForge."

Farah's eyes narrowed to an annoyed squint. "What did the creep do?"

No love lost there.

"He died," Bree said in a blunt voice.

Farah blinked. Shock erased her irritation. "What?"

"May we come in?" Matt asked.

Farah recovered and headed toward them. "Let's go up to the house. I'll get cold if I'm not moving." She turned off the space heater, changed her climbing shoes for rubber duck boots, and grabbed a jacket on the way out. They trooped across the clearing and entered the cabin through the back door into a mudroom. Farah sat on a boot bench and slipped off her duck boots. Standing, she removed her jacket and stepped into fuzzy slippers.

The combination kitchen and living space was the size of an average hotel room. Through a doorway, Bree could see a small bedroom. The inside of the cabin reflected its rustic exterior. The floor and walls were rough-hewn wood.

Inside, Farah added logs to a woodstove in the corner, then closed the door. Orange flames glowed in the small window, casting soft light on her face. Her features were strong, maybe Italian or Greek, and her olive complexion was free of makeup. She turned and stared at them, puzzled. "How——?" Realization changed her eyes. Her head tipped forward, and she squeezed her eyes shut for a few seconds. When she opened them, her expression was resigned. "It was him on the news last night. The murdered guy."

Bree nodded. "Yes."

"Well, shit." Farah backed up to an overstuffed chair and dropped into it. One arm curled around her waist. The other hand covered her mouth. Her eyes darted from side to side as if her mind were working.

Bree sat on a leather ottoman facing her. "When was the last time you saw Spencer?"

"Um. I don't know exactly. Let me check my calendar." Farah's hand dropped, and she shifted back in the chair to reach for a cell phone on an end table. She scrolled, then stopped. "I last saw him two weeks ago. He broke up with me in a text two days afterward."

Bree pulled out her notepad and jotted down the dates. "Did that make you mad?"

"Yes!" Farah snapped, then huffed. "Of course it did. It was a lousy thing to do, but in hindsight, all the signs were there that he was fucking around. I just wasn't paying attention."

"What do you mean?" Matt perched on the arm of a sturdy chair a few feet away.

"He was too smooth," Farah began. "He agreed with everything I said. If I told him I loved the color blue, he was like, 'Me too.' My favorite movies were also his favorites. It was as if he would say anything to make me like him, to connect with me. Of course, I didn't see any of this until afterward, but hindsight and all that, right?" She paused, her face creasing with resentment. "After the breakup text, I checked up on him. His profile was a lie. He didn't found his own digital-marketing firm. He didn't run his own business. He worked at the fucking Electronics Depot."

Bree tilted her head. "How did you find out?"

"I saw him there." Farah folded her arms.

"That's random," Bree said. "Do you go there often?"

"No." Farah folded her arms across her waist, one hand shooting to her mouth again.

Bree waited, letting the quiet grow like a silent crescendo.

Farah squirmed, but she held out.

"So you followed him," Bree said.

Farah looked away. "Yeah. I was sure he'd met someone else. I wanted to see who she was."

"Did you?" Matt asked.

Farah bit off a piece of her thumbnail. "Yes." She let out a huge puff of air. "Look, I was mad for about a day. I followed him. He went to the store. I thought he was going to buy something, but he didn't come out. I put on a hat and sunglasses and went inside. Can you imagine my surprise when I saw him wearing the blue vest and everything? So much for owning his own business." Her voice went bitter. "What a fucking liar."

"Did you confront him?" Matt asked.

Farah's head jerked in one abrupt nod. "But then I left."

Bree waited until her gaze lifted, then forced eye contact. "The manager didn't make you leave?"

Anger flared in Farah's eyes, and her jaw sawed back and forth. Instead of answering, she asked her own question. "How do you know?"

"The store has an incident report and surveillance video." Bree didn't blink.

Farah looked away. "I admit, it wasn't my proudest moment. I shouldn't have gone to his workplace. But he broke up with me in a *fucking text.*" She spit the final words out through gritted teeth. She took a deep breath. "I'm sorry. I was mad."

"Sounds like you're still mad," Matt said.

Farah shot him a look. "I left the store without issue."

But the story wasn't over. Bree could sense it. "So when did you see the other woman Spencer was dating?"

Farah studied her torn thumbnail without answering, but there were only two ways she could have seen Spencer out on a date: accidentally or purposefully. The odds of a random encounter were low.

"You followed him again," Matt prompted.

She picked at her cuticle with her other hand. "I followed him home after his shift. He changed clothes and headed out to the coffee shop an hour later." She lowered her hands to her lap and stared at them for a few seconds.

Neither Bree nor Matt said a word. They just waited for her to continue. She was reliving the memory—and seething.

She was definitely not over it.

"He went to the same coffee shop where we'd met the first time. I watched through the window. The woman looked a lot like me. A lot of things became real clear in about ten seconds. One, he was a douche. Two, I was better off without him. Three, he was going to do the same thing to her. He was working a pattern."

Bree leaned forward, invading Farah's space just a little, adding physical reinforcement to the verbal pressure. "What did you do next?"

"I bought brownies and ice cream, came home, and washed it all down with an entire bottle of prosecco." Farah lifted her eyes to meet Bree's. "I had a whopping hangover and permitted myself twenty-four hours to wallow in self-pity. Then I moved on. I'm dating again, and I've met several men since. They're all very different from Spencer. I'm over *him*."

It sounded as if she were trying to convince herself, because bitterness radiated from her like heat from the woodstove.

Bree paused before she asked the most important question. "Where were you yesterday from 4:30 to 5:30 p.m.?"

She blinked three times before answering. "Here."

Bree sought eye contact. "Was anyone with you?"

Their gazes locked for one long breath. Farah's phone vibrated on the table. A man's face and a name appeared on the lock screen. *Rhys.*

She quickly touched the side of the phone and the screen went blank. "My friend Rhys came over."

"What about before that?" Matt asked.

"I was here, alone. I'm writing a training manual. I work from home. Some days, I don't see anyone at all."

"What time did Rhys get here?" Bree pressed. If Farah was lying, she'd have to think fast and then remember all the details. Bree would ask the same questions again if a second interview was required.

"Around six, I think," Farah evaded. "I don't know exactly. I wasn't checking the time." Her jaw set.

Bree made a note in her notepad. "What did you two do?"

"Talked." Farah's thin shoulder lifted and poked through the oversize neck of her shirt.

"Did you eat dinner? Watch TV?" Bree continued to apply pressure. Lies would be caught in repetition.

"I said we talked." Farah enunciated each word as if she wanted to be sure they heard her.

"You didn't offer him a beverage?" Matt lifted a doubtful brow.

"He drinks tea." Farah's gaze shot to him like a thrown dagger.

"So, you made him tea?" Bree confirmed.

"Yes." Farah bit off the word. "He takes it with honey, in case you were wondering."

Well, that felt like the truth.

"Rhys is a good friend?" Matt asked.

"One of the best," Farah said. "We like all the same things. We have so much in common. I wish we had chemistry. He'd be the perfect life partner."

Bree made a show of writing more notes. Farah frowned.

A few seconds of silence ticked by. Then Bree asked, "Did Spencer own reptiles?"

"Yes." Farah's voice returned to normal. She was more comfortable moving away from the topic of her alibi. "He had some gorgeous snakes."

"He showed you?" Bree was surprised.

"He knew I have a gecko and like reptiles." Farah pointed to the kitchen counter, where a small aquarium sat. Inside, a five-inch lizard basked under a heat lamp.

"What kind of reptiles did Spencer have?" Matt asked. "Did you see his whole collection?"

"A whole room of them. He brought out this gorgeous, rare corn snake so I could hold it." She nodded toward her gecko. "Flash is cute and easy to care for. I don't have time for a high-maintenance pet."

"Did you see any rattlesnakes?" Bree asked.

Farah nodded. "Yes. He had three." She snorted. "I didn't hold any of those."

So, Spencer had recently owned three rattlesnakes. Now there were three empty spaces on his shelves and zero rattlesnakes in the collection. Had the killer taken the snakes?

Bree wanted to scream but kept her voice level. "Did you know it's illegal to keep a venomous snake in New York State without a special permit?"

Farah shrugged. "It never occurred to me to ask."

"This happened at his house?" Bree lifted her pen.

"Yes."

Truth.

"OK. That's all the questions I have right now." Bree tapped her pen on her notepad. "I'd like your cell phone number in case we need more information."

Farah gave it to her, then unfolded her long body and inched toward the door. Clearly, she couldn't wait to get rid of them.

Bree looked up and blinked innocently. "And a number for your friend Rhys? I'll need to confirm your alibi with him."

Farah balked. "Why?"

"Because you stalked Spencer shortly before he was killed. You had a public confrontation with him that was loud enough to warrant the store manager filling out an incident report and asking you to never return to the store. You threatened Spencer."

Farah's face went pale. "I never threatened him."

Bree flipped backward in her notepad to her notes from Todd's interview with the store manager. "You said, 'I'll get even with you. No one treats me like that.'"

Farah's lips parted. Her olive complexion turned ashy gray.

"So, how about giving me Rhys's number so I can verify your alibi?" Bree poised her pen over her paper.

Farah's voice sounded tight, almost robotic, as she read off a number.

Bree wrote it down. "His last name?"

"Blake," Farah said, her voice gaining strength, almost defiance.

"One more thing," Matt said. "Who owns that white Highlander outside?"

"My dad," Farah said. "He's working in Canada for a couple of months and didn't want to leave it unattended in his condo parking lot. Vehicles get broken into there."

"Do you drive it?" Matt asked.

Farah nodded. "Sometimes. He asked me to drive it once in a while."

Bree rose. "We'll get back to you with additional questions if necessary."

Matt stood and inclined his head. "Thank you for your cooperation."

Farah said nothing as she followed them to the door, but Bree heard the dead bolt slide home once they got outside.

She and Matt returned to the SUV.

Back in her vehicle, she blasted the heat. "Well, that was interesting."

"Talk about conflicting emotions." Matt spread his hands over the vents, flexing his fingers as if they were stiff. "She was confident in her alibi—until we asked for her friend's number to corroborate it."

"Either she didn't want to drag him into the investigation, or she was lying her head off. Whichever it is, I want to talk to Rhys ASAP."

"I'll call him now."

Bree backed down the narrow driveway. After she'd pulled onto the road, she handed Matt her notepad.

Matt flipped to the right page and dialed the number on speaker. It rang, with several skips in sound, as if Rhys were on another line and ignoring the call-waiting beeps.

"I'll bet she's warning him right now," Matt said.

"No doubt. It's what most people would do." Bree pressed on the gas pedal. "Give him ten minutes and try again."

They were halfway back to town when Matt got through to Rhys and explained that they'd like to speak with him.

"Sure." Rhys sounded stressed. "I've just finished with a client. Can you meet me at the Scarlet Café?" He gave them an address in Scarlet Falls.

"We can be there in ten minutes." Matt ended the call. He rubbed his hand, the one with the bullet scar. The cold always seemed to affect his old injury. "This should be interesting."

Bree had the same feeling.

CHAPTER EIGHTEEN

Bree headed toward Scarlet Falls's tiny retail section and found the Scarlet Café just off the main drag. The shops were surprisingly busy for late afternoon. Bree circled the block before parking in front of a bridal salon across the street.

Matt read from her vehicle laptop screen. "He lives in Grey's Hollow, near the train station. No outstanding warrants. He doesn't even have any parking tickets."

They got out of the car and walked toward the café. Inside, Bree scanned the dozen bistro tables. The café was empty except for two women huddled in the far corner. Rhys wasn't here yet.

Bree inhaled the scent of fresh baked goods.

"Hungry?" Matt asked.

Bree eyed a ham-and-cheese croissant sandwich. "Just coffee. Thanks." Her lack of exercise in the midst of a big case and Dana's pre-holiday baking spree were a dangerous combination. "I can feel my arteries hardening just smelling them."

She chose a table on the opposite side of the room from the other patrons. Matt went to the counter and returned with two coffees. The bell on the door rang, and a man of about thirty walked in. He wore dark jeans and a blue down jacket. The wispy ends of his blond hair poked out from under a gray beanie.

He scanned the room and spotted them. Bree's uniform identified her. Rhys headed for their table, held out a hand, and cleared his throat. "I'm Rhys Blake."

Bree introduced herself and Matt, then gestured toward an empty chair. "Please sit."

"Let me grab a tea." Rhys went to the counter and returned with a cardboard cup. He sat, unzipped his jacket, and removed the lid to his cup.

"Thank you for meeting us," Bree said in a low voice.

Frowning, Rhys dunked his tea bag. "I've never talked to the police before—let alone about a murder investigation."

Bree nodded in understanding. "We appreciate your cooperation. What do you do for a living?" She started with a few general questions to let him get comfortable.

"I'm an IT consultant."

"Are you self-employed?" Matt drank his coffee.

Rhys shook his head. "No. My employer provides IT services for special projects or for companies that don't have or want their own tech staff. We service a lot of small businesses."

"Do you like your job?" Bree asked.

"I do." He added a packet of honey to his tea and dissolved it with a wooden stirrer. "For the most part, I set my own schedule. I'm not stuck in one office. My jobs are varied, and I can work from home sometimes. It's a good balance. I'm never bored."

"Sounds like a good job." Bree picked up her coffee and took a sip, but it tasted burned.

"But you didn't ask to meet me to discuss the merits of my job." His eyes went grim.

"No." Bree set down her cup. "We're trying to verify your friend Farah's whereabouts on Tuesday evening."

Rhys shifted his butt in his chair and refused to make eye contact, two classic signs of discomfort. "She's not that close of a friend."

"No?" Matt pushed his cup a few inches away.

Rhys shrugged. "She's more of an acquaintance."

"How did you meet?" Bree asked.

"Through a dating app." Rhys removed his tea bag and set it inside the overturned lid. "When we got together in person, we had some good conversation, but there wasn't enough attraction between us."

"That happens," Matt said.

"Yeah," Rhys agreed, his gaze sliding to the wall for a few seconds. "But Farah decided, since we had a nice talk, she wanted to be friends. She keeps texting and calling me, wanting to meet for drinks or to hang out."

"You don't text her?" Bree asked. "Or want to get together?"

"I respond when she texts or calls, and we've gotten together a few times." He looked away again, studying the street outside the storefront window. "I don't know. I didn't join dating apps to make friends. I don't have anything against having platonic friendships with women, but I'm in a place in my life where I'm looking for more." He sighed. "I probably sound like a jerk."

"No," Matt assured him. "I get it. You're ready for a relationship, and you don't want to waste your time when there's no chance of one."

"Exactly." Rhys gave Matt an appreciative look. "Also, if I'm being totally honest, she's not interested in me romantically, but *I'm* a little attracted to *her*, so . . ." He trailed off. "We hung out at her place last week. It was weird."

"I can see how that would be uncomfortable for you," Matt empathized.

Rhys rubbed his thumb on the cardboard sleeve of his cup.

"How long have you been almost friends?" Matt asked.

"A few months," Rhys said.

Now that they'd established a rapport, Bree gently steered the conversation back to Farah. "Did you see Farah Tuesday night?"

A flash of anger lit Rhys's blue eyes. "No."

Bree and Matt exchanged a look. Matt's eyes took on the feral gleam that accompanied catching someone in a deception. Though chafing for details, Bree forced herself to wait. Even though they weren't besties, Rhys seemed reluctant to squeal on Farah. Best to let him skewer her at his own pace.

"She called me right after you left her place. She told me what she wanted—no, *expected*—me to say to you." He sighed and sipped his tea. "I shouldn't feel guilty about not lying for her. I'm more than a little mad that she would ask."

"So you weren't with her Tuesday evening?" Bree confirmed.

"No," Rhys said. "But she'd called me earlier that day. She knew I was planning to be home alone, so she said no one would be able to prove I wasn't with her." He shook his head and blew air out through his nostrils. "I don't want to lie to the sheriff for her. That's illegal, right?"

Matt nodded. "It's obstruction of justice."

Rhys's frown deepened.

"We appreciate your honesty, Mr. Blake," Bree said. "I'll need you to sign a formal statement."

"Really?" He rubbed the back of his neck, his face tight. "So, she'll know."

"Yes," Bree said.

Matt leaned forward and gripped his coffee cup between his palms. "Is there a reason you don't want her to know? Did you promise you would corroborate her story?"

"I was vague and noncommittal," Rhys said. "But I'm sure she heard my answer as an agreement. She assumes I'll do whatever she wants."

She sounded selfish, but Bree kept her opinion to herself and went with a less judgmental response. "Sometimes people see what they want to see."

"I totally get that," Matt sympathized in the man-to-man tone Bree had often heard him adopt when he was trying to establish a connection with a witness or suspect.

Bree pulled out a business card. "If she harasses you, call me."

"If she harasses me, I'll block her. I'm done with her." Rhys looked at the card as if it were a hairy spider. But after a few seconds, he put it in his pocket. "I really don't want to get involved with a murder investigation."

Bree didn't state the obvious. He was already involved.

"We understand," Matt commiserated. "But this is on her. It was unfair of her to ask you to lie—to commit a crime—for her. You're doing the right thing."

Rhys's nod wasn't reassuring, and Bree hoped she'd get that signed statement out of him. She'd need it to obtain a search warrant for Farah's phone records. Cell phones could potentially be tracked, and Bree really wanted to know where Farah had been on Tuesday evening. She'd get Rhys's records as well, to back up his statement.

Maybe Farah's could be tracked to Spencer's house when he was being killed.

Bree asked one last question. "Did Farah ever talk about Spencer?"

Rhys hesitated, then reluctantly answered, "She did."

"In what way?" Bree pressed.

Rhys picked at his napkin. "She was mad at him for the way he ended things. To be fair, dumping someone in a text is an asshole move. Sorry to speak badly of the dead and all, but the guy was a jerk."

Bree collected his address and arranged for him to come to the station the next morning to sign his statement. "I'll have it ready. Ask for Marge at the counter."

"I'll be there." Rhys nodded curtly. On the way out, he threw his empty teacup in the trash with unnecessary force.

Matt and Bree left the restaurant, carrying their coffees outside. They returned to the SUV and climbed in.

"Now what?" Matt fastened his seat belt.

Bree checked the time on the dashboard. "We go back to the station and see which reports are in and if we have any additional evidence to support Farah as our prime suspect."

"Lying and fake alibis usually put suspects at the top of my list."

"Stalking too," Bree added. "While we're doing that, I'll send a deputy to bring Farah to the station for a more formal interview. Maybe a ride in a patrol car and the knowledge that she's being recorded will make her more honest."

Bree's phone buzzed. She answered the call. "Sheriff Taggert."

A female voice said, "This is Officer Kaminski over at the juvenile detention center. Ricky Sanderling has requested to speak with you."

"We'll be there shortly." Bree ended the call and relayed the request to Matt.

"*Ricky* wants to talk to *you?*" Matt asked.

"Apparently." Bree changed direction, heading for juvie. "I can think of only one reason he wants to talk to me. He knows something he thinks will give him leverage against the charges."

CHAPTER NINETEEN

The juvenile detention center was an ugly concrete box built in the '70s, when all municipal buildings were designed to look like bunkers. Bree parked in the lot. Interest and dread warred inside her. She hated juvie. Hated seeing all the broken kids.

She sometimes wondered how her life could have turned out differently. If the old sheriff of Randolph County hadn't been the one to pull the traumatized Taggert siblings out from under the porch—if he hadn't been the first adult in her life to make her feel safe. He was the reason she'd turned to the law instead of against it. What if that chapter of her life had ended differently? She could have easily ended up here or worse.

They met Ricky in a small interview room. A metal table and four stools were bolted to the floor. Bree took the seat across from Ricky. Matt sat next to her. Clearly twitchy, Ricky picked at a track mark on the inside of his elbow. His posture was all self-pity and resentment.

"You remember Investigator Flynn," Bree said.

Fear flickered in Ricky's eyes as he glanced at Matt. "Yeah."

Matt pulled his phone out of his pocket. "Excuse me. I have to take this call." He got up and left the room.

Bree refocused on Ricky. She could have been harsh—the kid *had* shot at her, but with her own miserable childhood in the forefront of her mind, she chose compassion. "How are you?"

He stopped picking at the scab and squinted at her, as if trying to assess whether she was full of shit. "How do you think? Sucks in here."

Bree thought he'd probably spent the night in worse places, but she could see the pain behind his belligerence. He was lashing out. Unfortunately, the only person he was hurting was himself. "I'm sure it does."

His fingers found the scab again. This time he drew blood. "I'm supposed to go to rehab later. That'll suck worse."

Bree nodded. "I'm glad they found a spot for you."

He scoffed. "Won't matter. I'm gonna be in juvie for a long time. I don't have anywhere else to go anyway." His eyes were moist with tears he struggled to hold back. "I really fucked up this time."

"You did." She saw nothing but misery in his expression. The truth was that the court had flexibility in sentencing a juvenile offender, and Bree had some leeway with the prosecutor and the charges. She would rather Ricky receive substance abuse treatment than punitive sentencing. "Why did you want to talk?"

"I heard people talking about the murder of Jasper's brother." Ricky's eyes turned shrewd. "Do you think he did it?"

"We've just begun the investigation," Bree said.

"What if I know something about Jasper?"

"Then you'd better tell me."

His gaze dropped to his arm, and he ripped off another scab. "I want something in exchange: immunity."

Ricky clearly watched too much TV.

"That's not how this works," Bree said. "We're not asking you to testify against a major drug cartel." She paused, waiting until she caught his eye again before continuing. "I'm not a game player, Ricky. I'll be straight with you. Always. I expect the same in return. Here's the truth: rehab is your chance to turn your life around. Don't waste it. You won't be a juvenile much longer. If you think this is bad"—she waved her hand in a circle—"then you don't want to experience actual prison."

He contemplated the thought of prison with an expression that made her wonder if he'd ever really considered that was the direction he was heading. "Then what? My dad won't let me move home. My mom . . ."

Bree mentally filled in what he couldn't say. *Left him.* "That sucks."

His mouth turned down in a sullen frown. "But you won't help me?"

"If you volunteer information about Jasper, I will make sure the judge and prosecutor know you've been cooperative, but I won't make any promises."

He picked at another scab. "I went over to Jasper's place a few weeks ago. He was fighting with his brother on the phone. It got nasty."

"Do you know what they were fighting about?"

Ricky nodded. "He had the call on speaker. His brother sold him some rare kind of python and it died. Jasper was pissed. He accused his brother of selling him damaged merchandise. The brother said it wasn't his fault."

Bree couldn't imagine killing someone over a dead snake.

Ricky sniffed. "Jasper said, 'You owe me twenty-five grand.' And the brother was all, 'Like hell.' Then Jasper told him to go fuck himself."

"That's a lot of money for a snake."

"Right?" Ricky agreed. "Crazy." He sat back. Some of his resentment seemed to have faded. "You'll tell the judge I helped?"

"I will," Bree promised. "You'll give rehab a real go?"

His sigh deflated him. "Yeah."

"Good." Bree stood. Then she added, "I'll be checking up on you," just to let him know that someone actually gave a fuck.

She called for a guard to return Ricky to his pod. Then she found Matt outside.

"Who called?" she asked.

"No one. It felt like Ricky would talk more if I left."

"Good call." Bree summed up Ricky's info.

"Now we know why Jasper wouldn't tell us about the phone calls with his brother," Matt said.

"And we have twenty-five thousand reasons Jasper might want his brother dead."

CHAPTER TWENTY

It was approaching dinnertime when Matt fell into step beside Bree in the parking lot behind the sheriff's station. Wind whipped across the asphalt, sending a few dead leaves and an empty plastic water bottle tumbling into the base of the building. Matt veered aside to pick up the bottle.

Bree hunched against the arctic blast. "Your jacket isn't even zipped. Aren't you cold?"

"Not really."

"Must be that Scandinavian blood." She opened the door and they stepped inside. "I'm freezing."

Matt tossed the water bottle into the recycling bin.

Todd stopped them as they crossed the squad room. "Farah Rock declined our invitation to ride in a patrol car. When the deputy arrived at her house, her brother—who happens to be a lawyer—was there. They're coming to the station together."

"Thank you, Todd," Bree said. "Let's request dating app access for both Farah's and Monica's accounts. We don't need warrants for those."

"I'll have someone work on that." Todd turned toward a deputy sitting at a computer station.

Irritation flashed through Matt. "I know lawyers are integral to our system of justice, but they really get in the way of a good interview."

"No argument from me." Bree snorted as they continued into her office.

Marge appeared at the door as soon as they got inside. She waved a notepad in her hand and spoke while Bree and Matt took off their jackets. "The press has been calling about the murder case. Someone leaked details. They're asking if the victim was suffocated with plastic wrap."

"Ugh." Bree sank into her chair, her face locked in a frustrated frown. "How I hate leaks." She shook her head. "I'll hold a press conference today. We'll put some of the curiosity to rest and hope no one leaks the rest of the details."

Marge scanned Bree. "There's a clean uniform in your closet. You have dirt on your face, and is that hay in your hair?"

Bree reached up, felt the top of her head, and plucked out a wisp of hay. She tossed it into the trash can under her desk.

"She looks fine." Matt hadn't even noticed the hay.

Marge gave him a high school principal stare. "You're not a politician, and even if you were, you wouldn't get judged for wearing a wrinkled uniform. You have that ruggedly handsome thing working for you. Disheveled looks good on you."

He tried to look sorry but couldn't quite manage it. Nor could he prevent the corner of his mouth from ticking up. "Ruggedly handsome?"

Marge rolled her eyes. "But the public *will* judge the sheriff for her appearance." She turned back to Bree and scanned her with an assessing eye. "The dark circles are fine. Lets the public know you're working long hours to solve the case. Tired is one thing. Dirty is quite another."

"I'll clean up," Bree promised.

Matt coughed into his fist to cover a grin. Bree's idea of an accessory was her Glock. She didn't wear makeup unless she was on camera or they went out to a nicer restaurant. Don't get him wrong, she could clean up very nicely. But mostly, they were sweatpants, pizza, and Netflix people.

Marge gave them a serious look and left the office.

Bree leaned back in her chair, the mechanisms squeaking. Her phone went off, and she glanced at the screen. "It's a text from Luke." She read it aloud: "Vet stitched the wound. Beast was a good boy."

"Beast." Matt shook his head at the name Luke had used. "It's ridiculous."

"Then think of a better name." Bree's phone buzzed again, and she turned it around so he could see the screen. A photograph of the stitched gash came through, then a second picture of the giant horse nose-to-nose with Ladybug. Bree's dog stood on her hind legs, her paws on the horse's stall door.

The intercom buzzed. Bree pressed the "Answer" button. Marge's voice came across the speaker. "Miss Rock and her attorney are here. Do you want me to show them to the interview room?"

"Yes. Thank you, Marge." Bree released the button. She stood, empty coffee mug in hand. "I'm going to grab a refill on the way."

"Good idea." Matt picked up his own mug and followed her out of the office.

They stopped in the break room, where Todd was stirring a cup of coffee.

Bree filled her mug and turned to Todd. "I'd like you to watch the interview from the monitoring room. I want your take on her." She set the pot down. "We've already caught her in a lie."

Todd carried his coffee toward the door. "OK."

Matt changed his mind about coffee. He'd had enough. Acid already swirled around in his stomach. He rinsed out the stainless-steel mug and filled it with water.

They walked down the hallway. Todd went into the monitoring room.

"I'll be right there," Bree said, heading for the restroom.

"OK." Matt entered the interview room. At the table, a man and a woman sat next to each other facing the door.

"Ms. Rock." Matt inclined his head toward Farah.

Without getting up, Farah gestured to the man beside her. "This is my attorney—and brother—Benjamin Rock."

"I'm Criminal Investigator Flynn," Matt said.

Farah looked like a different person. Instead of her climbing attire, she wore dark jeans and a black sweater. Her shiny, dark hair was tied in a loose ponytail and pulled over her shoulder.

The family resemblance between Farah and the attorney was obvious. Like his sister, he was olive-skinned and ultra-fit. His tailored charcoal suit and blue silk tie screamed money. He was no ambulance chaser.

"What kind of law do you practice?" Matt asked.

"Criminal." Benjamin named a large, pricey firm from the city.

Fuck.

Matt had been hoping he was a corporate attorney who wouldn't be as familiar with the criminal justice system. No such luck.

"Thank you both for coming." Matt sat across from the lawyer. He'd let Bree have the chair opposite Farah. "The sheriff will join us in just a minute."

"I have a meeting, so I can't stay long." Farah pointedly touched the screen of her phone to read the displayed time.

"The sheriff will be here soon," Matt assured her.

"My sister already answered questions regarding Mr. LaForge's death." Benjamin rested his forearms on the edge of the table and interlocked his manicured fingers. "Which she shouldn't have done without an attorney present."

He was fishing for more information. Matt simply nodded.

The attorney scowled. "She wasn't Mirandized."

"She wasn't a suspect." Matt emphasized the past tense.

The attorney didn't flinch, and Matt knew he would challenge any information they'd obtained in Farah's first interview. Miranda warnings were required before questioning only if a suspect was in custody. But Benjamin wouldn't be the first attorney to argue his client didn't feel free to end the interview, which indicated they were actually in custody even if law enforcement hadn't expressed it verbally.

The law was on Bree and Matt's side, but much depended on the judge.

Bree walked into the room, took the seat across from Farah, and introduced herself. "Thank you for coming in, Ms. Rock."

Matt introduced the suit.

The lawyer huffed. "As I just said to Investigator Flynn, my sister already answered questions."

"Yes, and we appreciate her cooperation. Today's interview will be recorded." Bree started the video camera, gave the time, and listed everyone in the room. Then she read the Miranda rights and presented Farah with a form of acknowledgment to sign.

Alarm flashed in Farah's eyes. "Am I being arrested?"

"No," Bree answered. "The form is routine for all formal interviews."

Worried, she glanced at her brother. "Should I sign this?"

"Yes." The brother never took his eyes off Bree. "It means nothing. They recorded the sheriff reading you your rights. You can't deny it."

Farah signed with dramatic flourish. After setting down the pen, she shifted backward, folded her arms across her chest, and glared at Bree. "Why am I here?"

She sounded genuinely confused. Matt realized it hadn't occurred to her that Rhys wouldn't do what she asked. She assumed he'd follow her instructions. Was she accustomed to getting her way, to men doing what she wanted? Maybe she used their feelings for her to manipulate them.

Bree took the paper with a businesslike motion. "We have some follow-up questions to our earlier interview."

"I already told you everything," Farah whined.

"Yes." Bree held up a typed paper. "So you said."

The attorney leaned forward, his joined hands hitting the tabletop. "Would you get to the point, Sheriff?"

"Of course." Bree nodded. "You told us that you were at home on Tuesday evening and that your friend Rhys was with you. Is that correct?"

Farah glanced at her brother, the first suggestion of doubt creeping into her eyes. "Yes."

Bree dropped the bomb. "Rhys Blake says he wasn't with you Tuesday evening. He says you called him and asked him to lie for you."

Farah froze. Her mouth opened and remained gaped, like a fish struggling to breathe. "I—"

Benjamin cut her off, covering her hand with his. "Don't say anything."

Bree raised her brows. "Do you care to amend your statement? Lying to the police during a major investigation is obstruction of justice."

Farah's lips parted, but no words came out. She leaned closer to her brother, as if to whisper in his ear.

He shook his head to stop her. "Sheriff Taggert, does Mr. Blake have any proof of these accusations?"

Bree tilted her head. "His cell phone records will show he wasn't with your sister."

Benjamin smiled. "The records will prove where his phone was, not where he was."

"It will prove where he used it," Bree said.

"Where *someone* used it." Benjamin squeezed his sister's hand and turned his head to speak with her. "The sheriff doesn't have any evidence tying you to the murder. If she did, she wouldn't be fixated on disproving your alibi." He released Farah's hand. "You don't even need an alibi. You haven't been accused of a crime." He turned back to Bree. "Right?"

Bree bared her teeth. No one could confuse it with a smile. "Your sister lied to law enforcement in an official investigation."

"She could have been mistaken," Benjamin said. "Or Mr. Blake could be mistaken. Did you record your first interview?"

Bree's poker face didn't budge. "No."

"So, you have no evidence of anything my sister said," Benjamin said an *aha* voice. "Maybe *you* were mistaken."

Matt leaned in. "She wasn't mistaken. I was also present. Farah asked Blake to lie for her."

"So he says." Benjamin didn't sound concerned. "Or Mr. Blake is bitter because my sister rejected him and is getting even."

She'd told him everything. Matt studied Farah. Her lips were mashed together, as if she were afraid she'd blurt out the wrong thing. But she was smart enough to let her lawyer do the talking. Some suspects couldn't keep their mouths shut no matter what their counsel advised.

Benjamin lifted her hand an inch off the table. "Is my sister under arrest?"

"Not at this time," Bree said.

"Then we're leaving." Benjamin pressed both palms flat on the table, preparing to rise. "Let's go."

"But I—" Farah got to her feet.

"You are not answering any more questions." Her brother stood up. "They won't tell you this, but they can't make you. You are under no obligation to answer their questions. Unless you are under arrest, you are free to leave at any time. You came here voluntarily in a good-faith effort to help with their investigation." He gave Bree a hard stare. "That won't happen again."

He guided his sister toward the door with a gentle hand under her elbow. She glanced over her shoulder as they walked out. Matt read her expression as a mix of apprehension and anger.

Bree turned off the video recording. Todd stood in the doorway.

"What did you think?" Bree rose.

"She asked her buddy to lie for her. Definitely." Todd grimaced. "And she seemed really surprised that he didn't."

"That's the impression I got too." Matt stood.

Bree stretched her arms to the ceiling. "I wonder how she would have answered if she hadn't brought a lawyer."

"A question we will never know the answer to." Matt pushed his chair in. "But I think the fake alibi she gave us was an impulse. She didn't think it through, and she knows it was a mistake."

Bree lowered her hands and headed for the hallway. "She won't make the same mistake again. Her brother won't let her say a word."

They walked to the break room together.

Matt refilled his cup with water. "If I was her lawyer, I'd tell her to choose silence as well. She already dug herself into an unnecessary hole. She could have just said she was home alone. We hadn't accused her of anything."

"Her brother was right," Todd said. "She didn't need an alibi."

"So why would she invent one?" Bree asked. She contemplated the coffee machine, as if considering yet another cup.

Matt filled another cup with water and handed it to her. She needed actual sleep tonight, not coffee. She took the water but gazed longingly at the coffee as she drank.

"I can only think of one reason," Matt said.

Todd nodded. "Because she's guilty."

Bree drained the cup and refilled it at the tap. "Let's regroup in the conference room. Our impressions of her behavior don't mean squat. We need actual evidence. We all know high-profile trials are theatrical. Her lawyer is smooth, confident, and good-looking. Juries love those types. He'll convince everyone that we're taking advantage of an honest mistake and that we're trying to railroad her. She's pretty. No one will believe she committed a horrific crime without solid evidence."

"Juries want forensic shit like they see on TV," Todd said.

"That's pathetic but true." Bree set her mug in the sink.

Matt gestured toward the doorway. "Let's go check our reports on forensic shit."

CHAPTER TWENTY-ONE

Matt stared at a bag of nuts inside the vending machine. He was really sick of nuts. Why couldn't the vending machine dispense cheeseburgers? Grabbing a bottle of water, he retrieved the conference room key from Marge and unlocked the door. Bree brought her laptop and notepad. She held a mug in her hand. Matt smelled coffee.

He peered into her cup. "You're not going to sleep at all tonight. Your blood is ten percent caffeine at this point."

She nodded and sipped. "What can I say? I'm weak, but I'm also so tired that I doubt caffeine will be an issue."

"You'll be wired." Matt checked the time on his phone. "It's five thirty. Let's work for an hour, then quit for the day. You need a couple of hours to unwind, see your family, and get some sleep. You can't run flat-out for the entire investigation."

"I know." But she continued to drink the coffee.

Todd came in holding a manila file and a laptop. He took a chair and opened the computer. "I have a couple of updates. First, you should know that Jasper made bail."

Bree sighed. "Not a surprise. He didn't have any priors, he's lived in the area a long time, and his lawyer is street smart."

Todd nodded. "Next, a preliminary report from forensics on the crime scene is in. I emailed copies to both of you."

Matt opened the email on his phone and skimmed it. "They found a few long dark hairs in Spencer's bedroom."

"They could belong to Farah Rock or Monica Linfield," Todd suggested.

"Since it seems women with long dark hair were Spencer's type, the hairs could have come from other women as well," Matt said. "Spencer was a busy man."

"Unfortunately, both women already said they'd slept with him, so I'm not sure how that helps us solve the case." Bree massaged her temple.

But Matt knew if they made an arrest, physical evidence that officially placed the suspect inside the house was always good.

"Anything else interesting?" Bree asked.

Matt closed the email. "Nothing else is jumping out at me, but time will tell about the usefulness of the trace evidence forensics collected." If they gathered enough evidence on one of their suspects to obtain a search warrant, fibers, hair, soil, and DNA found at the scene could match those found at a suspect's home. "I'm liking Jasper. He had a recent argument with Spencer. Money is always a motive. Plus, the murder felt like rage, and families bring high emotion." In Matt's experience, no one could hate quite as hard as a loved one.

"We need to set up another interview with him." Bree made a note. "Let's move on to Farah Rock. She lied about her alibi and tried to get her friend Rhys Blake to also lie. She has access to a white SUV, her father's Highlander."

Matt raised a hand. "We still don't have any physical evidence tying her to the crime." But the lying bugged him.

"Which is why she's not in a jail cell." Bree sounded as if she'd really like to amend that.

"We didn't see a long-haired black cat at either Monica's or Farah's." Matt pictured each residence. "No cat at Jasper's place either. We didn't go to Avery Ledger's house. We interviewed her on scene."

"Because she found the body." Bree tapped a finger on the table. "Did the surveillance video from her employer confirm what time she left work?"

Todd nodded. "Juarez watched the video and verified she left at 4:56 in the afternoon."

"So, the video confirms her alibi." Matt envisioned the timeline of the murder. "It's possible but unlikely she would have had time to kill Spencer by five thirty."

"We'll move Avery to the bottom of the list," Bree agreed.

Todd said, "Next up, Monica Linfield. I assigned Juarez to watch the surveillance video you forwarded from the film studio. Monica Linfield was at the shoot all day, except she left at 4:44 p.m. and didn't return until after six."

Bree flattened her palms on the table. "And Monica drives a white Audi Q5."

"Which is a midsize SUV," Matt said. "Like the delivery driver spotted at the house next to Spencer's."

Bree nodded. "Let's bring Monica in for a formal interview too."

"I'll ask Juarez to pick her up," Todd said.

"Let's expand our search into Monica's background, including her dating app activity," Bree added.

Todd nodded and wrote notes in his file. "We've received Spencer's credit card and bank information. He was worse than broke. Between the renovations and his fancy taste, his debt is through the roof. He's been shuffling debts around, but he couldn't have kept that up for long."

Bree frowned. "Any sizable transactions in his bank account?"

"Are you thinking he borrowed from a loan shark?" Matt asked.

"Can't shuffle debts forever." Bree tapped a forefinger. "We haven't seen any sign of an extra twenty-five grand."

Matt wondered if Ricky had also been lying. Everyone else did. "Maybe Ricky made up that story."

"It's possible," Bree agreed. "But it didn't feel that way."

Matt didn't trust people who shot at him.

Todd shuffled papers. "I don't see any significant influx of cash, though he desperately needed it."

"What about his phone records?" Matt asked.

Todd said, "As we expected, his cell provider only keeps actual texts for five days. After that, messages are purged. I haven't had a chance to dig into the details yet. The techs in forensics are working on extracting data from Spencer's cell phone."

Matt thought about other online activity. "Did Spencer have social media accounts?"

"He did." Todd nodded. "But he didn't post. He followed other people, mostly women. As you would expect, his profile information was all BS."

"Just another tool for him to manipulate women. What a scumbag." Disgust filled Matt. "Have we found any friends?"

Todd shook his head. "Not yet. He seemed to have been a loner."

"Like Jasper said." Matt didn't trust Jasper any more than he trusted Ricky. He stared at the suspects' photos on the murder board. Avery was the only one they hadn't caught in a lie or significant omission.

"What about social media for Monica and Farah?" Bree asked.

"Monica's posts are mostly professional." Todd scrolled on his laptop. "Farah has accounts. She posts the occasional rock-climbing pictures, but again, she's not a big user either."

"Keep working the cell phone records angle," Bree said.

"OK if I take it home after the press conference?" Todd asked. "If not, I can ask Cady to feed and walk Goldie." He smiled. "Or she's going to eat her way out of her crate. That's Goldie—not Cady."

"It's fine." Bree waved toward the door. "Make sure you eat and get some sleep tonight too."

"Yes, ma'am." Todd gathered his files, closed his laptop, and left the room.

"Matt, you take the financials. I'll keep working the dating app angle." She checked her phone. "After the press conference, I'm going to head home to have dinner with the family, then work at home after the kids go to bed."

Matt didn't want to go home alone. "OK if I stop and see my new horse?"

"Of course." Bree smiled. "I'm sure there will be plenty of food, and you can eat whatever Dana baked today. If I eat any more pastries, I'm going to need new uniforms."

Matt's stomach growled. "Good. I'm starving." His own fridge was bare. He ate at Bree's or his parents' house a few nights a week. If he went home, he'd need to go grocery shopping or eat a sandwich for dinner. Neither appealed. Plus, he'd rather spend time at Bree's.

Bree checked the time. "Ten minutes to press conference." She pulled a small makeup kit out of her drawer. "I can't wait to actually have a women's locker room."

"Don't hold your breath," Matt said.

"It'll happen someday, but it's amazing how many details the county board of supervisors can argue over even after the funds have been approved." Bree had won a huge battle with county administration to have the station expanded and renovated. Before she had become sheriff, the department hadn't employed a single female deputy. Bree had corrected that and was attempting to modernize the building to include a women's locker room. A proposed plan had been drawn up, but the county board of supervisors seemed determined to argue over every light switch and screw, no doubt in an attempt to delay the spending of funds.

But Matt was sure it would happen. Much to the supervisors' dismay, Bree was relentless, patient, and ruthlessly polite. She left them with nothing to complain about.

She went to the closet. Her uniform was on a hanger, covered in a dry cleaning bag. She grabbed it and headed for the open door, presumably on her way to the restroom to clean up.

A few minutes later, Matt stood at Bree's side, a half step back as she faced the press in the lobby of the station in a fresh uniform. With only a single murder—and some fresh national political drama that Matt had no time to care about—only a half dozen news crews gathered to hear Bree. Matt recognized them as the usual locals. Reporters pushed to the front, with their cameramen working behind them.

Bree began with the facts. "The victim of Tuesday evening's murder has been identified as Grey's Hollow resident Spencer LaForge. Mr. LaForge died by violent asphyxiation."

Nick West from WSNY News asked, "Is it true he was suffocated with plastic wrap?"

"Yes," Bree acknowledged.

"Can you confirm a stun gun was used by the killer?" Nick asked.

"Yes. A stun gun was used to subdue the victim." Bree's voice remained cool, but a vein on her temple popped as if she were power-lifting. They'd known about the leak, but hearing the reporter blab all the key facts about the case still stoked Matt's anger.

Arrogant little creep.

An intense look passed between Bree and the young reporter. Matt could tell Nick understood that the sheriff was angry about his questions, but the reporter seemed undaunted. Matt suspected Nick would regret his decision.

Nick persisted. "Is it true the victim was bound with zip ties?"

"I cannot comment on the details without potentially compromising the investigation." Bree deliberately pointed to another reporter.

"Do you have any suspects?" the woman asked.

"We are pursuing all lines of investigation." Bree's tone remained neutral. "And are interviewing multiple persons of interest."

The woman continued. "But you haven't arrested anyone yet?"

"No." Only those who knew Bree very well would recognize the signs of irritation on her face. To anyone else, she was cool, collected, and professional.

A tall bald man pushed forward. "Is Investigator Flynn working on the case with you?" His mouth curled into a suggestive sneer. Bree and Matt's relationship was public knowledge, but some reporters continued to try and make it newsworthy.

Bree offered no excuses or explanations. She simply met the bald man's eyes with what Matt liked to think of as her signature no-bullshit stare. "Yes."

"And you don't think your personal relationship affects your ability to work together?" The bald reporter's tone suggested he did.

"No." Bree's tone left no room for argument. "Next?"

"Was the crime sexual?" a woman called out.

"There was no evidence of sexual assault." Bree looked for another question.

Nick West raised his hand again. "Should people be worried?"

Bree leaned closer to her microphone. "At this time, we have no reason to believe there's any threat to the community. That said, I will always recommend people lock their doors and pay attention to their personal safety."

Bree ended the conference. News crews separated to give their last sound bites. Bree and Matt retreated to her office.

Todd ducked in. "Juarez reported that Monica isn't home. Should he wait for her?"

"No. She could be anywhere. We'll track her down at the film studio in the morning. I've had enough. I'm going home." Bree shoved papers into her briefcase. She glanced up at Matt. "We can review more reports after dinner."

"Oh, joy." Matt slid into his jacket. "Do you mind if I stop for Brody?"

"He's always welcome," Bree said, sorting through more paperwork. "You go on ahead. I'll meet you there."

Matt left the station, stopped for his dog, and drove out to the farm. Brody's tail wagged as Matt turned into the driveway. Bree was just parking her SUV when he pulled up alongside her, got out of his Suburban, then helped Brody out of the back seat. After the older dog injured his shoulder, the vet forbade him from jumping in and out of the high vehicle.

Lights blazed in the barn. Snow drifted through a quiet sky. Bree walked next to Matt, while Brody trotted ahead.

Halfway across the backyard, Matt stopped to sniff the wood-smoke-scented air. "It's peaceful out here."

"It is." Bree reached for his hand.

He intertwined his fingers with hers. The more time he spent at Bree's farm, the less he enjoyed his own place. When he'd bought it, the ten acres had felt serene. He'd needed the space to come to terms with his injuries and the end of his career. Frankly, he hadn't been fit company much of the time that first year. But now that he had Bree and her family in his life, all the empty land felt, well, empty.

He pulled her closer for a kiss before they walked hand in hand to the barn.

The Standardbred was tied in the aisle. The kids were grooming him, and the horse looked considerably cleaner than when they'd brought him home earlier.

The Percheron stretched his head over the half door. He nickered and bobbed his nose. Matt walked closer and gave his forehead a rub. While looking around the animal's giant head, he saw a bandage circling the horse's back leg. But the big beast looked happy.

Dana sat on a bale of hay in the aisle, her hands shoved deep into her pockets. "I saved you some chicken piccata."

Matt patted his stomach. He'd eaten her piccata in the past. "Did you make linguine?"

"Of course, from scratch," Dana huffed, as if to suggest otherwise would be an affront. "Now that you're here to supervise, I'll go warm up the leftovers." She rose and brushed hay from her jeans. "Not that I was all that useful out here. My presence was mostly supportive and supervisory, if the supervisor can know less than those she is in charge of."

"That's often the case." Matt laughed.

"So true." Dana headed out of the barn. She was a bodyguard as much as a nanny. Whenever Bree was working a big case, Dana grew more protective over the kids.

Luke looked up from brushing the horse's foreleg. "It's too cold to give him a bath, so we're trying to clean off some of the dried mud."

Kayla worked a rubber curry in circles on the Standardbred's shoulder. A small cloud of dust billowed. "He needs to be pretty when he meets Uncle Adam."

"Was Uncle Adam pleased at the news?" Bree asked.

"He didn't call," Kayla said, disappointment heavy in her voice.

Bree froze for a second. Matt could see the tension in her posture. Her eyes met his. She shook her head. "I'm going to call him again."

"I'm sure it's fine." Luke stood. "You know how he gets when he's painting."

"I do." Bree smiled and ducked out of the barn. With a final pat to the Percheron's nose, Matt went outside. Bree was ten feet away, her back to him, her phone pressed to her ear. "Adam, are you there?" She paused, then said, "Please call me." Lowering the phone, she typed a text with her thumbs. "I'm officially worried. Lately, Adam has made an effort to call me back pretty quickly. If he's buried in his painting, he'll at least send me a quick text telling me so."

"He might have forgotten to charge his phone," Luke said from the doorway.

"That's possible." Bree nodded, but her expression told Matt the explanation didn't sit well.

"Let's eat. If he hasn't called back by the time we're done, then we'll drive over to his place," he suggested.

Bree glanced at her phone, then nodded. "I don't like this at all. It's not like him."

She'd lived through more tragedy than most people could comprehend, but Matt knew that everyone had limits.

CHAPTER
TWENTY-TWO

An hour later, Bree parked in front of Adam's place, a converted barn in the middle of a wide-open meadow. Mentally, she crossed her fingers.

Please be home.

"His truck is here." Matt pointed to the ancient Bronco held together with body putty and prayer, one more thing Adam could easily replace if he desired.

Her brother was very successful. He'd supported their sister and the kids for years. He'd set up trust funds for the kids. Bree didn't need to worry about paying for their educations.

He could afford to live in a much nicer home, but he chose to stay in this one. It met all his needs—light and isolation being the most important of those. His paintings had been hot on the art scene for a number of years, but his last work had been . . . She struggled to describe the raw emotions he'd captured on his canvas—a glimmer of hope amid violence and despair.

More than hope. His painting had made a promise: whatever darkness you'd experienced . . . something brighter was on the horizon.

Bree wasn't the artsy type. She lived in a world ruled by evidence, science, and fact. But that painting had drawn her in like no other. All

Adam's work called to her with their rawness of emotion. Darkness was in her soul. She'd been born with it, something she'd always worried about. But while his previous paintings had called to the bleakness inside her, the last one had banished it like sunlight drove out vampires.

It was brilliant.

The art world clearly agreed with Bree. A collector had snapped up the painting immediately and loaned it and a few of Adam's other works to a museum for an exhibition.

She and Matt stepped out of the vehicle. Clouds obscured the moon, casting the meadow in darkness broken only by the lights glowing in Adam's windows. Bree had lived in Philadelphia from the age of eight until this past January. It was never really dark in the city. Light pollution brightened everything. But night in the countryside could be stark and unrelenting.

A thin coating of snow dusted the ground. It crunched under her boots as she approached the front door. Bree couldn't explain how she knew, but the house felt empty. There was a stillness that stirred her anxiety and compressed her insides.

In the past, Adam had lost track of everything when he was in the middle of a project. He forgot to eat and sleep. He became obsessed with—no, possessed by—his work. Bree understood. She'd been the same way with homicide investigations in her previous life.

Before her sister's murder.

Before Bree had essentially become a parent.

Before she'd reconnected with Adam. They'd grown closer over the past eleven months. The desire to provide home and family to Luke and Kayla had forced them to leave their confirmed loner statuses behind. Adam had improved his communication skills, and he made time to see the kids regularly even when he was in the middle of a painting. He no longer completely disappeared into his art. He'd made room in his life for his family.

Bree had been separated from her siblings after their parents' deaths. After Erin died and Bree moved back to Grey's Hollow, she and Adam had worked hard to develop a real relationship. She'd never stopped loving her little brother, but she hadn't really known him. Now that she did, the thought of something happening to him made everything inside her go cold and queasy, like that hope—that light in his painting—would never shine again.

When Adam didn't answer the door, she knocked again. A gust of bitter wind swept across the meadow, carrying dead leaves and snow dust in a frigid cloud. The hairs on the back of Bree's neck lifted.

The lights are on. Adam is here. He's working.

She reached for the knob, then hesitated and looked over her shoulder at Matt. His face was grim in the harsh glare of the porch light. "I'm not sure what to do. He's an adult. He has the right to privacy."

"But he usually calls or texts you back, right?" Matt asked.

"Yes."

"Plus, his car is here and he's not answering the door. That's odd." Matt frowned. "Any chance he has a girl in there?"

"Ugh. I hadn't even thought of that." She raised her fist and pounded on the door. The sound reverberated across the empty meadow.

But the house remained still, and Bree's belly ached with worry.

"That's it. I'm going in." She reached into her pocket for her key ring and found Adam's key. She inserted it into the dead bolt. It turned with no resistance. Bree froze. "The door isn't locked."

Was Adam inside, or had he forgotten to lock the door? He could be incapacitated or with a woman. She and Adam had developed a decent relationship, but none of their conversations had covered this specific situation.

"Just go in already," Matt said.

Bree reached for the doorknob and turned it. She pushed open the door. Her right hand hovered above the butt of her weapon. "Adam?"

No one answered. They went inside and closed the door behind them. The house was one large room, with a partial wall that divided the living space from the studio. A light shone from the studio, casting half of the space in shadows. Bree flipped the wall switch in the kitchen, and the room went bright.

Empty Chinese takeout containers and discarded cans of Red Bull littered the coffee table. Pizza boxes were stacked on the floor. Dishes and cups filled the sink. The bedding was in disarray.

The bathroom door stood open. Bree peered inside. It was empty except for a pile of musty towels on the tile floor.

Matt ducked around the partial wall into the studio area. "He's not here."

Bree scanned the mess. With a neat person, this level of disorder could signal the home had been ransacked or that a struggle had taken place. In Adam's case, the chaos simply meant his current painting was progressing. After he'd finished with the project, he'd eat, sleep, and clean up his house. Then the process would start all over again.

"Now what?" Bree asked. "If a stranger came into my office to report their brother missing because he didn't return her call from earlier that same day, I wouldn't waste many man-hours investigating. In that short amount of time, I wouldn't even consider an adult missing without unusual circumstances or some sign of foul play."

"There's probably a simple explanation for why Adam hasn't responded to your messages."

"Probably, but how did he go out without his car?" Bree asked. Frantic dread burned in her chest. She pressed a hand to it, as if she could quell the fire behind her breastbone with her touch.

"Rideshare?" Matt suggested. "Maybe the Bronco is having mechanical problems, or he went out for drinks and didn't want to drive home."

"Both plausible," Bree said. "He's not much of a drinker, though." As children of an abusive alcoholic, neither she nor Adam had a taste for booze.

"I can't blame you for being worried. If this were Cady, I'd be uneasy too."

Bree racked her brain. She walked a circle around the kitchen, her fist still pressed to her chest. "We don't have a vehicle for deputies to look for him."

"Do you have the ability to locate his cell phone?"

"Yes!" Bree opened her Find My Phone app and selected Adam's cell. A gray circle appeared, signifying the phone's last known location. "His phone is either off or the battery is dead." If Adam's phone location were live, the circle would be green.

"Where was it last?"

Bree squinted at the map, then zoomed in. "He *was* in a bookshop in Grey's Hollow."

"Let's go."

They locked the door on the way out. Bree drove into town. Slowing the SUV, she cruised through the commercial area. She turned right and slid to the curb halfway down the block in front of Hollow Books. She and Matt hurried from the vehicle and into the shop.

Signs advertised upcoming readings and signings. Faded couches and chairs were scattered throughout the store. They sold coffee, tea, and short-bread from a small cart. Payments were collected on the honor system.

A young woman at the register looked up and called, "Can I help you, Sheriff? We close in ten minutes."

Bree nodded. She approached the counter and dug out her phone. She pulled up a recent photo of Adam and showed it to the woman, whose name tag read SHARLA. "Did you see this man tonight?"

Sharla tilted her head. "I don't know. We weren't very busy tonight, and I was in the back working on orders. Is something wrong?"

"I hope not," Bree said.

Sharla turned and called into the back of the shop. "Clarice, would you come out here for a minute?" She turned back to Bree. "Clarice is the owner."

An older redhead hustled through the doorway, wiping her hands on the legs of her jeans. Her eyebrows shot up as she took in Bree's uniform.

Sharla pointed toward the phone. "Did you see this man tonight?"

Clarice squinted, then reached into her pocket for a pair of readers. She set them on her nose. "He looks familiar. I think he was in tonight." She turned to Bree with excited eyes. "Is he wanted for something?"

"No. I just need to find him."

Clarice pursed her lips, almost seeming disappointed. "I don't remember what time he came in, maybe around seven?"

Bree checked the time. It was almost nine. "Was he alone?"

"No." Clarice shook her head. "He was with a woman. They sat in that corner." She pointed to a pair of leather chairs near the travel section.

That information should have eased Bree's worries, but it didn't. "Can you describe her?"

"She was pretty, with dark hair." Clarice propped a hand on her hip and stared at the ceiling. "The gentleman bought a book on artwork in the Vatican and a collection of Sherlock Holmes stories. The lady didn't make a purchase, so I didn't get a good look at her."

Matt studied the ceiling. "Do you have surveillance cameras?"

Clarice grimaced. "No. They broke years ago, and I can't afford to replace them."

"Thank you." Bree led the way out of the store.

Matt stood on the sidewalk and scanned the street. "I don't see any businesses close enough for their surveillance cameras to have captured the front of the store in their feed."

"No." Bree eyed the building across the street, a bridal shop. The entrance of the shop was located around the corner, on Main Street. If they had cameras, that's where they would be. "So, we don't have a picture of the woman he was with."

Matt took her hand. "They could have gone somewhere after the bookstore. At least you know he was fine two hours ago."

"Yes." She nodded. But it felt like steel bands encircled her chest. She wouldn't breathe easy until she'd talked to Adam. "I know I'm overly protective. He's an adult. He's entitled to a personal life."

"He is, and it's great that he's dating," Matt said. "I love your brother, but he can be forgetful, especially when he's deep into a project. He probably forgot to charge his phone. Try not to worry too much."

But Bree knew that wasn't possible. She always imagined the worst.

CHAPTER

TWENTY-THREE

I steer my vehicle down a side street. The roads are wet and slick. I avoid a patch of black ice. An accident would ruin my evening.

Grey's Hollow is a small town. Not much happens at night. Flurries drift through the halos of streetlamps. Taillights glow at the next intersection, in front of the only open business, a chain drugstore.

A quarter mile down the road, I slow to read the numbers on the houses. I can't check my location on my map app because I've left my phone at home. I don't want to be tracked. Not tonight.

The sheriff said they were investigating persons of interest. The sheriff is blowing smoke out her ass. She's fucking with me, trying to pretend she has real leads when she has nothing. That reporter knows as much as she does.

What I don't fully understand is why her cluelessness bugs me. I should be glad, right?

Instead, I'm irritated, which is extremely fucked up. Whatever. I have a surprise in store for the sheriff. I'll expose her incompetence.

As I drive, I read the numbers on the mailboxes. Twenty-seven, twenty-nine. I'm going to house thirty-three. I've been here before, but the houses on this street are close together and look alike, all old and narrow. I glide to the curb when the house comes into view, making sure to park in the darkest location between streetlamps.

Like most houses in town, this one is Colonial in style. The facade is comprised of a small front porch and attached garage. The living area is in the back of the first floor. Spencer's bedroom was also at the back of the house, but upstairs. The windows above the garage look into the spare bedroom, currently outfitted as a home office.

The windows of the house are dark. It doesn't appear as if anyone is home yet, but the homeowner should be here any minute.

My second target is Julius Northcott. He's the kind of man who puts a capital *A* in *Asshole*. Everything about him is douchey. Unlike Spencer, who dumped women after fucking them a couple of times, Julius prefers to juggle many women at once. He isn't just a liar; he's also a cheat. He doesn't bother to actually break up with any of them. To him, they are interchangeable. If they catch him cheating, he doesn't care. If they become demanding, he loses interest. Then he ghosts them.

Tonight, Julius is going to get ghosted—literally.

I turn off the engine, zip my jacket, and slide down in the seat. Without the heater running, cold seeps into the car, but I won't have to wait long. The auto dealership where Julius works closes at eight. It's nearly nine now. He'll be home soon.

Headlights approach. The giant black truck pulls into Julius's driveway. I snort out loud. I'll bet five hundred bucks Julius has never driven the vehicle off-road. Not even once. Don't get me wrong—it's a useful vehicle for a contractor or a farmer, a real workhorse. But it's a ridiculous choice for Julius. He doesn't even mow his own grass.

There's no PIN pad entry system, so I can't slip in and lie in wait for him. I've watched the exterior of his home multiple times, but I've been inside only once. Two weeks ago, I slipped in while the house cleaner was working upstairs. She wears earbuds and sings while she cleans. She never heard a thing and made it easy to avoid her. Getting into the house undetected tonight will be a little more challenging, but I have a plan.

I always have a plan.

I step out of my vehicle and shrug into my backpack. I've turned off the dome light. Not that Julius would even notice me. He's usually very focused on himself. I jog across two lawns and press my back to the side of Julius's house just as the pickup pulls into the garage. The engine quiets. I hear Julius get out of his truck. Hard-soled shoes clomp across the concrete floor away from me. The overhead door begins to rattle down. An interior door squeaks open, then closes. Julius never waits until the door is fully down before going into the house.

I wait until it's nearly closed, then hit the ground and roll under it. I'm in.

The door touches down with a metallic thud. I crouch between the truck and the wall. A few minutes later, the light goes out. I sit on the concrete and check my watch. I need to wait for thirty minutes. Julius has a sex addiction problem. If he isn't having sex, he's watching it. On nights he doesn't have a date, he stays in with his porn. He'll grab a bite to eat, pour a double scotch on the rocks, and settle in the den in front of his big-screen TV.

I know this because his den looks over the backyard, and his blinds are inadequate.

As I wait in the cold, I run through my plan over and over in my head. Excitement rushes through my veins, keeping me warm. My plan is so perfect.

So utterly appropriate.

And after I finish with Julius, I have a surprise in store for the sheriff. Several, actually. I rub my palms together, anticipating how the evening and next day or so will play out. The half hour passes so slowly. I feel like a child waiting for Santa to come.

Finally, it's time. I get up, stretch, and loosen up my muscles. A cramp at the wrong time could ruin everything. I open my backpack and push aside the knife to remove the stun gun and zip ties. Shoving them into my pocket, I press onward.

I go to the interior door of the garage, which Julius never locks. He's too lazy to bother with a key every day. I tug on my gloves and make sure my knit hat covers my hair. Then I turn the knob slowly, minimizing noise. A gentle push opens the door.

The house isn't big. Julius's man cave is just down the hall. I can hear the TV—at least I hope the groaning and the wet slap of flesh on flesh is from the movie.

But whatever.

Julius's nasty habits are why I'm here, right? He's gonna do what he's gonna do. The only thing I know for certain is that he'll be adequately distracted.

Light flickers from the TV. I creep down the hall, placing each footfall slowly and carefully. I pass the kitchen on my right. At the open doorway on the left, I peer around the arched frame. The couch faces away from me, but I can see Julius's reflection in the glass doors of the fireplace. The flat-screen is mounted over it. Julius lies back, his sweatpants around his knees, stroking himself.

I pull the stun gun out of my pocket and walk on my toes to approach Julius from the back. His attention is riveted on the screen, where a man and woman writhe and groan. Wait. There's more than one woman, and they're burning each other with hot wax. I ignore the movie. The ridiculous dialogue and moaning fade to background noise as I focus on my prey.

Julius pauses midstroke. His head cocks slightly, as if he hears me breathing. His head whirls around, his erection popping free of his grasp. I lunge forward. With my thumb on the switch, I shove the stun gun into the base of his neck. It crackles. His body jerks and goes stiff. He cries out in a garbled scream as I silently count five Mississippis.

Five seconds of charge should incapacitate him for a minute or so. I release the switch and walk around the couch to stand in front of him. His twitching body falls sideways, stiff like a felled tree. Before he can recover, I can't resist shoving the weapon into his groin for a second, vindictive zap.

Two shocks have left him limp and sweating. He whimpers as I fasten zip ties around his wrists and ankles. A single word rasps out of his mouth. "Please."

"Shut up!" I fish in my backpack for the duct tape. I rip off a piece and slap it over his mouth.

Satisfied that I don't have to listen to him, I step away.

The next zap is just for my own satisfaction. His eyes roll back in his head. His inhuman grunt makes me happier than it should. I recognize that I'm not a good person. But neither is Julius. At least I only prey on those who need to be punished. Julius targets the innocent.

I glance at the TV screen, where the kink continues.

There's nothing innocent about Julius.

With my target restrained, I can take my time. I open my backpack and pull out the plastic wrap. Julius's eyes open wide. He's wheezing, his chest pumping. His limbs jerk randomly, like he's having partial, random seizures.

I was going to find a new way to kill, but this method worked so well for Spencer. No blood to get on my clothes. I appreciate the neatness of the kill.

Julius's whole body trembles. Does he know what I'm going to do? It feels wrong to drag out the murder. I should be humane and put him down quickly. But we've already established that I'm no saint. Julius and I share one thing in common: we don't care about our shortcomings. We are comfortable with our sins.

So I tell him exactly how it's going to go. He whimpers and squirms, pulling at his bonds, as I lay out the details of my plan. His muscle control is returning, but it doesn't matter. He can't get out of the plastic binds. I'm not sure if the trembling of his limbs is caused by electrical shock or fear.

I'm not sure I care. Either way, I'm enjoying the hell out of his discomfort. Tears and snot run down Julius's face as I begin to unwind the plastic wrap.

CHAPTER TWENTY-FOUR

Matt paced the small patch of floor in the film studio's kitchenette. A ray of morning sun slid through a gap in the blinds and speared him in the eyes. He squinted against the glare and pivoted again. There was barely room for him to take three steps in each direction, but he couldn't sit still.

While he walked off his frustration, Bree leaned against the wall and watched him with patient eyes. Unlike him, she didn't waste energy fidgeting. She sipped coffee from a paper cup, having made use of the pod-style machine on the counter when they'd been asked to wait until Monica was finished filming a particular segment.

She still hadn't heard from Adam, and evidence of a sleepless night showed in the dark circles under her eyes. She lifted her coffee to her mouth, tilting her head back to drain its contents. Then she tossed the empty cup in a trash can.

"Sheriff?" A man holding a clipboard—someone's assistant—stood in the doorway. About thirty years old, he wore round, thick tortoiseshell glasses, an untucked plaid shirt, and red skinny jeans. "Monica's ready for you." His snotty tone suggested Bree and Matt weren't welcome.

A microscopic hint of annoyance flickered in Bree's eyes before she covered her reaction with a professional nod.

"This way." The assistant performed a sharp pivot. He didn't wait for them but strode away without even glancing over his shoulder to ensure they were behind him.

They walked down a hallway into the main studio. People milled around the cameras, lights, and backdrops. A half dozen models dressed like metallic chess pawns clustered around an older woman wielding a can of hair spray like a weapon. Matt didn't see Monica.

"You can talk in here." The assistant stood aside and waved toward a room the size of a walk-in closet. He checked his watch. "But we need Monica back on set in twenty."

Bree didn't respond. Matt followed her into the tiny space, which had been set up for hair and makeup. A barstool-height director's chair faced a vanity and mirror. Cases of makeup, brushes, and hair gadgets cluttered the vanity. With no other seats, Matt leaned against the wall facing the chair. Bree rested a hip on the vanity.

Monica came in and closed the door behind her. Bree gestured toward the chair, and Monica perched carefully on the front edge of the stretched canvas, as if afraid to get too comfortable. Not that comfortable looked possible in her dramatic costume. The gold skin suit fit like body paint. Her hair was slicked down in a dark, shimmery fall. Her face glowed, not in a healthy way, but with a metallic sheen. Her cheekbones were accented with bronze, and her lips were painted silver, as were her eyelids. Enormous fake eyelashes framed her eyes. How did she even lift her eyelids?

Matt eyed her shoes. Gold—of course—with ice-pick heels that had to be five inches high. "What kind of commercial are you shooting?"

"Perfume." Monica gestured to her skin suit. "The concepts are always weird." She looked to Bree. "Why are you here?" The question was blunt, but her tone wasn't rude.

"We have a few follow-up questions from yesterday's interview," Bree began.

"I already answered your questions," Monica complained.

"But you were one of the last people to date Spencer," Matt explained. "Your statements are important."

"OK." She sighed. "But I don't have a lot of time." She lowered her voice to a whisper. "The director is in a *mood*. Again."

"We'll be brief." Bree whipped out her notepad. "You told us you were here shooting a commercial all day on Tuesday."

"That's correct." Monica nodded. "Same director. He doesn't let up, but the money is good, so . . ." She made a *whatever* gesture.

Bree flipped some pages, then made direct eye contact with Monica. "But the surveillance video actually shows that you left the building at 4:44 p.m. and didn't return until six."

Monica scooted her butt backward and sat up a little straighter, her movements restless. When she broke eye contact, Matt predicted her next words would be a lie.

She couldn't deny she'd left. They had her on video.

"I forgot about that." The lie rolled smoothly off her lips. "I was upset." She returned her gaze to Bree's. "I know Spencer broke up with me, but I still liked him. I always like men who treat me like garbage. It's something I need to work on."

Matt sensed her last admission was the truth. Monica still pined for Spencer, even though she admitted he had been a terrible person. Some people were drawn to drama and addicted to heartache.

"Where did you go?" Bree asked.

Monica blinked but didn't hesitate. "There's a convenience store down the street. I don't usually eat during a shoot, except maybe a protein bar. I don't want a bloated stomach. The camera already adds pounds. I told everyone I was getting a Red Bull—which I did—but I also bought a doughnut." She whispered the last part, as if she'd said *heroin* instead of *doughnut*.

"You were shooting for thirteen hours," Matt said. "Surely you need more than a protein bar."

Monica lifted a shoulder. "It's part of the job. I'm used to it. But Tuesday was so freaking loooong." She cast a rueful glance at the door. "So much yelling."

"You didn't mention this foray to the convenience store when we talked to you yesterday," Bree said.

"I just said I forgot." Monica's eyes misted. She jumped to her feet. "I can't cry. The director would be so mad if I ruin this makeup." She pinched the bridge of her nose for a few seconds. Then she reached for a tissue from a box on the vanity and, leaning close to the mirror, carefully dabbed at the corners of her eyes. "This makeup took forever. I was here before dawn." She assessed her reflection, seemed satisfied, then turned to them. "I need to get back to work."

"Just another minute." Matt held up a hand. "Did you eat the doughnut at the store?" He hoped he could trip her up. He could sense she was still holding something back. But what?

"No." Monica sank back into the chair. Her gaze darted to Matt, her expression guarded. She cleared her throat. "I took it back to my car."

Bree cocked her head. "It was cold. Why did you eat in your car?"

"I didn't want anyone to see me. I didn't just eat it. I scarfed it down in two bites." Monica looked ashamed. "I know food isn't the answer to stress. I can't let it be." She motioned to her long, lean body. "I *have* to look like this. There's always an eighteen-year-old waiting to take my place. I know I sound superficial, but I don't have a fallback career. I need to milk this one as long as possible. I'm pretty, not smart."

Matt thought she was savvy, though. "I get it. It's your job."

"Yes." Monica batted her weirdly long eyelashes at him.

He resisted the urge to roll his eyes. Did she really think a little attention from her would make him drop her from their suspect list? Or forget her omission? It was so cliché. And also, really weird in that makeup. It was like having a robot flirt with him.

"You were gone for an hour and fifteen minutes," Bree interrupted. "It doesn't take that long to eat a doughnut."

Monica turned off her seductive act like she threw a switch. Her gaze returned to Bree's. "I needed some alone time. I sat in the car and listened to music. It was a rough day."

Bree didn't respond but continued to study Monica, who squirmed under the intensity of her scrutiny. Monica looked back at Matt, as if she could convince him to take her side. If she could play the flirty cliché, then Matt and Bree could work with a good cop, bad cop theme.

Matt played along, nodding. "Everyone needs alone time."

"Exactly." Monica sat back, one eyebrow rising in a haughty expression as she looked back at Bree.

"Do you have a receipt for the Coke and doughnut?" Bree asked.

"Red Bull," Monica said pointedly.

Bree acknowledged the correction. "Do you have a receipt for the Red Bull and doughnut?"

Monica shook her head.

"Did anyone see you there?" Matt applied pressure and tried to trip her up again. "Did your friends go with you?"

"No. No one went with me. That was the whole point." Monica shot him a betrayed look. "I just said I wanted to be alone."

Bree nodded. "Did you pay with cash or credit?"

"Cash," Monica said.

"What's the name of the store?" Matt asked. "I'm sure they'll remember you." He used a tone that suggested she was memorable.

But Monica wasn't flattered. She shot him a sharp glare he couldn't interpret, but it didn't seem grateful. She gave him the name of the store. "But they were very busy."

Was she providing an excuse for them not remembering her?

"It's a shame you don't have a receipt," Bree commented, her tone regretful. "Do you want to know what time Spencer was killed?"

The color drained from Monica's face, but she didn't ask.

Matt supplied the answer. He couldn't help it. "Between 4:30 and 5:30."

Her eyes widened slightly, but her face barely moved. She was smart enough not to respond.

"We'll check with the convenience store," Bree said. "I'm sure they have video surveillance as well. Everyone does these days."

Monica's eyes narrowed a millimeter. She was smarter than she pretended not to be. Without saying another word, she rose, applied fresh lipstick, and put a tissue between her lips and smacked them together. Crumpling the tissue, she tossed it into the wastepaper basket.

After she disappeared through the doorway, Matt pushed off the wall. "This is the kind of moment when I want to say, 'Don't leave town' like a TV cop." In reality, they had no authority to limit a suspect's movement.

"If we were on TV, we could get DNA results in an hour." Bree removed an evidence bag from her pocket. She put on a glove and retrieved the lipstick tissue from the trash can.

Matt grinned. "Gotta love free DNA."

"Cops do love to trash pick." Bree bagged and tagged the tissue.

Matt jerked his head toward Bree's thick boots. "If we were TV cops, you'd have to wear stilettos, though."

Bree shrugged, as if unconcerned. "Not for long. The case would be solved in under an hour."

"So true." Matt led the way out of the studio.

After the bustle of the crew and models, the cold air outside felt refreshing. They returned to the sheriff's vehicle. Inside, she started the engine and turned on the heat.

"What did you think?" Bree asked.

"People who are being honest don't have to think of their answers." Matt held his hands in front of the vent, but the air was still cold. "Her face is hard to read. Her eyes are expressive, but she has one hell of a poker face. Feels almost like an emotional disconnect."

Bree looked at him, then shook her head. "Probably Botox."

"What?" Matt pulled his head back.

"It's a shot in the face to prevent wrinkles," Bree said.

"I know what it is," Matt said. "I thought cosmetic surgery was mostly confined to Hollywood. I've never met anyone who used it before."

"I'm sure you have." Bree laughed. "Plenty of regular people use it."

"Seriously?"

"Yes. It's very mainstream, though I saw more of it in the city than here. Usually, docs are subtle about it. Being a model very concerned about stretching her career for as long as possible, Monica might get a higher dose." Bree pointed to her forehead. "Her forehead doesn't move at all. Her eyebrows are practically frozen in place, and there isn't a single crinkle in the corners of her eyes."

Matt snorted. "That would explain the disconnect between her eyes and her facial expressions. But her body language still suggests she wasn't being entirely truthful."

"I agree." Bree cocked her head to listen to a quick burst of radio chatter. But it was just a traffic stop. "Let's see if we can verify any parts of Monica's story. I'll send a deputy to the convenience store with a photo of her. See if anyone remembers her. If they have surveillance video, we'll get a copy."

Bree's phone buzzed. "It's dispatch." She'd turned off the radio on her duty belt during the interview. She answered the call on speakerphone.

"Sheriff," the dispatcher said, "I just took a call about a dead homeowner." He read off an address. "Deputies are en route. ETA five minutes. The caller was near hysterical but kept saying his face was covered in plastic."

Chapter Twenty-Five

Bree couldn't keep an image of Adam out of her mind as she and Matt raced toward the scene. She swerved around a pothole, and her stomach lurched.

It's not him.

"I know what you're thinking, but it's not Adam." Matt read her mind from the passenger seat. He reached behind the seat for his body-armor vest. Shrugging into it, he fastened the Velcro straps. "The caller said the dead guy is the homeowner."

Bree wore her vest beneath her uniform. "I know." But with plastic covering the victim's face, how could the caller be certain it was him? Logically, Bree knew the chances were less than one in a million, but logic didn't always prevail over emotions, especially when worry about a loved one was concerned. "But I can't help but think of the worst that can happen."

"Because you've actually seen the worst that can happen." Both of her hands were on the wheel, but Matt reached over and gave her shoulder a quick squeeze. He turned back to the computer. "The residence is owned by Julius Northcott, age forty-two. Northcott has a few speeding tickets but no criminal record."

Bree turned down a side street and sped to the address. Ahead, the swirling lights of two patrol cars flashed. She pulled to the curb behind her deputies' vehicles. An older-model Toyota sedan was parked in the street. A deputy crouched in the open vehicle door, speaking with a person in the driver's seat. A second deputy was stepping out of his patrol vehicle.

Forcing her personal paranoia from her mind, Bree jumped out of her vehicle, opened the rear hatch, and retrieved her AR-15 from the lockbox. She handed it to Matt. There was no one she trusted more to watch her back.

Carrying the weapon across his chest, Matt kept pace with her.

The deputy stepped away from the Toyota and faced Bree. "Sheriff," he began in a low voice. He nodded toward the sedan. "This is Susan Muckell. She came to clean the house, found the body, and called 911."

Bree crouched until she was eye level with the witness. She felt Matt stop behind her.

An ultra-thin woman in her midthirties turned her shocked face toward Bree. Susan wore black yoga pants with bleached-out splotches and a ratty army-green parka. "Mr. Northcott is dead." Her words and breaths came fast, as if she were going to hyperventilate.

"Is there *any* chance he's alive?" Bree asked.

Susan met Bree's gaze, and her head moved in a slow shake. "His skin was cold. Cold and gray. And his face was covered in plastic. You can't breathe through plastic." Her eyes reflected pure horror.

"Are you sure it's Mr. Northcott?" Bree asked.

Susan's face went blank, as if she hadn't thought of the question. "I can't be a hundred percent sure because his face was covered, but I didn't have any doubt until you just asked."

"Did you see anyone else inside?" Matt asked over Bree's shoulder. Susan shook her head.

"Where is Mr. Northcott?" Bree asked.

"You go through the front door, straight back," Susan said. "The den is on the left."

Bree stepped away from Susan. Matt and her two deputies gathered in a circle.

"Have you cleared the house yet?" Bree asked her deputies.

"No, ma'am," the first deputy said. "We arrived about a minute before you."

"OK." Bree pointed to the deputies. "You two go around back. We'll take the front door."

Bree headed up the walkway. She bent to examine the lock. "No sign of forced entry here."

Matt moved to the opposite side of the doorway. "If I was going to break in, I'd use the back door, where no one would see me." He looked up and down the street. "This feels visible."

Bree moved into position. "Agreed."

They shared a bracing look as they opened the front door. A nasty smell drifted out. Of one mind, they each took a deep breath of fresh air before they stepped into the house. Leading with her weapon, Bree scanned the foyer. The vacuum, cleaning supplies, and purse piled by the door likely belonged to Susan.

Bree gestured toward a door on her left. From its position, she assumed it led to the garage. Matt moved into place, and she opened the door to reveal a black pickup truck. Matt took a quick tour around the truck. Bree glanced under it. Empty.

They returned to the foyer.

Matt scanned the walls. "I don't see—or hear—a security system."

A feminine groan emanated from the back of the house. Matt lifted his brows. Glock raised, Bree followed the sound. With Matt just behind her left shoulder, they went down the hall.

The hallway ended in a T, with an eat-in kitchen on the right. Sliding glass doors behind the kitchen table overlooked a small fenced-in yard. Bree's deputies were at the back door.

Matt veered to the sliders. "They're locked from the inside, and the security bar is in place."

The fixed bar prevented a break-in by lifting the sliding glass door out of its tracks.

Not wanting to disturb the door, she gestured for the deputies to return to the front of the house.

On the left, an arched doorway framed the death scene in the den. Matt checked a closet. There wasn't another place large enough for an adult to hide. The front door opened. Her deputies came down the hall, and she sent them upstairs to clear the second floor.

Then she regripped her weapon and approached the couch. Craning her neck, she peered over the back. The body lay on its side facing a fireplace and big-screen TV. The victim's hands were bound behind his back, and his pants were around his knees. Blinds covered a long window on the right. Light slanted through the tilted slats, forming lines on the carpet. She identified the source of the moaning. A porn movie played on the TV.

But the victim wasn't watching it, not through the layers of plastic wrap encasing his head. Bree leaned over the back of the couch and pressed two fingers to the victim's neck. No pulse, and Susan had been correct. He was corpse cold.

In the doorway, Matt grimaced, but Bree exhaled in relief, glad the one-in-a-million odds had been reduced to zero. The victim was definitely not Adam. Once she'd put that aside, her insides twisted as she registered multiple glaring similarities to Spencer LaForge's murder. A Post-it note was stuck to the chest. She turned her head to read the block print aloud. "Watch your step, Sheriff."

"A personal note from the killer is never good."

A quick shiver rippled through Bree's bones. "No."

Matt turned in a circle, rifle at his hip, scanning the rooms.

"Does the body fit Mr. Northcott's description?" Bree asked.

Matt said, "Five eleven, one eighty, brown and brown."

Bree couldn't see the color of his eyes, but the hair above the plastic wrapping was medium brown shot with a few strands of gray.

Bree spotted a long, curved purple mark on the back of the victim's neck. "Is that mark on his neck an injury? Could he have been hit over the back of the head?"

Matt leaned over the body. "I don't know. I don't think it's a bruise. Looks more like a birthmark."

Bree pulled out her phone. She snapped a picture of the mark. "I'll notify the ME."

Matt started taking pictures of the scene with his phone. "I see stun gun burns." He pointed to a pair of marks on the victim's neck and another on his groin.

Bree pressed her phone to her ear and made the calls. "The ME will be here soon. Forensics is on the way."

Matt snapped a photo of the room. "Unfortunately, this looks very much like Spencer's death." He echoed her initial impression.

"Yep." Bree didn't want to say the words *serial killer*, but that's what her brain was screaming.

"Could be a copycat," Matt said.

There were reasons police withheld crime details from the public. You couldn't copy a crime if you didn't know the specifics.

"Too many details were leaked to the press." At that moment, Bree could have choked Nick West for giving away the plastic wrap, stun gun, and zip tie details. "I wish I knew who leaked the information."

"Think of how many people are involved with the case from your office, forensics, the medical examiner. Deputies, techs, administrative personnel. Hell, even cleaning crews could see a file."

"I know." Bree rubbed her temple. "It's still frustrating." She dropped her hand. Sunlight glinted on something behind a fake potted plant. "What's that?" She walked around the couch to get a better view.

A glass tank sat on the floor in the corner of the room. Its mesh lid lay half-askew. A small pile of hand-warmer packets, the disposable ones that went in your pockets, were piled on the carpet next to the lid. It took her a second to process the sight. Then the hairs on the back of her neck snapped upright like soldiers.

Movement on her right caught her attention. A sixth sense commanded her to freeze. Something rattled. Slowly, she turned her head. Her heartbeats echoed in her ears, and her breathing shifted to quiet and shallow for a reason she didn't understand. Every fiber in her warned that she was in grave danger.

She tracked the rattling sound and spotted the snake coiled on the floor maybe four feet away. Not just a snake.

A rattlesnake.

For a few seconds, she couldn't believe what she was seeing. Even though they'd suspected snakes had been stolen, the sight of it felt unreal. She squeezed her eyes closed for a second, then reopened them. The snake was still there.

"Matt?" Bree called in a soft voice.

"Yeah." He moved toward her.

"No. Stay still." She moved her eyeballs to glance at him.

He frowned. "What is it?" He couldn't see the animal from where he stood.

"A rattlesnake." She returned her attention to the reptile. She knew there wasn't anything inherently bad about snakes. They were just as nature had designed them. But the creature just *looked* evil. The tip of its tail quivered, reproducing the rattling sound.

Matt froze, clearly tuning into the sound. A soft curse sounded under his breath. "Fuck."

The rattler's triangular head lifted, and it stared right at her. She could feel its focus. Bree wanted to scream, but self-control squeezed her throat like a strong hand, strangling her voice before it could emerge. She knew next to nothing about rattlesnakes but would treat it like any other dangerous predator. No sudden movements. No loud noises.

"Can you ease away slowly?" Matt asked, his voice barely a breath.

"I'm going to try." She shifted her weight. A floorboard squeaked. Bree lifted one foot and painstakingly placed it a few inches behind her. As her body followed, the snake's rattle shivered. Bree eased her hand toward her weapon as she took a second step back.

The snake hissed. The head turned a few degrees as the beady eyes followed her movement. Its tail trembled harder, rattling louder.

Slowly.

Fear rose in Bree's throat, burning like bile. Her next breath rasped through her tight chest. The snake seemed to tense, and Bree froze for a few seconds. Her pulse thrummed in her ears. Her vision tunneled down until all she could see was the reptile. Would it perceive direct eye contact as a threat? It didn't matter. She couldn't look away.

The same instinct telling her not to move also warned her that the snake was alarmed. It was going to strike. She sensed the impending attack a split second before the snake shot forward in a blur of motion.

She flung her body backward. The mouth clamped onto her boot as her tailbone rang on the hard floor. She kicked at the snake. *Fuck.* Was that the head? The brown body fell away. She scrambled down the hall on her ass. Her hands and boots clawed at the wood, pulling herself backward like a drunken crab.

Matt got in front of her, putting his body in between her and the den. He leveled the rifle. "Where is it?"

"I don't know, but it's mad! Just get out!" Bree managed to get upright. Her brain scrambled as she paused to wrench her Glock from its holster. Survival instinct took over. She was an animal, trying not to be killed by another animal.

Her head pivoted as she retreated. Her brain screamed *Where is it?* over and over. She scanned the floor, the doorway, the area rug, all the while easing toward the door. Matt was at her side, the rifle aimed in the same direction as her handgun. Though the snake had moved so fast, she couldn't have gotten off a shot. She radioed her deputies to warn them.

Bree never took her eyes off the end of the hall as Matt pulled her outside. He closed the door. Bree fell on her butt on the step just as her deputies raced out of the house.

Kneeling in front of her, Matt ripped at her laces and yanked off her boot. He stripped off her sock and held her foot up. He inspected the bottom of her foot and between her toes. "Where did it bite you?"

"I don't feel anything." She'd felt the impact of the strike and the weight of the animal suspended from her boot, but the adrenaline flooding her body could have blocked any pain. Her lungs locked. She couldn't breathe. Her pulse skyrocketed out of control, the wild cadence of her heartbeat turning her stomach. Was that the venom working its way through her body?

How long did it take to die from a rattlesnake bite?

CHAPTER TWENTY-SIX

Bree stared down at her bare foot. "I don't see a bite."

Matt rolled her pant leg to her knee and examined her calf. "Me neither. Do you have any pain?"

"No." Bree reached for her boot and turned it over. She pointed to a pair of punctures on the thick sole of the boot. *Damn.* Those fangs were long and sharp. "Here's where it got me."

"Are you sure?" He took the boot and turned it over, his expression doubtful. "How do you feel?"

"Fine."

"Maybe you should go to the ER anyway, just to be safe."

"Because it almost bit me?"

"I guess not." Matt sat back on his haunches, relief showing in his eyes. "Want me to call animal control?"

Bree nodded. "We have a guy who's good with snakes, but I don't know if he can handle one that's venomous."

"If not, I'll call the zoo." Matt opened his phone.

Bree scrubbed both hands down her face. She shivered. Despite the cold, a layer of adrenaline sweat had soaked into her uniform. More deputies had arrived, along with an EMT unit. Bree addressed the EMT. "The victim is dead. Nothing you can do for him."

"There's a rattlesnake inside," Matt said.

The EMT's eyebrows rose. "Seriously?"

"Yep." Matt gestured toward Bree. "It struck the sheriff's boot. Could she have a bite and not know it?"

The EMT frowned. "You'd likely see puncture marks, but watch for pain, swelling, nausea, dizziness, numbness or tingling of your fingers, rapid heart rate . . . If you feel weird in any way, head to the ER."

Bree nodded, though she was feeling half of those symptoms from adrenaline overload. She put her sock and boot back on. From now on, these were her lucky boots.

The EMT returned to his vehicle.

Bree tied her laces. "I'm going to talk to the witness again."

Matt stepped away and spoke into his phone. Bree called Dana and put her on high alert. The note from the killer to her was a personal threat. Dana would stick close to the kids until he or she was caught. Bree called Adam again. When his voice mail answered, she left another message. Worry for him crawled through her. *Where is he?*

Bree paused for a few steadying, head-clearing gulps of cold air before walking toward Susan. Two more patrol cars had arrived. Todd and Juarez conferred with the two responding deputies.

Bree headed for the Toyota. Susan had closed the door, and the engine was running. When Bree approached, Susan motioned for her to get into the car. Bree slid into the passenger seat and closed the door.

Susan drank from a bottle of water. She adjusted the dashboard vents to aim at Bree.

Bree was grateful for the heat.

Susan reached behind the seat and produced a water bottle. She handed it to Bree. "You look like you need this."

"Thanks." Bree twisted off the cap and took a long swallow.

"What happened in there?" Susan set her own bottle in the cup holder.

Bree sipped more water. "When you were inside, did you see an aquarium in the corner of the den?"

Susan cocked her head. "An aquarium?"

Bree nodded.

"No," Susan said. "Mr. Northcott doesn't have fish."

"This one was outfitted for a reptile."

"Mr. Northcott doesn't—didn't—have any pets."

"There's a snake loose inside the house."

"A snake?" Susan shuddered. "Did you kill it?"

"No." Bree didn't get any more specific about the type of snake, though there was no way she'd be able to keep the rattlesnake's presence a secret. "Walk me through your movements when you arrived here."

Susan emitted a quivery sigh. "I came to clean a few minutes before eight, like I do every other week. I let myself in and dumped my stuff by the door." She paused for a pained breath. "I knew something was off. For one, the TV was on." She summed up walking through the house, finding Northcott, and freaking out. By the time she got to the end of the story, she looked as if she were going to be sick.

"How often do you clean this house?" Bree nodded toward the residence.

"Every other week." Crossing her arms, Susan rubbed her own biceps.

The car was toasty inside, but a chill had settled into Bree's bones. "And how long has Mr. Northcott been your client?"

"About a year, but he's never here when I come. We've only met in person twice."

"He met you twice and gave you a key?"

Susan nodded. "I have great references. Most of my clients have been with me for years."

"How did he become a client?" Bree asked.

Susan swiped a gloved hand under her nose. "I clean three other houses on this street. Mr. Northcott saw me unloading my mops and stuff one day and asked about my rates. I started cleaning for him the next week."

"Do you ever talk to him?"

Susan adjusted her seat. "We text. I let him know if I need to move his cleaning day. He does the same."

"Have you seen anyone hanging around the house recently?"

Susan shook her head. "No."

"Do you know of any threats to Mr. Northcott? Do the neighbors like him?"

Susan looked up at Bree. "No. The house is empty when I come. The most personal information I know is that he uses Preparation H, has a prescription shampoo for thinning hair, and likes porn. Other than that . . ." She shrugged. "I clean four houses a day. I don't have time to snoop on my clients, and honestly—I don't want to know their secrets. I just don't. I have enough drama in my own life."

"Don't we all," Bree said.

An animal control vehicle pulled up to the curb. Bree reached for the door handle and said to Susan, "We'll contact you if we have more questions. Also, we'll ask you to come to the station and sign a formal statement in a day or so."

"OK. Can I go?" Susan asked.

"Yes," Bree said. "Please don't talk about what you've seen. We'd like to contact Mr. Northcott's family before they learn about his death accidentally."

"I don't want to talk about it to anyone." Susan rubbed her hands together. "I excel at two things: cleaning and minding my own business."

"Thank you for your cooperation." Bree stepped out. After the warmth of the car, the cold outside air hit her like a slap. Drying sweat under her uniform and body armor had left her clammy.

Bree recognized the animal control officer as Cody Pinter. She had worked with him before, but typically they responded to aggressive dogs and feral cat complaints. As the sheriff, Bree was responsible for everything from the county jail to the animal shelter.

Bree met him behind his vehicle. "You're comfortable catching a rattlesnake?"

Cody nodded. "We just have to be careful not to agitate it. The snake will probably find somewhere to hide. They're usually only aggressive if they feel threatened."

"I must have startled it." Bree gave him a quick rundown.

"I'm wearing my snake boots." Cody tapped a toe.

"Indeed." Bree paused. "Fair warning: there's also a dead body in the house. This is a crime scene, so the less you disturb the scene, the better."

"And I thought my morning was going to be dull." Cody paused, thoughtful. "Snakes should be hibernating this time of year. Do you have any idea how it got inside the house?"

Bree said, "Someone put it there."

Cody's head snapped around. "That's crazy."

"No argument," Bree agreed.

Cody retrieved a plastic storage bin with tiny holes poked in the sides from the cargo area of his vehicle. Next, he lifted out two long poles with metal hooks at the end. He carried his equipment toward the house. Bree followed.

"I'll go with you, just in case." She pulled out her Glock. The last thing she wanted to do was go back into the house, but keeping her employees safe was her responsibility.

Cody frowned at the gun. "Let's hope you don't need that."

"Always," Bree said. "But it already tried to bite me. I won't take any chances."

"A rattlesnake bite isn't usually fatal as long as you get treatment. FYI, don't use a tourniquet or suck on the wound. Just be as still as possible. The faster your heart beats, the quicker the venom is pumped through your body. I don't want to get bitten, but it's not usually a death sentence with prompt medical treatment." Cody sounded rational.

Bree felt less so. "Good to know." She wiped a sweaty palm on her leg. She could ask Matt or another deputy to have Cody's back, but passing off a dangerous duty didn't feel right. She was learning to delegate and trust her officers with responsibility. But she would not ask them to perform a duty because she was too afraid to do her damned job.

At the door, Cody held up one hand. "Move slowly."

Fresh sweat trickled down Bree's back. "The snake was in the den, which is at the end of the hall on the left."

Cody eased forward. He stopped a few feet shy of the kitchen and tilted his head as if he were listening. Bree strained her ears, but she heard no slithering, hissing, or rattling, just her heart doing an *are you crazy?* dance.

He stood in the doorway to the den for a few long minutes. He paid no attention to the body but scanned the floor. A *gotcha* smile curled the corners of his mouth. "I see it. Timber rattler."

Bree tensed. "Where?"

"Other side of the room, next to its tank. He or she might be looking for heat. Snakes can't maintain their body temperature without help. They get sluggish in the cold."

Cody walked around the couch. He set down the container and removed the lid. Bree stayed put, but she aimed her gun at the reptile. The snake slithered farther into the corner. Was it afraid? Or did it sense the presence of someone it couldn't intimidate?

Cody used a long-handled hook to lift the snake a few inches off the ground, but it slithered out of the hook and struck at the wooden stick. It hissed and coiled backward.

Bree made a startled noise.

"Easy there, little buddy," Cody soothed. "I want to get you somewhere warm."

Little buddy?

Cody blocked the snake's forward movement with the rounded back of the hook, not letting it come any closer. "It's important to be calm. Animals can sense tension."

"Seems like."

Cody chuckled. "I guarantee that snake is more scared of us than we are of it."

Bree thought Cody could speak for himself. Part of her didn't want to hurt the creature. The other part wanted to shoot it until it was completely obliterated.

"His striking distance is only about half the length of his body." Either Cody was completely confident in his ability, or he was one hell of an actor.

More sweat trickled down Bree's back.

Before she could breathe, Cody scooped up the snake, deftly juggled it between the two hooks as it tried to slither away, and placed it in the container. He snapped the lid into place with a smile. "There we go." He patted the top of the tub almost as if he were petting the snake.

"I owe you." Bree's muscles loosened as her tension ebbed.

"Nah. It's what I do." Cody turned toward the body, his expression shifting from triumph to grim, as if he were just taking in the details now that the snake had been captured. "You have the harder job. I'll take animals over humans any day. Animals aren't evil."

Bree didn't argue. "Can I carry something? Not the snake."

Cody handed her the hooks while he hefted the container. At the end of the hall, she opened the door for him, and he carried the plastic tub to his vehicle.

"How did it go?" Matt scanned them both. "No one got bit?"

Cody laughed and nodded toward the container. "We got him. He was just scared."

"There was no *we*." Bree swallowed. "Cody gets a hundred percent of the credit."

"I couldn't get a hold of the zookeeper. I left a message," Matt said.

Cody lifted his container. "I'll find a home for it."

"You can't just release it?" Bree eyed the closed container.

"No," Cody said. "For one, it's too cold. The snake wouldn't have time to find a place to hibernate. Second, it could be carrying a virus or parasite. We wouldn't want to compromise the local snake population. Considering the timber rattler is a threatened species, a zoo might want it. I'd better get it out of the cold." He closed the cargo door of his vehicle.

After he drove away, Matt leaned closer. "How did it really go?"

"Rattlesnake. One star. Do not recommend." Bree gave herself a little shake. "Now let's get back to the body."

Todd joined them.

Bree said, "As soon as we have an approximate window for time of death, we'll start knocking on doors. Houses are close together in this neighborhood. Chances are, someone saw something."

News vans parked on the street. Within minutes, reporters went on air. They stayed off the property, so there wasn't anything Bree could do about their presence.

"News got out fast," she said to Matt.

He made an unhappy, slightly aggressive sound in his throat.

They spent the next hour photographing and searching the house. There was no sign of forced entry or burglary. When the ME arrived, Bree and Matt walked her back to the den. Bree told Dr. Jones about the rattlesnake.

"Everyone knows about it." Carrying her kit, Dr. Jones stood in the entry to the den.

"Impossible to keep something that weird under wraps," Matt said. "The press has been here for a while. No doubt they saw the animal control van."

"We had some neighborhood lookie-loos too," Bree grumbled.

After a few minutes of intense scrutiny of the overall scene, Dr. Jones approached the body. "Normally, when a death presents with a clear sexual element, I'd consider sexual motives or causes. BDSM comes to mind here, as well as erotic electrostimulation, even accidental death from autoerotic asphyxiation." She looked up at Bree. "Do you have any concrete evidence this case is linked to the last one?"

"Just the obvious similarities." Bree gestured toward the body.

"OK. Let's see what we have." With a gloved hand, Dr. Jones pointed to the victim's side that was in contact with the sofa. "Lividity is well underway and suggests he was killed here." After the heart stopped beating, gravity caused blood to sink to the lowest part of the body, turning the skin purple.

She grasped a limb, but the body resisted. "He's in full rigor." In general, the body stiffened for twelve hours, remained that way for another twelve, and then the muscles slowly became flexible again between twenty-four and thirty-six hours after death. So, Julius was in the second phase, between twelve and twenty-four hours postmortem.

The ME used a scalpel to make a small incision to take the body temperature via the liver. She checked the thermometer, then did a calculation. "Based on body condition and temperature"—she checked her watch—"time of death was likely between nine and eleven last evening." She peeled off her gloves. "I can't tell you much else until I get him on the table. I'll do the autopsy ASAP. I know you want to get ahead of"—she paused and motioned to the victim's plastic-wrapped face—"speculation."

As if that were possible.

"We do," Bree said.

The ME stepped back and gestured for her assistant to begin photographing the scene. Bree and Matt walked outside, giving them room to work.

Todd met them in the driveway. Bree summoned him over. "Assign deputies to knock on doors. See if any of the neighbors know Julius

Northcott, if suspicious persons or vehicles have been spotted in the area, or if anyone saw activity at the house last night between nine and eleven."

Todd moved off to execute her orders.

A Mercedes pulled up to the curb behind the police cars. A thin white-haired man in his midsixties leaped out and ran toward the house. The deputy in charge of the crime scene log stepped in front of him, blocking his access with his body.

"Get out of my way," the man yelled. His face was impending-stroke red.

Instinct had Bree moving toward him.

He tried to push past the deputy. "That's my son's house. You can't keep me away."

The deputy was a rookie but showed good judgment and restraint. He didn't let the man pass, using a firm but level voice in an attempt to deescalate the man's understandably high emotion. "What's your name, sir?"

But the man was in a state of near hysteria and not in the frame of mind to think clearly. He thumped both fists on the deputy's chest and yelled, "You can't stop me!" His voice was shrill, but Bree recognized that his aggression was fueled by fear. He puffed up his chest and stabbed a forefinger at the deputy. "Who's in charge here?"

Bree stepped in. "I'm Sheriff Taggert. Let's step aside and talk."

"I don't want to talk," the man yelled in her face. "I want to see my son."

Pity squeezed Bree's heart. She was about to ruin this man's life—and he knew it too. It showed in the panicked haze in his eyes. She looked around for privacy, but the man's shouts had already alerted the media. Reporters' heads were turning as they focused on the drama, like dogs that smelled meat.

Bree did not let him pass. "I'm sorry, sir. I can't let you in. This is a crime scene."

"Crime scene? What happened to my son?" The man lunged forward, one hand reaching forward to shove her aside. "I demand you let me through. This is private property!" He was a half head taller than her and tried to bulldoze past her.

She blocked his arm, spinning him around. Instead of putting him in an arm bar, she wrapped an arm around his shoulders. "Please, sir," she said in a low voice in his ear. "Let's go somewhere private."

He stopped resisting. "Is my son dead?" His voice dropped to a hoarse whisper.

Bree steered him to the side of the house, out of sight of the media. She turned him to face her, then released him. The pain in his eyes brought back the moment when she'd learned of her sister's murder. She didn't want to give him the terrible news here, but he needed to know. Delaying would be torture.

Direct was best.

"The medical examiner has not officially identified the victim, but we believe it's your son," she said.

His knees buckled, and the moan in his throat was one of a wounded animal, a soul-deep anguish. His grief amplified the emotion buried inside Bree.

"It can't be," the man cried. "I need to see him."

"I know, and you will, just not right now." Bree could not take him into the house. He might think he wanted to see his son, but she would not allow him to live with that nightmarish image as his final memory of Julius. She knew what it was like to have a family member murdered—but to have your child die . . . Now that she had the kids . . . No. She blocked the thought. She couldn't even go there for a second. Yes, she understood what he was feeling.

She took hold of his forearm and steadied him. "What's your name?"

"Fred. Fred Northcott."

"OK. Mr. Northcott, I'm going to have one of my deputies take care of you. I'm going to need to talk to you shortly."

He nodded, and his whole body sagged, as if all the fight had left him. He seemed to have aged ten years in a few minutes.

Bree led him back to the front yard, using her body to shield him from view. She waved to a deputy. "Take Mr. Northcott home and stay with him. Don't let anyone bother him."

The deputy took the older man by the arm and led him to a patrol car. The vehicle was barely out of view when the ME and her assistant wheeled their body-bag-laden gurney out the front door.

Bree also knew from experience that Dr. Jones would attempt to make Julius look presentable before allowing his father to view his body. The ME's compassion—and the respect she'd shown Erin's body—had made a difference.

Bree's insides went hollow as she wondered if the killer had carved anything into Julius's forehead.

CHAPTER

TWENTY-SEVEN

Matt would rather face an armed killer than the grief-stricken family of a murder victim. He sat next to Bree on an old leather sofa in Fred Northcott's living room. The room was appropriately dim, with the blinds closed against curiosity. So far, the street was quiet, but the media would find him soon enough. Dust motes floated in the rays of light that seeped in around the edges of the window frame.

In the wing chair angled toward them, Julius's father wavered between a stunned look of utter disbelief and helpless sorrow.

Mr. Northcott rubbed both hands down his face, leaving red marks on his skin. "You're sure it's Julius?" The question sounded robotic. His voice didn't hold any real hope.

"As I said before, the medical examiner hasn't issued an official ID yet, but you can help." Bree tapped on her phone. Matt could see the photo on the screen, a close-up of the crescent-shaped birthmark on the victim's neck. The image was carefully cropped to not reveal the condition of the body. "Does Julius have any distinguishing birthmarks or tattoos?"

"He has a strawberry mark on the back of his neck. Looks like a quarter moon."

She turned the screen toward Mr. Northcott. "Is this it?"

Mr. Northcott glanced at the screen. His face crumpled, and he buried it in his hands. His shoulders shook. Silent pain radiated from him like fog from dry ice.

Bree glanced at Matt. Her eyes reflected Mr. Northcott's suffering. More than anyone, she would empathize. Matt had no doubt she was reliving her sister's death. He pressed his shoulder to hers. By mutual agreement, they'd agreed that public displays of affection were not acceptable while they were on duty. But he hoped the small amount of physical contact brought her some comfort. Her eyes softened with gratitude before she turned back to Mr. Northcott. "We're very sorry for your loss."

The man's shoulders gave a quick shudder. "How did he die?"

"The medical examiner hasn't issued a cause of death," Bree said.

Mr. Northcott paused, as if he wanted to insist, then changed his mind.

Matt knew Bree didn't want to tell the father the horrors that had been inflicted upon his son. Julius's last moments had been terrifying and cruel. He'd been tortured. His father didn't need details he'd relive every time he closed his eyes. No doubt he'd learn some of those details in the coming weeks. But there was only so much misery a person could absorb in one moment.

Mr. Northcott sat up, wiping his face with his sleeve. "You'll find the person who did this?"

"We will do everything we can." Bree's voice hardened.

Mr. Northcott read her face and nodded. "I believe you will."

Bree leaned forward. Connecting with victim's families took a huge toll on an investigator. But Bree would never shy away from the most difficult of tasks. She was all in, no matter what the personal cost. "But we could use your help."

"Anything." Mr. Northcott's chin jutted forward, terrified but determined.

Matt said, "Some of our questions might be difficult for you to answer, but we need to know as much about your son as possible in order to find the person responsible. Don't hold back."

Mr. Northcott nodded once, hard, his face set.

Matt began. "What did Julius do for a living?"

"He sold cars and trucks." Mr. Northcott's eye took on a faraway look. "He loved pickup trucks. The bigger, the better. He's one of the top salesmen in the dealership. That's why he scored that monster demo to drive." Fresh tears welled in his eyes. "He was so excited to get that truck."

"Did Julius have plans last night?" Bree asked.

Mr. Northcott lifted a helpless shoulder. "I don't know. I don't think so."

"Did Julius have friends?"

"He has some guys from work he hung around with once in a while to watch a hockey game or grab a beer, but I wouldn't call them best friends." Mr. Northcott waggled a hand. "Julius preferred to spend his time with women. He used to say he didn't have time for a sausage fest." He closed his mouth quickly. His gaze darted to Bree. "I'm sorry if that was inappropriate, ma'am."

"I need to hear the truth, Mr. Northcott," Bree assured him. "Trust me. I've heard much worse."

"I guess you have." Mr. Northcott scratched his stubbled jaw.

"We'll be talking to his coworkers," Matt said. "What about hobbies?"

Mr. Northcott shrugged. "He went to the gym, stayed fit. We watched hockey together. That's about it."

Bree frowned. "What about a girlfriend?"

Mr. Northcott sighed. "He had lots of them. My Julius is—was—quite the ladies' man." A hint of sad pride edged his voice.

"But no one special?" Matt pressed.

"He was still playing the field." Mr. Northcott shook his head. "He wasn't ready to settle down. He was having too much fun."

"Did he mention any specific women recently?" Bree asked.

"Not really." Mr. Northcott pursed his lips, as if solving a difficult math problem. "He talked about his dates, but he didn't mention names very often. There were too many to keep track of anyway."

"Did any of the women have things in common?" Bree asked.

"Julius only dates—dated"—his voice hitched—"beautiful women." More of that masculine pride edged Mr. Northcott's voice.

"Did you meet any of them?" Matt asked.

"No." Mr. Northcott shook his head. "He showed me pictures on his phone. He used dating apps."

And there's the link, thought Matt. "Do you know which apps?"

"No." Mr. Northcott snorted. "Julius tried to get me to use them, but they're not for me. I'm just learning to use the camera and get directions on my phone. I'm not tech savvy like Julius. He used to come over here and fix my Wi-Fi once a week." His gaze drifted to the tightly closed blinds, his expression confused. "I keep forgetting he's gone. How can I forget?" His eyes went lost.

Bree cleared her throat. "Did anything unusual happen recently?"

Mr. Northcott lifted one palm. "I can't think of anything. Like I said, he didn't want to settle down. He didn't like to stay with any one woman long enough for her to develop expectations."

"Expectations?" Bree cocked her head.

"Some women think if they go out with a man a few times, he owes them something." Mr. Northcott jerked his eyes away from Bree, then back again. "Not all women, but some. A man has to be careful."

Matt thought that was bullshit, but he didn't say it. Fred Northcott was on the brink of shattering like an ice sculpture. Matt wouldn't be the hammer. Deep down, he knew that Northcott's grief would break him.

"Do you know the passcode for Julius's phone?" Matt mentally crossed his fingers. They could save a day or two if they could directly access Julius's apps and other phone data.

"Yeah." Mr. Northcott sniffed and ran a hand beneath his nose. "He used my birthday." He recited six digits.

Bree pulled out her notepad and wrote them down. "That's going to be a big help."

Mr. Northcott rapped a fist on his knee but didn't respond. Matt could hear the sorrow rattling in the man's chest.

"When did you last see Julius?" Matt asked.

"Monday. We met for breakfast before he went to work." Mr. Northcott drew a shuddering breath. "He had an egg white omelet. He should have had steak and eggs." Tears leaked from his eyes and dripped down his cheeks. He didn't bother to wipe them away.

"Did you talk to him since then?" Bree asked.

Mr. Northcott shook his head. He was fighting for control. The cords on the sides of his neck stood out, and his jaw sawed from side to side until it seemed he could crack a molar.

Matt didn't want to leave him alone.

Bree touched the older man's forearm. "Is there someone we can call for you?"

Mr. Northcott shook his head. "No. I'm used to being alone. Julius's mother ran out on us when he was two. After that, I never could trust a woman enough to get close." He clenched his fists on his thighs. "It was just me and Julius. We were best friends. I don't know what I'm going to do without him." He broke down, sobbing.

Broken.

He would never be the same. A lifetime of memories, of work, of joy . . . had been erased.

"Parents shouldn't outlive their children," Northcott moaned. "It's not natural."

They left him in emotional pieces.

Matt slid into the passenger seat. Bree sat behind the wheel, making no move to start the engine.

"Sometimes, this job is the worst." She stared out the windshield, clearly not focusing on the residential street in front of them.

"Julius would have been murdered whether or not we got his case." Matt reached across the console and took her hand. "People will always kill other people. You and I know that, and there isn't anything we can do to stop it. The very best we can do is to bring killers to justice and prevent them from committing future murders. That's all we have."

"You're right." Bree breathed. "We can't stop a murder before it happens. Solving them is second best, but it's our job."

"It's an important job." Matt squeezed her hand. "We need to lock up the ones that kill."

"So, we're sure the same killer murdered Spencer and Julius?"

"As sure as we can be," Matt qualified.

Bree nodded. "We need to stop them before they claim another life. Because they will. We both know it."

"We're not going to say the words."

"You mean, *serial killer*?" Matt asked.

"Yeah. We're not going to say those words."

Matt exhaled. "We have two extremely similar murders occurring only one day apart. That's beyond escalation."

"You're right." Bree's eyes narrowed. "This isn't some nutter who thinks bathing himself in the blood of virgins will give him immortality. I'm not sensing any insanity at these scenes."

"What about the rattlesnake?"

Bree considered. "It felt like window dressing. Something added on to throw us off. The murders were planned. Every step of the process executed with precision. The killer easily overpowered two healthy, strong men without leaving any signs of a struggle. They brought a stun gun, zip ties, and plastic wrap. They encountered no real difficulty. Mentally unstable people can't follow precise methodology."

She was right.

Matt considered the snake. "Jasper would be comfortable handling a rattler."

"Yes, but we'd need to find a link between Jasper and Julius. So far, the biggest connection between the murders is the use of dating apps."

"The stun gun and zip ties are practical."

Bree nodded.

"What about the plastic wrap?"

Bree's head bobbed from side to side. "Also practical. These kills were bloodless. No mess. No fuss. The victim is incapacitated and restrained. Then they're at the killer's mercy."

Of which he clearly had none.

Bree continued. "No blood means less evidence the killer can track home."

"The Tidy Killer?"

"I doubt the media will use that nickname." Bree snorted. "But a neat killer is smart. Sloppiness leads to evidence. Evidence leads to conviction. This killer won't be caught that easily. He or she committed two murders in two days. No one saw. No one stopped them. No one had a clue."

Matt's blood chilled. "How do we catch a smart killer?"

Bree wrapped her fingers around the steering wheel. "By being smarter."

CHAPTER

TWENTY-EIGHT

Todd stood on the old woman's porch. The door was open to the end of its security chain. A pair of sharp gray eyes squinted at him through the three-inch gap. Near Todd's boots, a dog snuffled on the other side of the door. "I'm Chief Deputy Harvey, ma'am. May I speak with you?"

Her gaze turned suspicious. "How do I know you are who you say you are?"

Todd gestured to the street behind him, where emergency vehicles clogged the street. "I'm with them."

Her eyes crinkled with humor. "OK. I guess you're legit." She pronounced *legit* like she'd been watching reruns of 1960s cop shows. She opened the door and waved him inside. "Don't let the dog—or the heat—out."

He hurried through the opening and closed the door behind him. He stopped dead as he took in the dog, a gray pit bull with a fireplug body, cropped ears, and battle scars. She stuffed her nose into his crotch and wagged furiously.

"I'm Edna Zimmerman, and that's Missy. She's a rescue and friendly with almost everyone."

Todd dropped to one knee to greet the dog. "That's a good girl."

Missy wagged and licked his face.

Todd stood and waited for warmth to hit him but quickly realized the inside of the house was freezing.

"I have strudel." The old woman turned and shuffled toward the back of the house. She wore a hat and coat over purple sweatpants. Missy ambled along beside the old woman.

As he walked through the living room, Todd glanced at the thermostat. The temperature read 55 degrees.

He walked past a cat tree, where a long-haired white cat gave him a quiet hiss. An orange tabby wound around his ankles. The cat bumped against the pit bull, who gave it an amicable sniff.

In the kitchen, Mrs. Zimmerman reached for a teapot on the counter. In her midseventies, she was less than five feet tall and couldn't have weighed a hundred pounds. The hair tucked under her knit cap was fluffy and white. She was thin, but not frail, and resembled a Q-tip. "Sit down. You'll have tea." She issued commands like a much larger person.

"I don't have time—"

"Sit."

Todd dropped into a chair like a well-trained retriever. Missy planted her butt on the floor.

"I just made a pot." Mrs. Zimmerman set a china cup of tea and a plate of pastry in front of him. She laid a cloth napkin on the table next to the plate and set a fork on it. "You look cold. Eat. Then we'll talk."

Todd dug into the pastry, thinking eating it was the fastest way to get his information. The taste of cinnamon and apples flooded his tongue. "This is incredible."

"I know." No pride, just matter-of-fact confidence, filled her words. "Now"—she sat across from him with her own steaming cup—"you're here about the wickedness next door."

"Yes, ma'am." Todd wasn't a tea guy, but the thought was appreciated. "Did you see anything unusual in the neighborhood last night, particularly at Mr. Northcott's house?"

The tabby jumped into her lap, and she shifted back to make room. "There was a white SUV parked a few houses down. It doesn't belong to anyone on the block." She gave Todd a direct stare. "I know everyone."

"I'm sure you do." Todd had no doubt. "But people get visitors."

She scratched under the tabby's ear, and he began to purr. "It was cold last night, and the person in the SUV sat behind the wheel for a while." She set the cat on the floor, walked to the window, and pointed. "It was right there, in between the streetlamps." She turned back to Todd. "Where it's the darkest."

Strudel gone, Todd got up and stood behind her.

"It was about fifteen feet in front of the fire hydrant."

With a good line of sight on the Northcott house, thought Todd. "Do you know the make or model of the SUV?"

"I don't know much about cars," she said. "I didn't get a good look at the person either. It was too dark, and they were hunched down in the seat, as if they were hiding." She added drama to the last part.

"You've never seen the vehicle before?"

"No."

Todd returned to his chair. "Would you recognize the SUV if I showed it to you?"

She considered his question with a tilt of her head. "Maybe? I can't say for sure."

"How well do you know Mr. Northcott?"

"Well enough to not want to get better acquainted." Mrs. Zimmerman returned to her chair. The cat immediately reclaimed his spot on her lap.

"He wasn't a good neighbor?" Todd asked.

Mrs. Zimmerman shrugged. "He kept to himself, which wasn't the problem." She pointed to the opposite side of her house. "The Andersons live on the other side. Kyle Anderson is a nice young man. He always shovels my walk when it snows. He drags my trash cans to and from the curb too. I never have to ask. In exchange, I bake them cookies, and when they go on vacation, I feed the cat and collect their mail. Other folks on the street keep an eye on each other's houses. That sort of thing." She paused. "But his lack of friendliness wasn't the issue with Northcott."

"Then what was?" Todd asked.

"Mr. Northcott was a pervert."

Todd hadn't expected that and had no response.

"It was a constant parade of women in and out of that house." She held up a hand. "I'm not a prude. I believe sex is a healthy part of an adult relationship. But *adult* is the key to that. I have two granddaughters. The oldest is only fourteen, and Northcott looked at her in a way that a man of his age should not look at a child." Her hand drifted to the pit bull's head. "He's the only person Missy has ever growled at. I believe dogs are good judges of character, don't you?"

"Yes, ma'am, I do. Did you ever confront him?"

"Damned straight I did!" Bright spots of color flooded her parchment-like cheeks. "He denied it, of course. Then he laughed at me and said I was just a powerless old lady. I told him that a bullet fired by an old lady would leave him just as dead as one fired by a young person. And if he ever looked at my girls like that again, I'd shoot him and feed his carcass to my pets." Her gray eyes went cold, and Todd had no doubt she would be willing to kill to protect her grandchildren.

Then he thought about how *that* would read in his report.

"We told him, didn't we?" Mrs. Zimmerman reached down and patted the dog's head again. "After that day, I never let the girls outside without me—and Missy. He was terrified of her."

Missy thumped her tail on the floor.

"You're a good girl," Mrs. Zimmerman crooned.

Todd couldn't think of any questions to top that story. He stood. "Thank you for the strudel."

"You are very welcome." She smiled, and there was no sign of the lady who'd threatened to shoot her neighbor and turn him into pet food.

"Is it always this cold in here?"

She wrapped both hands around her mug. "Not in the summer."

"Fair enough."

She toyed with the mug handle. "Someone threw a rock through my back window. Kyle from next door nailed plywood over it, but the cold gets in. The window glazier can't get out until next week to install new glass." She lifted her mug. "I'll survive. I'll bake a lot."

"Do you have any idea who broke the glass?"

She shook her head. "I have ideas, but without proof they're meaningless."

"True."

Anyone could speculate.

Had Northcott thrown the rock? Had he resented her threats and wanted to teach her a lesson?

"Don't you have anyone you can stay with for a few days?" he asked.

She stroked the old cat's head. "If it gets too cold, I can go to my son's. But I'd rather stay here. They have a small house, and it gets crowded. I love them, but I like to sleep in my own bed at night."

"One more thing." Todd pulled out his phone. "Do you recognize any of these women?" He scrolled through pictures of Avery Ledger, Monica Linfield, and Farah Rock.

"She looks familiar." Mrs. Zimmerman tapped on Farah's photo. "I think she was one of Northcott's floozies."

Which would link Farah to both victims.

Despite the quick zip of excitement, Todd kept his voice level. "You saw her at his house?"

"I think so."

"Do you remember when?" Todd asked.

Her face scrunched in thought. "Four weeks ago? Six?" Her face relaxed. "I can't say for sure."

Todd showed her a picture of Spencer LaForge. "Do you recognize this man?"

She nodded. "He was on the news. He was murdered." Her gaze caught his, and her eyes brightened. "Are the murders related?"

Todd gave her the usual brush-off. "We can't say at this time."

But she was sharp, and he wasn't fooling her.

"Thank you for your time." He gave the dog a final pat before he left the house, full of strudel and suspicions.

Mrs. Zimmerman wasn't a serious suspect, but had Northcott offended other parents of teenage girls?

Had he done worse?

CHAPTER TWENTY-NINE

It was afternoon before Bree and Matt made it back to the sheriff's station. Bree's empty stomach swirled with hunger pangs and coffee.

Matt carried a bag of sandwiches from a local deli. "I'll take these into the conference room. Please come and eat before you get sucked into anything else."

"I will," Bree promised. She veered to her office to drop off her coat and check her messages. Most of her correspondence came in through email and voice mail, but there were still some people who insisted on speaking to and leaving a message with a human being.

Marge greeted her at the door. "The media is going ballistic. You need to make a statement."

"I know." Bree hurried past the squad room into her office. "I'm hoping to get updated information, but the public has a right to know what's going on. Tell the press I'll make a statement and take questions within the hour."

"Will do." Marge nodded. "Go eat. The rest of your messages can wait."

"You're the best. Seriously." Bree meant every word.

Her phone went off, and she glanced at the screen.

Adam!

She answered the call. "Hey."

"I'm sorry I didn't call you back," Adam began. He sounded out of breath. "I had a date last night, and my phone battery stopped charging yesterday. I replaced it today."

"Thanks for calling me back." Relief sang through Bree. "Who was your date?"

"Her name is Rachel." He didn't sound very interested.

"Going to see her again?" Bree asked.

"Probably not. She doesn't like art or books." Which were Adam's main interests. "What kind of person goes to a bookstore and doesn't buy anything?"

Bree laughed. "I stopped at your place last night. I got worried when your Bronco was there and you weren't."

"I'm sorry. The Bronco is having issues. I bought a new vehicle yesterday."

"Seriously?"

"Yeah."

"You bought a new car and a new phone. What brought on this desire to be part of the modern world?"

Adam chuckled. "I went on a date last week, and the Bronco had a moment, which made me late. Then it wouldn't start afterward. I had to use her car to jump-start mine. No shock she doesn't want to see me again. I felt like such a loser."

"I'll bet. What kind of car did you buy?"

"It's a little embarrassing. I totally got sucked into an impulse."

"What is it?" Bree teased.

"A Porsche Cayenne."

"You bought a Porsche?" Bree asked. Adam forgot to comb his hair, put no thought into his appearance, and he usually dressed like he was homeless. "Who are you and what have you done with my brother?" She couldn't believe how much he'd changed.

Adam chuckled.

"You deserve it. You've given so much to the kids. You supported them and Erin for years. It's time you treated yourself." Bree was happy for him. "Will I see you before Sunday?"

He paused. "I doubt it. I was stuck on my painting. I thought I was going in the wrong direction, but I'm feeling the urge to get back to it." His voice drifted off. She recognized his distracted tone. He would be buried in his art for days.

"I love you," Bree said.

"Love you back." Adam ended the call.

Bree felt better for about three seconds, until she remembered her plastic-wrap killer had struck again. The prospect of a serial killer in Grey's Hollow—one who had taken a personal interest in Bree—started her nerves churning again. She checked in with Dana by text. After being assured all was OK at home, she headed for the conference room. She wasn't hungry, but her body needed food. Matt was staring at the murder board and chowing down on a foot-long meatball sub. He'd updated notes and added printouts of digital photos. She told him about Adam.

Matt wiped his mouth with a napkin. "That's great. You must be relieved."

"Definitely." She sat across from him and looked up at the murder board. Photos of the suspects and not-so-lucky victims stared down at her.

Matt handed her a white-paper-wrapped turkey sub that was half the size of his sandwich. She unwrapped her food. The first bite tasted like paste. But the meal improved the more she ate. She finished the last bite, crumpled the wrapper, and tossed it into the waste can.

Matt did the same. "That's better."

"I need to update the press, which is about the last thing I want to do."

"The reporters will want to use the *serial killer* label."

"They might be right."

Matt reached for the evidence bag that contained Julius's cell phone and slid it toward him. "I know."

"That sums it up," Bree agreed. "Do we have any updates? I hate to take questions when I have so few answers."

"Still waiting on reports." Matt tapped the bagged phone. "I'll call forensics and dig into Julius's phone."

Bree nodded. Matt stepped out of the room. Bree's own phone buzzed on the table, and she read the screen. The ME. Grateful, she snatched up the phone. "Sheriff Taggert."

Dr. Jones wasted no time. "I finished the autopsy on Julius Northcott." The sound of the doctor tapping on a computer keyboard came over the line. "The cause of death is asphyxia due to suffocation. He was smothered by plastic wrap. Under the plastic wrap we found duct tape over his mouth and the word *cheat* carved into his forehead with a sharp blade. The mutilation occurred antemortem."

All of it. The same as Spencer.

Dr. Jones continued. "I found multiple sites of stun gun burns on the neck and torso. Despite the sexual elements at the scene, there is no evidence of sexual assault. I'll send you a written preliminary report."

"Thank you." Bree ended the call.

Matt hurried back in. "Forensics found one cat hair in the plastic wrap, and they're checking some dust recovered from the duct tape on the victim's mouth. They'll get back to me as soon as they know what it is."

"OK." Bree rubbed her temples with both hands and repeated the information from Dr. Jones. "It doesn't feel like we've made enough progress on two murders in two days."

"The lab and forensics techs are working nonstop." Matt slid the phone out of the bag. It had already been fingerprinted and swabbed for DNA. Therefore, the device could be handled.

"I know," Bree said. "If there's another murder, we'll need assistance." She had no issue with calling the state police or FBI if necessary. "We might need to form a task force. We can't process the sheer volume of evidence fast enough." Bree's rural county simply didn't have the resources for an investigation of this magnitude.

"Maybe I can help." Todd stood in the doorway.

"You have something?" Bree dropped her hands.

"I do." He summed up his interview with Julius's neighbor. "She saw a white SUV and recognized Farah Rock as one of Julius's 'floozies.' Her word, not mine. She also said she caught him leering at her teenage granddaughter and threatened to shoot him and feed his carcass to her pets."

"How old is this neighbor?" Bree asked.

"About seventy-five." Todd grinned and held his hand about five feet above the floor. "And about this tall."

"Are we adding her to the suspect list?" Matt deadpanned.

Bree snorted. "In my mind, Farah has moved to the top slot. Jasper is still in the running, but unless we establish a connection between him and Julius, Farah looks more promising. Northcott's father gave us the passcode to his cell phone, so we can access his dating apps, text messages, et cetera." She gestured toward the cell phone in Matt's hands. "While we're doing that, let's get Farah's financials and phone records. We know she dated Spencer. We have a witness who says she dated Julius. She lied and tried to convince a friend to lie for her as well."

"I'll get the warrant," Todd said.

"Where is the access to Farah's dating app profiles?" Bree asked.

"I'll check on that status as well." Todd made a note. "Also, we found a receipt near the aquarium that we believe was used to transport the snake to the victim's house."

"A receipt?" Interest warmed Bree's veins.

"Yes." Todd nodded. "It's a credit card receipt."

"Oooo." Bree liked receipts. "Maybe it's traceable."

"Juarez is working on it." Todd smiled. "Some of the ink ran from the snake's water bowl, so we can't read the name of the store. The transaction number is legible, and the amount and date. I'm optimistic."

Bree held up crossed fingers. "I need to talk to the press." She stood. "I'd like you both to come with me. We need to show we have all resources on this case."

Todd rose. "Will you mention the idea of forming a task force?"

Bree shook her head. "Not until I talk to BCI." The process wasn't as simple as making a declaration. Other agencies had to agree to dedicate manpower to her case. Also, she had mixed feelings about her last experience with an investigator from the New York State Police Bureau of Criminal Investigation. He'd tried to pin a murder on her. In the end, he'd come around to her side, but Bree had lost some faith. "We all need to be on the same page before I wave them in front of the press."

Marge appeared in the doorway. "What is that smell?"

Bree sniffed her arm. "I believe that's us." Their clothes had absorbed odors at the death scene, but they'd been inside long enough to become scent-blind to their own stink. "What's up?"

Marge grimaced. "Brace yourself."

Bree did. "What?"

Marge sighed. "Madeline Jager is in the lobby."

Fuck.

Matt rolled his eyes to the ceiling in a *give me a break* expression. "Fuck."

Bree tapped her forehead on the table. This was not the first time the county administrator had barged into the station. "I really don't want to talk to her, but I will not give her the satisfaction of running me off my turf. I assume she was in front of the press when she demanded to see me."

"You know it. She would never pass up the chance for PR." Marge paused. "I could tell her you're not here," she offered. Her lips curled in a sly grin. "Or have one of the deputies toss her out on her ass."

"I'd pay money to see that," Matt said.

Bree imagined the scene, and it was glorious.

Madeline had been a dagger between Bree's shoulder blades since the county supervisor had been elevated to administrator. Madeline was a politician to her core. She and Bree were orange juice and toothpaste. Jager was one of the few people who could make Bree lose her temper. She pushed Bree's buttons like a six-year-old in an elevator. Marge had once said that Jager would eat her own young for good PR, and she was so right.

"I have to play nice," Bree grumbled. Reality was a bitch.

Marge sobered. "Do you want me to take her to your office?"

"No." Bree glanced at the murder board and all its full-color horror. She knew from experience that the crime scene photos would throw off Jager, and Bree was not above using whatever means necessary to discourage future surprise visits. "Bring her in here. I'm sure she wants information about the case, and it's all right here."

Marge glanced at the murder board. "That's mean." But the corner of her mouth tilted up.

"She should have called first." Bree shrugged.

Marge returned a couple of minutes later with the politician in tow. Madeline Jager fought aging hard—too hard. Her hair was freshly dyed in a shade of red that had never been natural on anyone, and she looked like she'd been stung on the lips by a bee. Filler, maybe. Definitely. She hesitated on her way through the door. Her nose wrinkled, but being a politician, she didn't ask who smelled. She saw the murder board, then quickly averted her eyes.

"Ms. Jager." Bree gestured toward Matt. "You remember Investigator Flynn and my chief deputy, Todd Harvey." Bree motioned toward a chair. "Please have a seat."

Jager barely acknowledged Matt and Todd with a single nod. She kept her focus on Bree. Instead of sitting, she leaned forward and pressed her hands flat on the table. "Reporters are talking about a serial killer in Grey's Hollow. What are you doing about that?"

Bree ignored the attempt to loom over her and invade her space. The normal reaction would be to shift backward and reestablish her boundaries. But Bree did neither. She sat completely still, refusing to allow her body posture to shift even a millimeter—as if Jager's belligerence had zero effect. "About the murders or about the reporters?"

"Both," Jager snapped. "We can't have this here." She stabbed the table with a forefinger. "This is a nice, wholesome small town. We didn't have killers here before you took over."

"Well, actually, you did." Bree had come back to her hometown to solve her sister's murder.

Jager's face flushed. "What are you doing about the murders?"

Bree motioned to the murder board, then the table covered with files, reports, and photos. "We're investigating. We've had two murders in two days. We're still processing evidence."

"You need to solve this case!" Jager demanded, rapping her knuckles on the table once.

Bree reached for the murder book and shoved it toward Jager. It slid across the tabletop, stopping in front of Jager. "There's the evidence we have so far. Do you want to take a crack at it?"

Jager straightened and looked at the binder as if it were a scorpion. "That's *your* job, not mine."

"This is true," Bree said. "And I'd like to get back to it."

Jager's temper flared in her eyes. "The board of supervisors would like an update on the investigation." The words came out clipped and precisely enunciated, as if it were taking all Jager's self-control not to scream at Bree. "Do you have a suspect?"

Bree considered Farah Rock. "We have a person of interest."

"Who?" Jager jutted one hip and propped a fist on it.

Bree shook her head. "We're waiting on a couple of key pieces of evidence. Once those are in, *if* they confirm our hypothesis, *then* we'll apply for a search and/or arrest warrant. We have rules and procedures we must follow. You know that. Every suspect is innocent until we prove them guilty. If we skip any legal hoops, we risk losing in court and potentially having a killer go free."

"But you're close?" Jager shifted her weight to the other leg. "You think you know who it is?"

"We have a strong suspicion." Bree weighed her words carefully. "Much will depend on those key pieces of evidence. Thoughts, feelings, and gut instinct don't mean anything to a judge. I won't jeopardize this case with speculation."

Jager digested Bree's words, then nodded. "The board would like regular updates."

"Certainly," Bree agreed without committing to any particular intervals.

Jager tipped her head back. "And you need to nix this serial killer rumor."

"How would I do that?" Bree asked.

"Just deny it." Jager lifted one bony shoulder.

"What if it's true?"

"People will panic."

"Will they?" Bree didn't think so. "I find people panic less when they feel they're being kept informed. They need to trust us. Lying will not facilitate that trust."

"You don't have to lie," Jager hedged. "Just be vague, change the subject, don't actually answer a direct question. It's not that hard to be evasive. You're clever. I'm sure you'll manage."

Jager pivoted on one ice-pick heel and stomped out of the room.

Except lying to the public went against every molecule in Bree's body. The people needed to know they could rely on her to protect them. That's what would keep them from panicking. She would not lie. Nor would she withhold information she thought the public needed. She worked for the people. Not the other way around. And while the board of supervisors controlled Bree indirectly through the budget, she answered to the people of Randolph County.

She wouldn't let politics affect her integrity, even if it put her job at risk.

Bree waited until Jager was long gone before turning to Matt and Todd, neither of whom had uttered a word during the exchange. Neither of them had even breathed loudly. "You two were quiet."

"Damned straight," Matt said. "I am *not* a politician."

"What he said." Todd jerked a thumb at Matt. "She's unhinged."

Matt agreed with a nod. "She's ridiculous, like a Disney villain." Over the past few months, Matt's knowledge of all things Disney had increased tenfold. "A redheaded Cruella de Vil."

"Great." Bree rubbed her eyes, as if the gesture would erase the mental image. It didn't help that Jager was cartoonish, and Matt's comparison was spot-on. "Now every time I see Jager, that's what I'm going to picture."

"Happy to help." Matt stood and headed for the door. "Now, you'd better see the press before Jager does."

"Shit. You're right." She stopped in the restroom for two minutes and used the facilities. Washing her hands, she evaluated her reflection and shoved a stray piece of hair back into her bun. She didn't bother changing into a fresh uniform, although Marge had likely replenished the spare in her office. Her admin was efficient as hell. Bree had no time to worry about her appearance. She found Matt and Todd in the hallway, waiting. They walked as a team—a cohesive unit—through the station.

Reporters crowded the lobby. Matt and Todd stood behind Bree as she gave a basic statement. "This morning, the body of Julius Northcott was discovered at his residence." Bree spotted reporter Nick West in the front row. He already knew the details of the case. She could tell by the smug look in his eye. She'd beat him to the punch. "Mr. Northcott was subdued with a stun gun and smothered by plastic wrap."

Murmurs moved across the crowd. A camera flash made Bree see spots. She blinked them away.

Nick West raised his microphone. "In your last press conference, you said there was no threat to the community. Now that a second man has been killed in the same way as the first, would you like to revise your community statement?"

Bree debated which details to reveal and decided to make any information public that might help people protect themselves. "Both of our victims are in their forties, they were both killed in their own residences, and they both used dating apps—"

"Is the killer tracking people on dating apps?" a reporter yelled.

Bree continued. "All we know is that both victims were heavy users of this technology. But causation and correlation are not the same thing." She scanned the group. "Neither home showed any sign of forced entry."

"Is a serial killer on a murder spree in Grey's Hollow?" Nick asked.

The room went silent.

The real answer to his question was *probably*. A copycat was still a possibility but looking less and less likely. Jager and the other county supervisors would lose their ever-loving minds if Bree admitted there was a serial killer in town. But could she live with herself if she didn't? She pictured herself as the police chief in *Jaws*. There was no political win in this situation for her. If she made light of the danger, and someone else died, the supervisors would blame her and call out her failure.

And someone would be dead.

If she alarmed the public, they'd do the same, but at least people would be warned. The most important thing was that no one else died. Politics would be the death of her career. Some days, that thought sounded appealing.

If her career tanked, she would go down with a clear conscience, but she would compromise and not use the *S* word. "It's likely that the same killer murdered both victims. My advice to the community is to keep your doors locked. If you have an alarm system, use it. Don't let anyone into your home whom you don't know well. Be wary of strangers you met online. Be careful with dating apps. Don't give out your personal information. It would be sensible to be extra cautious at the current time." Bree made eye contact with some of the reporters but also with the cameras. "Rest assured that when I have more information, I will bring it to you, and I'm going to ask the public to do the same. If you have any information, if you see something that isn't right, call us. We want to know. The sheriff's department is working night and day to find the person responsible for these terrible crimes."

CHAPTER THIRTY

Matt rubbed an eye as he studied the email from forensics. The words were blurring on the screen, but he could feel excitement stirring as the case against Farah Rock began to take shape.

Across from Matt, Bree extracted data from Julius's cell phone. "Julius and Farah definitely dated via the Cool Beans app."

"But that was a month or so ago, right?" At the other end of the table, Todd looked up from his laptop. "Their messages would be purged."

"True, but they communicated via text as well." Bree tapped the phone screen with a forefinger. "And Julius never deleted her texts." She slid a finger down the screen. "Listen to this exchange." She read aloud. "Farah: 'How many women are you fucking?' Julius: 'We never said we were exclusive.' Farah: 'Answer the Q.' Julius: 'A few.'" Bree rolled her hand in the air. "They go back and forth with a few insults. Then, Farah texts: 'You're a horrible person. Karma is a bitch, and she will come for you.' That sounds like a threat to me." Bree sat back in her chair.

"Agreed," Matt said. "Did Monica date Julius?"

Bree held up the phone. "There's no mention of her in the dating apps Julius used. I'll keep her on the suspect list, but there's no evidence to move her up."

"What about Spencer's brother, Jasper?" Matt asked. "Have we ruled him out as a suspect? He was bailed out Wednesday afternoon, and Julius was killed Wednesday night."

Bree tilted her head. "We haven't found any connection between him and Julius."

"We have an update from forensics." Matt rolled a stiff shoulder. "The powder found on the duct tape across Julius's mouth is chalk."

"Chalk?" Todd asked. "Like blackboard chalk? Don't tell me we have a schoolteacher killing people."

"They don't use chalk at Kayla's school." Bree interlaced her fingers and rotated her joined hands for a stretch. "It can trigger asthma and allergies."

"Doesn't matter. This isn't the same kind." Matt read from the report. "Blackboard chalk is made of calcium carbonate or calcium sulfate. This is magnesium carbonate, which is the kind used by weight lifters, gymnasts, rock climbers, et cetera."

"Rock climbers?" Bree steepled her fingers and brought the tips to her chin, almost as if she were praying. "Farah is a climber."

"Yes, she is." Matt felt their case building, the pieces snapping into place like LEGOs.

"Are there different types of this chalk? Is there any way to differentiate one kind from another?" Bree asked.

"Maybe." Matt skimmed the text. "Some brands are finer or coarser than others. There's natural chalk. Other kinds have drying additives that claim to improve grip. Climbers have personal preferences. I don't know if that would be significant, but if the type found on Julius's body matched the type Farah used, it would certainly strengthen our case."

"OK." Bree dropped her hands to the table. "Do we have anything else?"

"We do," Todd began. "Juarez successfully traced the receipt found near the rattlesnake's empty aquarium to Farah Rock. She purchased a smoothie and power bowl at the Green Works one week ago. She used her credit card. Juarez was able to confirm the transaction on her credit card statement."

"Send a deputy to the Green Works for a copy of the surveillance camera feed," Bree said. "Farah and Julius haven't dated in a month or so. This receipt was dated last week."

"Then she dropped it at the scene?" Matt got up to pace.

Bree closed her eyes, clearly visualizing. "Say Farah killed Julius. She wants to plant the snake for some weird, unknown reason. She'd wait to bring the snake in until after he was dead. I can't see wanting to set loose a venomous snake until the deed was done and she was on her way out the door."

Matt rubbed his beard. "That would explain the hand warmers next to the tank. She could have used them to keep the snake's habitat warm in the car."

"OK," Bree continued. "She set down the tank and piled the hand warmers around it. But she wouldn't want to remove the lid with her hand. She'd be too close. The snake might bite her. She uses a stick or pole to push off the lid. She does, and the snake reacts. It hisses, rattles, startles her. She jumps backward and the receipt falls out of her pocket. With her adrenaline running, she might not have noticed, and she wouldn't have wanted to stick around after the rattler was loose."

Matt paced to the end of the table and back. "I can see that. She could plan everything except the snake's reaction. That was the risky move, the addition that ruined her perfect crime."

Bree's eyes gleamed with exhaustion and fervor. "Let's get a search warrant for her house. Do we have enough for an arrest warrant?"

Matt ticked the evidence off on his fingers. "She dated both men. She threatened Julius via text. She lied to us about her whereabouts, and she asked someone else to lie as well. Chalk was found on Julius's body, and a receipt belonging to Farah was found at the scene near his body."

Bree added, "She also stalked Spencer and threatened him in the presence of his store manager."

Todd added, "Don't forget the white SUV observed at both scenes by two different witnesses. Farah has access to her father's white Highlander."

"Let's get the search warrant to start. We'll bring Farah in for questioning while it's being executed. We can hold her for forty-eight hours before filing charges. With the amount of evidence we have, her attorney won't be able to do anything about it." Bree folded her hands. "I want her off the street before she kills again."

"I wouldn't count the case as closed just yet." Matt stood. "We haven't caught her yet, and she's proven to be extremely dangerous."

CHAPTER

THIRTY-ONE

It was after ten p.m. before the warrants were in place. At the end of Farah's dark driveway, Bree and her team gathered in the darkness. She ignored a trickle of sweat that raced down her spine. Behind her sternum, nerves swarmed like angry hornets.

Bree drew her Glock. Wearing his body-armor vest over his shirt, Matt hefted an AR-15.

The forensics tech waited in his van.

With a wave of her hand, she headed up the gravel driveway. Matt and her deputies fell in behind her. They crept through the darkness. At the edge of the clearing, Bree assessed the situation. No sign of Farah's blue Subaru, but the white Highlander was here. The windows in the cabin and barn were dark.

Was she home? If not, where was she, and what was she doing?

Bree's dread gathered. She should have moved faster. She could have tried for a search warrant earlier. Two men had died in two days. This was day three. Farah could be out stalking another victim.

Bree's team gathered behind her. They'd made a plan and were simply waiting for Bree's signal.

She made a chopping motion with one hand. They split into assigned groups. She and Matt jogged to the front door. Two deputies flanked them for backup. Todd took two more deputies around the back of the cabin to cut off any escape attempt. Another trio of armed deputies headed for the barn / homemade climbing gym behind the cabin.

Bree took two breaths, getting her heart rate under control. She looked at Matt. Their eyes met. He gave her a slight nod.

She stood to the side—out of the direct line of fire—and knocked. "Sheriff!"

Matt leaned a shoulder against the doorframe on the opposite side. He tilted his ear toward the house. Bree did the same, listening hard. She heard nothing. No TV. No music. No voices. No approaching footsteps.

Inside, the cabin was dead quiet.

Bree knocked again, louder. "Ms. Rock, this is Sheriff Taggert. We have a warrant to search the premises."

She knocked a third time. "Ms. Rock. Open the door or we're going to break it in."

Nothing.

Bree signaled for a deputy to come forward with the battering ram. She pulled her flashlight from her pocket. Matt switched on the light mounted on the AR-15. A deputy swung the ram, striking the door next to the dead bolt. The wood cracked and splintered. The door burst open and bounced off the wall with an earsplitting *crack*.

Bree was the first one through the entry. Her senses went on full alert, her heartbeat echoing in her head. Holding her light above and away from her head, she covered the left side of the space. Matt charged through the door behind her, his light sweeping over the right side of the cabin.

Light shone from the range hood over the stove. Embers glowed faintly in the window of the woodstove. The rest of the room was dark.

They made a quick turn around the open space, checking any places large enough to conceal a human being.

Tucking her flashlight under one arm, Bree opened the closet door. Empty. There was no other spot large enough to conceal anyone over the age of six. The main rooms were clear.

Bree led the way to the bedroom. She and Matt took the same positions as with the front door. They'd worked together long enough that they operated smoothly as a team. They went through the doorway. Bree checked under the bed. No one there.

Matt ducked into the adjoining bath. Bree heard the metallic zing of a shower curtain being swept open. Matt reappeared, the rifle across his chest. "Bathroom is clear."

She exhaled, her pulse slowing, the adrenaline rush in her veins ebbing. The night wasn't close to being over, but no one had opened fire on them, and they hadn't encountered a loose rattlesnake.

It's the little things.

Bree pivoted, scanning the room. "Where did she stash the snakes? Those aquariums took up some room."

"They're not here," Matt said.

Bree used her earpiece to communicate with Todd as she returned to the main living area. "Inside is clear. No sign of the suspect. What's your status?"

"Barn is clear," Todd said in her ear. "Two deputies are searching the barn gym space for evidence now. Two more are sweeping the surrounding woods. I'm headed back to the cabin."

There weren't many hiding spaces in the homemade gym. Bree needed Todd to help search Farah's personal space, where they were more likely to find trace evidence that might match that found at one of the crime scenes. Without a full hazmat suit, it was damned hard not to leave anything behind after committing a major crime. People shed skin cells and hair everywhere they went.

"Make sure they bag and tag the climbing chalk," Bree said. "We'll need it for comparison to the chalk found on Julius Northcott. I want the forensics tech in the Highlander. That's the vehicle likely spotted at both scenes."

"Yes, ma'am." Two minutes later, Todd came through the front door.

Bree holstered her weapon, snapped on gloves, and shifted into search mode. She flipped a wall switch and turned on the lights. "Let's get cracking. I'll take the kitchen area."

"I'll take the bedroom," Matt said.

Todd headed for the living room space. He sat on an ottoman and opened the top drawer of a credenza.

Bree pulled out her flashlight and opened a kitchen cabinet. "Be careful. Last time we tried to search a house, we found a rattlesnake."

Todd froze for a second. Flashlight in hand, he turned back to the drawers with more caution.

Bree spotted a box of plastic wrap in the kitchen. She bagged and tagged it, though Farah would certainly have a separate box of plastic wrap for committing murders. She wouldn't just grab the box on the way out of the kitchen. Not two nights in a row. But she might buy the same brand of wrap out of habit.

Farah would have prepared. She would have packed a bag with her stun gun, zip ties, plastic wrap, gloves, et cetera. Neither Spencer's nor Julius's murder had been impulsive.

No. Their deaths required planning. Detailed planning.

Todd stood. "These drawers are mostly full of spare cables, the empty boxes her electronic devices came in, and some user manuals for appliances. Nothing even remotely interesting."

"Why don't you check with the deputies in the barn?" she suggested.

"Will do." He left through the back door.

Bree finished the kitchen and circled the living area. Snapshots lined a bookshelf. From appearances, she thought the people in the photos were Farah's parents and younger sister. Bree studied a photo of the family at the sister's college graduation and another of the same people, much younger, at a campsite in front of a lake. Farah and her sister had clearly been raised camping, hiking, and skiing.

Stepping sideways, Bree moved on to the next wall and a photo collage. She studied the pictures, doubt wriggling inside her like a worm on a hook.

Matt walked out of the bedroom and joined her. "You look like you're thinking."

Bree nodded toward the collage.

Matt scanned the photos. "Interesting. Didn't Rhys say they weren't that close?"

"He did." Bree's gaze moved from picture to picture: Rhys and Farah at a fair of some kind, Rhys and Farah sitting in front of a campfire, Rhys and Farah smiling in front of a brilliant blue sky. Her brain started down a new path, hacking away at former deductions like a machete through the jungle.

"That's a lot of joint activities for two people who are barely acquainted." Clearly, Matt was thinking the same thing.

"It is," Bree agreed. "Seems like Farah was telling the truth about them having a lot in common and spending time together."

"Why would Rhys lie about their relationship?" Matt asked. "Maybe he wanted to distance himself from a murder suspect?"

"Or maybe this was all of their activities, and she documented each and every one. Whichever it is, I think we should ask him." Bree pointed to the collage.

Matt frowned. "Spencer lied. Farah lied. Rhys refused to lie for Farah but lied to us anyway."

Bree rocked back on her heels. "Is there anyone in this case who *isn't* lying?"

"I don't know, but what someone lies about can be as telling as the truth," Matt said. "I see two options here. One, Farah killing men she dated because they rejected her."

"I can see a motive for her to kill Rhys. He denied her alibi."

"She's definitely angry." Matt contemplated the photos. "Regardless of how he feels, she thought they were best friends."

"She's going to feel betrayed." Dread tightened Bree's throat. "Maybe she'll want to get even, which gives her motive to kill Rhys. Plus, Spencer and Julius rejected her."

"*Or* our answer is the exact opposite," Matt said. "Which brings me to option two."

Bree picked up his train of logic. "Rhys killing the men Farah dated out of jealousy."

"He admitted to still having feelings for her."

Bree let the idea roll around in her head. "We have physical evidence against Farah. The chalk, the receipt . . ."

"True."

"Sometimes, you can't fathom what goes on in a person's head." Bree had worked one case where a man claimed his cat convinced him to beat his wife to death with a hammer. "We know Farah has a short temper and threatened both Spencer and Julius."

"Yep." Matt waved at the photos of Farah and Rhys. "Rhys could have picked up some chalk dust on his person while he was here, and if they went out together, it would be easy enough for him to grab the wrong receipt."

Bree looked around the room. "Farah's short fuse and impulsiveness make her feel hostile. But it's possible she's just a bitch and not a killer. So, is she out killing someone?"

"Or is *she* missing?" Matt finished. "And he planted the evidence to frame Farah."

Bree nodded. "In which case, Farah could be in danger. There's only one way to get the answers we need. Let's go talk to Rhys." She checked the time. "It's almost midnight." They had no time to waste.

"We need to find them both."

"Ma'am?" Todd called as he walked in the back door. "Deputies are still working on the barn. They bagged the chalk dust. No sign of a cat." He paused. "But Juarez at the station called. Farah's phone records just came in. At 9:45, Rhys Blake called her, and they spoke for fifty-five seconds."

"*He* called *her*?" Bree asked.

"Yes," Todd said.

"He said he didn't want anything to do with her," Matt said. "Why would he call her?"

"I can't think of any innocent reason," Bree said to Matt, then turned back to Todd. "Can we track her location via her phone?"

"On it," Todd said.

"It's Rhys." Bree knew it in every cell in her body.

"I agree," Matt said. "The evidence can be interpreted in two ways. Sometimes, you have to rely on your gut."

Bree looked back at the photos of Farah and Rhys and wondered if both of them were still alive.

Chapter Thirty-Two

I hear the knock on my back door. An electric thrill rushes over my skin. I've been waiting for her. I almost can't believe she came, but then, I played my part well.

Farah. Beautiful Farah. You think you're so smart.

But I'm smarter.

I open the door, putting an apologetic mask on my face. "Hey, thanks for coming."

She smiles but not with her normal exuberance. Instead, her expression is pained, the smile fake, reminding me that she isn't here for a date.

Reminding me why I summoned her.

But if she can act, so can I.

I focus on looking sincere. Stepping back, I gesture for her to come in. She enters my kitchen. She's been here many times before, but tonight, she doesn't toss her keys on the counter or hang her jacket on the back of a chair. She doesn't even remove the jacket. She doesn't intend to be here long. That's obvious.

She keeps her keys in her hand, toying with them. "I'm glad you called." But she looks anything but glad to be here.

"Can I make you some tea?" I ask.

She shakes her head. "I can't stay."

"OK." I shove my hands into the pockets of my hoodie. The silence stretches out into awkwardness reminiscent of middle school.

She jingles the keys. She clearly can't wait to leave.

"I wanted to apologize," I begin. "I didn't mean to mess up your alibi. That sheriff . . . She kept firing questions at me. She threatened me . . ." I close my eyes and exhale through my nose, as if the experience were humiliating. "I got confused, then there was no going back."

In reality, the cops are stupid. I have laid them a trail, and they are following it like hounds on the dragged scent in a fake fox hunt. They will go where I have sent them. They will believe whatever I wish them to believe.

Her eyes soften, just a little. "The sheriff *is* a bitch." She swallows. "But I shouldn't have asked you to lie. The sheriff kept at me too. She made me feel like I needed an alibi. I didn't kill anyone. I didn't do anything wrong, but she sure made me feel like I should worry. I panicked."

Because I made Sheriff Taggert suspect you.

My face remains passive, but inside I'm gloating. I want to tell her everything. I put the chalk on the bodies. I left the receipt at Julius's house. I nurtured her anger with both men and encouraged her to confront them.

She looks away for a minute, her face tight. When she turns back to me, there's a new look in her eyes. Something final, and I realize she's going to say goodbye. My apology wasn't good enough.

I'm not good enough.

Love and hate war inside me. There are parts of her I can't get enough of. That fit, toned body. Her strong features. The long, thick hair I want to bury my face in. I want to inhale her, to love and cherish her, to have and to hold. I want the whole package.

But she will not have me.

And I can't bear for anyone else to have her.

It's vicious and destructive and selfish. But then, so am I. This is where the hate takes over. I hate the power she has over me, the way that I cannot get her out of my system.

"Anyway, this whole thing has made me rethink our relationship." Her gaze finds and grips mine. I see something akin to empathy in her eyes. "What I've been doing isn't fair to you. I know how you feel about me."

Oh, do you? You think you know everything.

She probably expects me to disengage, to be embarrassed and distance myself from the conversation, but I don't break eye contact. I hold it, my gaze steady. She seems disconcerted by my unexpected reaction.

She looks away. "I, um, wish I felt the same way. I really do. I enjoy your company. You're a great friend. We have a lot of fun together. I hate for it to end. But I can't force a romantic connection to happen. I can't make myself be attracted to you, and you can't stop feeling the way you do. For me, the chemistry is either there or it isn't."

But she's right about one thing: I can't stop wanting her. I have no control over my emotions, and my lack of self-control fuels my rage. I will not be at any bitch's mercy. No woman is worth sacrificing my self-respect.

I hate her just as much as I love her.

Of course, I say none of this. I shuffle my feet, as if I'm uncomfortable instead of angry. "I get it. I appreciate you being up front with me."

She nods, and the single, abrupt movement feels final. "Take care of yourself, OK? You're a great guy. Some woman is going to be really lucky to have you."

You condescending bitch.

I swallow my response. Soon—very soon—she'll learn an important lesson about stringing men along. For now, I mirror the curt, final nod she gave me. She turns to leave. As she reaches for the door, I pull the stun gun from my pocket and thrust it at her torso, aiming for the largest target for the initial strike. Once she's weakened, I can zap her wherever I choose. But she sees my motion out of the corner of her eye. She twists her shoulders, and I miss.

Surprise stops me for two seconds. I can't believe it. I never miss. My first two kills went off without a hitch. But then, Farah is fitter and quicker than either Spencer or Julius. They were gym-fit. Farah climbs walls and hangs off cliffs.

Her eyes go wild, and I can see her brain connecting all the important dots. I shake off my shock, and I see her do the same. She needs to go down. She cannot escape, not after I've given myself away. Tonight's plan is a must win. There is no plan B. If she gets away, she'll go right to the sheriff. I'll be done.

Can't have that.

She takes a defensive stance, hands in front of her body, one foot slightly ahead of the other. Her balance shifts to the balls of her feet.

I lunge, the stun gun extended. She pivots sideways, again evading me. She doesn't bother yelling, questioning, or asking for explanations because she is also smarter than either Spencer or Julius. Words are a waste of breath at this point. She knows exactly what is happening. She reads my intention and doesn't question her deduction.

Farah is a survivor.

She eases back a step, wary as a deer facing a wolf. We circle like that for a few seconds, sizing each other up, each of us seeing the other in a new way. There's respect in her eyes. Finally. This pleases me. I shift my grip on the stun gun. My hand is sweating. I should have foreseen her resilience. I should have known she would fight back. A person who is willing to scale the face of a cliff won't give up easily.

I feint a direct thrust, then go wide. She doesn't buy it. She reaches for a basket of mail and throws it at me. I bat it out of the way. In my peripheral vision, I see the basket hit the floor, the mail spill out.

Farah darts left, tries to run for the door. I cut her off. She reaches for the drainboard. A few dishes stand upright in the rack, drying. One at a time, she flings them at my head. I dodge the flying discs and ignore the crashes of shattering ceramic. There isn't much else on the counter. She's running out of ammunition.

I try again, lunging forward. She thrusts a chair in my path. I shove it aside and resume my charge. Her back hits the counter. She's in the corner, but still, even trapped she doesn't give up. I move in. She grabs my wrist, holding the stun gun away from her body. I push, but she is strong. We're both panting from exertion. Her breath smells like coffee and chocolate. Our altercation feels as intimate as sex, maybe even more.

The space is too tight—our bodies are too close together for punching and kicking. She drives a knee toward my groin, but I turn my hips and take the blow on my thigh. Pain zings up my leg, but adrenaline quickly suppresses it.

I have her now. There's nowhere for her to go. She can't escape. She is trapped. I yank my arm downward, breaking her grip on my wrist and shoving the stun gun at her body.

Her shoulders twist. Where there is no room to extend her arm for a punch, she uses her elbow in a downward arc, circling her shoulder for maximum force. The hard bone strikes my nose at the same moment the stun gun finds a target against her ribs. Despite the spray of blood from my face, as soon as the device makes contact with her body, I know I've won. I press hard, hold the device steady, and count to five. Her body jolts, stiffens, and quivers as the current rushes through her nerves.

Blood runs down my face onto my shirt and drips onto the floor. It tastes metallic and salty as it passes over my lips. I ignore it. A battle wound. Satisfaction surges through me. But I can't count my win as final yet. She is strong. She will recover quickly. I have to focus. I have to move fast.

Sweat soaks my shirt. My heart jackhammers. I can't hear anything else. My nose is clogged, the nasal passages already swelling, forcing me to breathe through my mouth.

I zap her a second time, just to be safe. Her body seizes and topples. On the way to the floor, her head glances off the edge of the granite countertop. As she goes down, blood gushes from a gash on her temple. Between my nose and her head wound, blood slicks the floor. I fumble, trying to shove the stun gun into my pocket. My shoe slides. My kneecap rings on tile. I catch myself with a hand on the floor. Panic crawls over me. My lungs go tight. My field of vision narrows. Light-headedness swirls in my brain.

This is not how this was supposed to go. I should be in control. She is at *my* mercy now.

Don't fuck this up. Breathe.

She's down. I have a minute or two, at least, before she begins to regain muscle control.

After taking ten seconds to get my shit together, I yank the zip ties from my pocket, roll her on her side, and press my knee into her hip. With her pinned, I fasten her hands behind her back. I bind her ankles too. No doubt she can knee and kick as well as she can use her elbow.

Ironically, relief makes me almost as light-headed as the panic. But I have her now.

I sit back on my heels to catch my breath. My hands are shaking. My nose is full of blood, so my gasps sound wet and gurgling. It's humiliating, definitely not the most masculine sound. This whole scene didn't pan out the way I'd planned. I grab a clean dish towel from the drawer, hold it to my nose, and assess Farah.

Her cheek is pressed into the floor. With her hands and feet bound, she has no leverage. My knee and weight on her side keep her face mashed down. A trickle of bright blood runs into her eye and onto the floor.

"What the fuck, Rhys?" She doesn't have full mobility of her jaw and mouth, so her words come out a bit garbled.

I lift the dish towel from my face. "You condescending bitch. Did you think you could just reject me, parade other men in front of me, then walk away?"

She doesn't answer. Just stares. I see her digesting the full ramifications of what just happened. Defiance fades from her eyes. Fear slides in.

Triumph blooms in my heart. "That's right. I'm in control now. You're about to learn all about respect and manners. You're going to learn the hard way, and so is your new lover boy."

She shakes her head. "I don't have—"

Her words cut off abruptly as I zap her. "Shut up!"

She writhes, her body simultaneously stiff and quaking. A moan slips through her clenched teeth. It sounds almost feral. Before she dies, I'm going to take her to rock bottom. I'm going to strip away her humanity. She will become nothing.

I lean close, so she can feel my breath on her face. "Don't lie to me. I saw you with him."

Blood drips from the corner of her mouth. She must have bitten her tongue. When she opens her mouth, it stains her teeth.

I dab her face with the dish towel. A few strands of her hair are stuck in the blood. I brush them away. She's still beautiful. I bet she'll even be beautiful dead.

I smile. This is the first time I've been truly happy in a long time. "I started planning this weeks and weeks ago. Remember how you stalked Spencer? You were so focused that you didn't see me following you."

Her eyes open wider. A tear slips from her eye, mixes with the blood on her face, and falls to the tile. It spreads, a watery, pink circle of liquid.

That's better. She's humbled.

I stand, wet the dish towel under the faucet, and mop my face. My clothes are ruined. The bleeding from my nose has slowed to a drip. Maybe it's not broken. I drop the dish towel on the floor and use it to clean the blood. But Farah's head has left quite the puddle. I learned years ago, after a car accident, that head wounds bleed copiously. Her wound might not be too serious. She's conscious and aware. The terror in her eyes is lucid.

I press a fresh towel to her head. I don't want her to make a mess in the car. Her little Subaru isn't big enough to transport Farah and a glass tank, so I can't use her vehicle. I reach into her jacket pocket, retrieve her cell phone, and put it in my own pocket.

"Here's where I'm supposed to say, 'If you cooperate, you'll be fine.' But unlike you, I'm not going to lie. Here's what's really going to happen. I'm going to kill you tonight. But first, you're going to watch your new boyfriend die."

CHAPTER THIRTY-THREE

Matt studied Rhys Blake's place, a Cape Cod–style house on a quiet street a few blocks from the train station. The house was dark gray or blue. It was hard to tell in the dark. As was typical for homes in town, the lots were small and covered with mature trees and shrubs. Broad oaks lined the street, their thick branches winter-bare. Looking down the driveway that ran alongside the house, Matt could see a detached two-car garage at the back of the small lot.

Bree parked at the curb. "Windows are dark."

"He could be asleep."

"Let's hope." She popped the lock on her seat belt.

A patrol vehicle parked behind them. Bree had left Todd in charge of completing the search of Farah's house.

Matt slid out of the SUV into the shadow of an oak tree. The side-walk was buckled and twisted from overgrown tree roots. Cold wind down-blasted the street, sending dead leaves tumbling in the gutter.

Bree walked to the driver's-side door of the patrol vehicle. "Wait here, but look sharp."

Bree and Matt walked up two brick steps to the front stoop. She rang the bell. The chime sounded behind the red door. When no one answered, she rang it again. But the house remained silent and still.

Matt stepped into the front flower bed and sidled behind a squared-off hedge. Glare from the streetlight reflected on the window. He cupped his hands over his eyes and peered into the house. The curtains weren't closed, and he could see into a dark living room. Dim light shone through a doorway at the back of the room, and Matt could see a skinny slice of kitchen. Nothing looked out of the ordinary. "I don't see anyone."

"Let's check around back." Bree started around the side of the house.

Matt followed. The narrow driveway led to the detached garage. A single lamp on the garage exterior cast weak light over the backyard. The lawn was no bigger than a volleyball court. Outdoor furniture consisted of a single chair at the edge of the patio.

Bree walked to the garage and pointed to a small window above their heads. "Boost me?"

"Sure." Matt interlaced his fingers and leaned over.

Bree put the toe of her boot into his improvised step.

He lifted her off the ground. "See anything?"

Steadying herself with one hand on the building, she shaded her eyes with the other. "Yes. An SUV."

"Rhys's Cherokee?"

"No. It's dark colored. I need a better view. Let's try the other window."

Matt lowered her to the ground. They moved back about a dozen feet to the next window and repeated the process. Bree pulled her flashlight from her duty belt and shined it through the glass. "Oh!" She glanced down at him. "It's a blue Subaru."

"Farah's vehicle?"

"Let's find out." She used her lapel mic to call dispatch and read off the license plate number.

Matt brought her back down. In a couple of minutes, dispatch confirmed the vehicle was registered to Farah Rock.

"So, she is or was here." And Matt didn't like it one bit. "Where is Rhys's Jeep?"

"Good question." Bree walked to the back patio. She peered through the sliding glass doors. "Eating area and family room. Both empty."

"Careful. We've already been shot at once," Matt warned.

"Like I could forget," Bree said.

He crossed to a small window high on the exterior wall and rose onto his toes. Pulling his own flashlight from his jacket pocket, he shined it into a mudroom, which was dark and empty. He moved to the next window and looked into a small, neat kitchen. Moving the beam of his light, he scanned the counters. "Hold on."

"What?"

Broken shards of ceramic gleamed on pale gray floor tiles. A few feet away, the drainboard lay upside down. A few oranges and an apple sat in the middle of the mess. A basket had been flung across the room, its contents—mail—strewn around it. A kitchen chair lay on its side.

"Definitely signs of a struggle." Bree pressed her own flashlight to the glass. "Look at the edge of the counter. What is that?"

Matt followed the beam of her light to a dark smear on the edge of the counter. The cabinets were white, and a thin line of dark liquid had dripped down the side. "Looks like blood, otherwise known as exigent circumstances."

"I agree." She turned away from the window and headed around the house. She broke into a jog. Matt stayed close. When they reached the front yard, she motioned for her deputies to join them and used her radio to update dispatch.

While she communicated with her department, Matt grabbed the AR-15 from the SUV and summed up the situation for the deputies. "We have signs of a struggle and what appears to be blood in the kitchen. We're going in."

Bree joined them, drawing her Glock. "Tread carefully. Keep your eyes open, not just for an injured or deceased homeowner, but for Farah as well. Her car is in the garage—oh, and watch out for rattlesnakes."

Matt was pretty sure he heard a softly muttered *fuck* from one of the deputies, and he wholeheartedly agreed with the assessment.

"Matt and I will go through the front door," Bree said. "You two watch the back of the house and the garage in case our killer is still in there and tries to run out the back."

With a quick nod, the deputies jogged down the driveway. Bree and Matt went to the front door. Bree tried the knob, but the door was locked. She used the butt end of her metal flashlight to break the small pane of glass next to the door. Then she ran the flashlight around the edges of the window frame to clear sharp points of glass. Shards fell to the floor. Reaching through, she unlocked the door. She pushed it open and stepped inside.

The interior was dark. Matt flipped the wall switch, turning on recessed lights in the ceiling.

He kept one eye on the floor as they moved through the rooms. Rhys's furnishings were minimal, and he wasn't prone to clutter, so the search went quickly. Methodically, they searched the living and dining rooms. They turned on lights as they went through the house. No one wanted to encounter a venomous snake in the dark. A hall closet and a half bath were cleared. They moved on to the kitchen. Matt checked the pantry.

Bree glanced at the debris on the tile. "I see some dark stains on the grout. It looks like there was more blood and someone did a quick mop-up."

"Thankfully, grout's a bitch to get blood out of."

A stairwell led to the second floor. Matt took point, the rifle pressed firmly into his shoulder. Two doors—one open, one closed—flanked the upstairs landing. Bree turned into the open doorway on the right. Matt opened the door on the left. Light from the ceiling fixture on the landing spilled into the room. Matt could see a desk and chair. Home office. A rattling sound stopped him cold. Sweat trickled down his spine as an irritated hiss followed the rattle.

CHAPTER

THIRTY-FOUR

Bree turned on the bedroom light. Gun extended, she scanned the room, freezing for a second as she spotted a form on the bed.

A long-haired black cat.

The feline lifted its head and turned toward her, its bright yellow eyes taking her in for two seconds before tucking its nose under its fluffy tail and resuming its nap.

Coincidence?

Bree wasn't a big believer in those, but she put her suspicions aside to finish clearing the house. There were two doors on the near wall. Putting a shoulder behind the frame, she jerked open the first door to reveal a walk-in closet the size of an elevator. She shifted clothes to ensure no one was hiding behind them. Then she went into the bathroom, sidled to the tub, and pulled back the shower curtain. Empty. Satisfied the room was clear, she headed for the hall, casting one last glance at the cat.

"Bree?" Matt called from the room on the other side of the landing.

"Primary bedroom is clear." She walked across the landing and froze at the sound of an angry rattle emanating from the room. She peered around the doorframe.

Matt stood in the middle of the room, staring at an aquarium on the floor of a home office. Inside the tank, a fat brown snake lifted its thick head and hissed. The tip of its tail quivered.

"Whoa." Bree stepped into the doorway.

"Right?"

Her brain did a one-eighty. "It's in a tank."

"Yep," Matt said.

She studied it in silence for a long minute, processing what the snake's presence meant. "Guess what's in the bedroom?"

"What?" Matt asked.

"A long-haired black cat."

They stared at each other. Then they turned and stared at the snake.

"We were right," Bree asked. "He has a white SUV and a long-haired black cat."

"He stole the snakes." Matt motioned toward the tank.

"But we need a warrant to search deeper and to get forensics in here," Bree said.

Police generally needed a search warrant to enter a private residence, but there were exceptions to this requirement. They'd broken into Rhys's house under the legal exemption of exigent circumstances. They'd had good reason to believe someone was injured, dead, or otherwise in danger inside the house. The blood and evidence of a fight supported that assumption. But exigent circumstances could be challenged in court, especially if the evidence wasn't in plain sight. Obtaining a search warrant was always preferable to ensure any evidence recovered was admissible.

"So where *is* Farah?" Matt asked. "Her vehicle is here."

"We have to assume he took her—somewhere." Bree nodded. "The blood says she didn't go willingly. We assume he kidnapped her." And that's the case she would need to lay out for the judge.

"We need to find them before he kills her."

"I'll talk to the judge." Bree's mind spun. She snapped a picture of the rattlesnake.

"I'll put forensics on notice," Matt added.

With two murders and two separate crime scenes, everyone was working 24/7, forensics and the lab techs included.

They went downstairs. Bree motioned through the glass doors for the deputies to meet them out front. "We'll need Rhys's cell provider and financial records too. Call Juarez and have him get the paperwork ready to send in as soon as the warrant is signed." She updated her deputies and ordered them to put out BOLO—be on the lookout—alerts for Rhys and Farah. Then she went to her vehicle to apply for an electronic search warrant. Bree had dealt with the on-call judge before. She outlined the evidence, emphasizing the blood and signs of a struggle in the kitchen, and her belief that Rhys had kidnapped Farah with the intention of killing her. Given the nature and pattern of the two previous murders, the judge agreed to the warrant, with the usual dire warning that Bree had better not be wrong or it would be the last warrant he signed for her.

In reality, he was telling Bree that if the night went sideways, he would throw her under an entire fleet of buses. But Bree would take that responsibility. She would do anything to stop this killer.

"I'm trusting you, Sheriff," the judge said. "Get this guy off our streets."

She made all the appropriate sounds of appreciation and assurance and crossed her fingers she could make her promises come true. With the necessary digital paperwork completed, she jumped from her vehicle. "We're in."

Matt lifted his phone. "Juarez is working on the requests for cell provider and financial records."

She donned gloves as she hurried toward the front door.

"A forensics tech will be here ASAP." Gloving up, Matt was right at her heels. They walked through the house again, this time looking for anything that might indicate where Rhys had taken Farah.

"Where do you think he did his planning?" Bree asked. "Because he planned these murders."

"In detail," Matt agreed, heading for the steps. "Let's start with the office. I didn't see any loose papers on the desk, which makes me think he's a paperless guy."

"Let's hope we can hack into his computer."

The snake rattled at them as they entered the office. Bree went to the desk. With a gloved hand, she opened a slim laptop. The screen woke, asking for a password.

Matt pulled out his phone. "No Facebook. No Instagram. He's on Twitter, mostly as an observer." He scrolled. "He's posted a few pictures of his cat. His name is Dexter."

Bree typed the name. "That's not it." She tried a variety of Rhys's key numbers—street address, zip code, birthday, et cetera—with and without the cat's name. None worked.

Matt began opening drawers and sifting through their contents. "He's organized and uncluttered. That helps."

Bree got locked out of the laptop. "Damn it!" She closed the lid.

"It was a long shot," Matt said. "He's a computer guy. He's going to have his machine protected."

"I know. The computer techs will get into his machine eventually." But that would take time, and Bree had wanted information *now*. She shifted her attention to the desk drawers. She slid open the top drawer and found a stun gun box. In order to preserve fingerprints, she used a pen to flip up the hinged lid. Nestled in the molded plastic were a charging cord and storage case.

"Look what I found." Matt set a black leather journal on the desk and opened it. Inside, Rhys had documented someone's comings and goings. "He has at least a dozen pages on the daily activities of 'the Liar.' He doesn't give a real name or address, but I think we can assume the Liar is Spencer."

"Yes." Bree leaned in for a better view. "He went to work at Electronics Depot, trips to the gym, runs."

Matt flipped more pages. "This section is for 'the Cheat.' That has to be Julius. Yep. Rhys has noted the times Julius arrived and left the auto dealership, among other daily activities." He turned over another page and froze. "There's another section."

"Shit." The nerves in Bree's stomach knotted tighter. "He isn't just going to kill Farah. He has another target in mind."

"Killing two people tonight would be a grand finale." Matt turned another page. "He calls the new guy 'the Flake.'"

"Because he flaked on Farah? Or because he's odd?"

Matt shrugged. "It doesn't say. But Rhys has only been watching him for about a week."

"He must be someone Farah dated recently."

"The Flake works at home, and doesn't go out much." Matt turned back to the beginning of the section. "Here's the initial meet between Farah and the Flake."

"Farah must have told Rhys about the date."

"Then Rhys followed him home."

Bree leaned back in the office chair. "I'll bet when we get our hands on his phone, we'll find lots of pictures. Stalkers love to take pictures."

"He might have a cloud account the techs can access."

"That'll take time." Bree rubbed the hollow dread in her gut. "I have a feeling he's going to kill someone tonight. I realize we can't form a pattern or make predictions based on two incidents, but . . ."

"Yeah. I feel it too."

Bree's phone buzzed with a text. "The forensics tech is here." She stood.

Matt set the journal on the desk. "I'll see what I can find in the bedroom."

Bree went downstairs. The forensics tech wore a Tyvek suit. He was taking pictures of the chaos in the kitchen. Bree pointed out the blood stains and drips, then let him go to work. While he did his thing, Bree went over the living room again, but all signs pointed to the violence being limited to the kitchen. The living room was perfect, as if Rhys didn't use it much.

In the laundry room, she opened the washer to find laundry that had been washed but not dried. She saw several dish towels, one of which seemed to carry a faded red stain.

The forensics tech called out, "Sheriff?"

"Yes." Bree returned to the kitchen. "It looks like he mopped up the blood and washed the towels."

The tech shrugged. "You can launder items multiple times, and I can still find the blood."

Matt came down and waited with Bree.

The tech turned back to the counter and tile floor. "I've photographed and sampled the blood stains as is. I'm about to use the reagent." The tech had set up a camera on a tripod to record the luminescence of the bloodstain. He gestured to a few evidence bags lined up on the counter. "I also found the top half of two torn fingernails—painted red—and six long dark hairs that appeared to have been ripped out from the root. The nails have blood on them, possibly skin as well."

"Farah was wearing red nail polish when we interviewed her," Bree said.

Matt nodded. "She fought back."

The blood and skin on the nails could help ID her killer through DNA, but it wouldn't save her life tonight.

He removed a spray bottle from his kit. "Here we go."

Bree stepped back. The tech pulled down his goggles, sprayed, and lit up the kitchen in a bright blue fluorescent glow. Bree could see a small puddle of blue where blood had pooled beneath a smear on the edge of the counter.

Matt pointed to the blue smudge directly above the puddle. "I would bet someone—maybe Farah—hit her head on the edge of the counter."

Bree crouched to get a better view of the floor. She moved her hand to indicate a round swirl where blood had pooled. "She went down. Maybe lay here for a few minutes, bleeding."

The blood smeared in a side-to-side pattern. Matt gestured over it. "He wiped up the blood with towels."

Bree followed a thin trail of blue streaks to the back door. "She was still bleeding when he took her out."

"The stains look all smeared here too," Matt said. "He took her out to his Jeep, then came back inside, did a quick mop-up, and tossed the towels in the washer."

Bree stared at the glowing blue swirls. "That's quite a bit of blood."

"The first two murders were bloodless," Matt said. "Why did he change his MO for Farah?"

"The two male victims were killed in their residences. Rhys called Farah to come here. Why? Why change everything?" Bree shook her head.

"We'll figure out the answers later. We need to find them." They already had state, county, and local law enforcement on alert.

Bree called Juarez, who was still working at the station. "I need you to search tax records. See if Rhys Blake owns any other properties."

"I was just going to call you." Juarez sounded strange.

"What's wrong?"

"I got access to Farah Rock's dating app activity."

"OK."

"Last week she went on dates with two men. One of them was your brother, Adam."

Bree couldn't breathe. Her chest locked tight, like her ribs were carved out of granite. She started for the door, leaving a deputy in charge of the search. Shaking off her shock, she lowered the phone and relayed the information to Matt.

"Ma'am?" Juarez called over the phone.

She lifted the phone and answered, "Put out BOLOs on both men, and let's do well-being checks." But she knew the target was Adam. "Do we have a patrol car near my brother's residence?" Bree spouted off the address, but even as she gave the rural route info, she knew it was a long shot. Adam lived in an isolated area.

Isolated enough for Rhys to do as he pleased. There were no neighbors to see or hear anything.

She could hear Juarez's breathing change. He was moving, probably heading to check with the dispatcher. She heard mumbling, then Juarez came back on the line. "There's no one closer than you. Most of our deputies are being utilized at the two property searches."

"I'm on my way. Send backup." She ended her call with Juarez as she ran out the door. On the way to her vehicle, she gave the most senior deputy a few quick instructions. Turning away, she broke into a run.

Matt jogged at her side. This time, he didn't tell her that everything would be fine, that the danger was in her imagination.

Because it was all too real.

"You drive." Bree's hands were shaking.

Matt slid behind the wheel. She rode shotgun, dialing her brother's number as she fastened her seat belt.

Every unanswered ring tightened the spool of dread building inside her. "He's not answering." The call switched to voice mail, and she left a message. "Adam, please call me. It's important." She hung up and sent him a text. If he was in an area with poor reception, a text message might go through when a call would not.

Matt drove away from Rhys's house. Bree pressed a hand to the center of her chest, where a hollow ache surrounded her heart.

She'd buried a sibling—a victim of murder—earlier this year. She couldn't do it again.

CHAPTER
THIRTY-FIVE

"Did you know that rattlesnake venom can take days to kill victims the size of adult humans, and some people might not die, even without medical treatment?" At a stop sign, I brake. The Jeep comes to a stop with a slight jolt.

A protesting rattle and hiss sound from the rear of the vehicle.

I lower the window. The cold night air blows in, carrying the scent of burning wood. Someone is enjoying a fire tonight. I pull Farah's phone from my pocket and heave it out the window. It bounces across the asphalt into the grass on the opposite side of the road.

A distraction for the sheriff and her deputies.

I close the window before the car turns too cool. I've piled some hand warmers and blankets around the aquarium to keep the habitat warm. It's important to maintain the snake's body temperature. I don't want it to become lethargic. I need it to be aggressive and angry when the sheriff finally arrives.

Then I turn in my seat to check on my passengers. The rear seats are folded flat, so the cargo area is one big space. Farah lies on her side. Zip ties fasten her wrists behind her back and bind her ankles. Additional ties connect her wrists to her feet. Her body is bent in a backward bow.

I've basically hog-tied her. Of course, I've tucked cloth under the ties to pad them. I wouldn't want ligature marks to mar that pretty skin. The sheriff needs to believe Farah died by suicide.

A soft gag fills that smart mouth. Can't leave duct tape residue for the medical examiner to discover. I watch *CSI*. But I can still hear her whimpering. The sound grates on my nerves like a whetstone.

"Will you shut up!" My command feels pointless. She clearly can't stop. Tears and snot run down her face. Her eyes are swollen and red. But my heart still pings as I look at her, and I hate her for that.

Her face is about ten inches from the snake's tank, and the rattler is not happy. His tail is twitching, he's coiled in the far corner of his habitat, and his head is drawn back. Because of her proximity, the snake sees Farah as a threat. Another bit of irony. Farah isn't in a position to be a threat to anyone.

I turn forward and touch the gas pedal. The Jeep creeps forward in the dark. My house is in civilization, but Farah's latest boyfriend lives in the middle of nowhere.

On the bright side, there are no neighbors within sight.

The Jeep runs over a pothole, and the snake emits another angry hiss. Farah whimpers again.

I glance in the rearview mirror.

She's fully recovered from being stunned, so why does she look woozy? I didn't think her head wound was too terrible, but maybe I was wrong. Not that it will matter in the long run. She'll be dead before morning regardless. But I would like to do the deed with my own two hands. In order to move on, I need closure, the up-front and personal kind.

A sheet of plastic covers my cargo hatch, and her head lies on a towel, so she doesn't make a mess. Blood mats her hair from where she struck the edge of my kitchen counter. Can the snake smell it? The scent of blood attracts most predators. Always looking for an easy meal, they seek the wounded and weak. But snakes swallow their prey alive and whole. Maybe blood means nothing to them.

My headlights sweep to the right as I make a turn onto the rural road. We're almost there. Excitement rushes through me. This is it. The night I've been waiting and planning for. My endgame.

Technically, Farah and the Flake's endgame. *Finale* is a better word.

I try to take a deep, calming breath, but my nasal passages have swollen closed, forcing me to suck in air through my mouth. I should have iced it but didn't want to take the time.

I slow the Jeep as we approach the driveway. Meadows flank the narrow lane all the way to the converted barn. With my previous victims, I planned how I would get into the house undetected. But the flaky artist hardly ever leaves. Tonight's entry will need to be more direct. But that's OK. I'm feeling ballsy. I ease off the gas and let the vehicle come to a stop where I can see the front and side of the barn in the distance. I raise my binoculars and scan the front of the building. His new vehicle is hot. Too bad he won't be around to enjoy it for long.

The big windows that provide him the perfect light for painting are the same windows that allow me a view of his studio. With the studio lights on full blast, I can see him now. He stands before his easel, paintbrush in hand, swirling and stroking color onto the canvas in layers.

I haven't watched him as long as the others, but I don't think it's necessary. I don't expect him to be much of a challenge. Artists aren't intimidating. He's the sheriff's brother, but I've never seen him with a weapon. He doesn't run or go to the gym. At times, he barely eats or sleeps.

He paints.

I focus in on the window. He is utterly absorbed by his work. I bet I could walk right up to him without him noticing. For a few minutes, I watch him work, not for the first time. I've been closer. Close enough to see the details in his work. The process by which the painting takes shape is fascinating. He builds his image, layer by layer, nuance on top of nuance. It's an intricate procedure. He doesn't seem to plan. Does he see the finished product in his mind's eye before he begins, or does he paint by instinct?

Maybe I'll ask him before I kill him.

I switch off my headlights and turn into the driveway. But I'm not afraid he'll notice me. He doesn't even remember to lock his doors. I ease the Jeep around the side of his house opposite from the studio, so it isn't visible from the road. After shutting down the engine, I haul my backpack from the passenger seat. I unzip it and check my supplies. Gloves, stun gun, zip ties, plastic wrap.

Handgun.

Now that I've done this twice, I'm developing a system. I just have to get into the house. Once I zap him the first time, it'll be game over.

Incapacitate, restrain, suffocate.

It's an alarmingly easy and neat kill. No bloody mess. Farah's head wound and my bloody nose were enough to make me appreciate a clean kill. No mess, no fuss, over in a couple of minutes. I slip out of the vehicle. The freezing night air feels like I'm inhaling glass shards. My face aches. Though I'm wearing gloves, my hands quickly stiffen. The cold seeps from the ground through the soles of my shoes.

Pinpricks tingle in my toes as I bounce. I flex my fingers and shake my wrists to keep my blood circulating.

I feel like the sheriff and I have developed a relationship over the past few days. I kill someone, and she tries to catch me. But she isn't even close to solving this case.

I lean back into the car. "She thinks you killed Spencer and Julius."

Farah snivels and sniffs.

"She's going to think you killed the Flake, then yourself," I add. "I have it all planned out. Sadly, I won't be able to suffocate you, though. People have used plastic bags to commit suicide, but I feel that would be difficult for me to pull off believably." I touch the outside of my jacket pocket, where the gun is a solid, reassuring weight. "No. Your death will be a quick and painless bullet to the head. It's almost a shame, really. The men you fuck die slow, agonizing deaths because of you, yet you get the easy end. This night is just filled with irony."

I hope Farah's current head wound doesn't add confusion. I'll have to make sure she shoots herself in the same temple to cover the gash and bruising. Thankfully, the gash is on the correct side.

My luck holds.

"You two wait here." I snicker at my joke. "I won't be long. Once he's restrained, I'll bring you in. You're going to have a front-row seat to his death."

She moans low in her throat, a desperate and almost feral sound of hopelessness. She's moved beyond terror and accepted her fate. I can see the resignation in her eyes.

I'm not worried about Farah getting loose. I have her trussed tightly. She can't move more than an inch. I tug on my gloves and hat and head around the corner of the barn. The wind howls as it sweeps across the open ground. The clear landscape ensures I'll see anyone coming long before they get here. I creep to the front door, my breath fogging into the night. The knob doesn't turn. He remembered to lock his door.

Disappointed—annoyed—I creep back to the shadows. Of course, I've made a contingency plan. The interior of the barn is one open room, with only a partial wall to separate the studio from the living quarters. There is just one window where I can enter and not be seen. I return to the Jeep for my stepladder. It's only two steps, but that's all I need. I unfold it under the window and climb up. I stop next to the bathroom window and take off my backpack. When I took my unsupervised tour of the barn the other day, I unlocked this window. No one checks the locks on their windows unless they open them. And Adam surely didn't open his windows this week. The temperature has barely reached freezing.

Holding my breath, I push up on the frame. The window slides up easily. When I unlocked it, I also applied a bit of WD-40 to ensure a noiseless entry. I push the backpack through, then slip my upper body into the opening. My jacket and shirt ride up, letting the bitter cold slide around my waist. This is the tricky part. I wait for the wind to kick up in a good, loud howl before I drop the backpack and wiggle through. My hands crawl down the wall onto the floor. I slide the rest of the way like a baby giraffe slipping out of the birth canal.

Not wasting time, I ease to my feet and gently shut the window. Then I stand stock-still for a few breaths, listening and hoping Adam doesn't have to pee before I'm ready. But nothing moves. It's almost as if the barn is empty.

I unzip my backpack, grab a handful of zip ties, and shove them into my left jacket pocket. The pistol occupies the right one.

I grip the stun gun in my hand. I flex my stiff fingers a few times to warm them. That's all I need for the first step: immobilization. The rest of my supplies can stay here.

I crack the door an inch. The living quarters are dark. He's probably been working in the studio since before sunset and didn't bother to turn on lights elsewhere. Outside, the wind assails the walls and rattles the windows. Inside, near silence crushes the air. A brush sweeps over canvas. Fabric rustles. The door swings open at the touch of my fingertip, and I step through the opening.

Dirty laundry litters the floor, as if the hamper exploded. The bedding cascades onto the floor. Disgusted, I make my way across the main room. The studio light is stadium bright. I approach the half wall, pausing in the shadows for a second. Adam stands before his easel, brush in hand, studying his work. Brushes, tools, his palette, and tubes of paint are strewn on a table next to him. For a few seconds, the painting in progress rivets me. Emotions shift on the canvas, the colors and layers at once simple and complex. Texture builds nuance. The reds and blacks elicit anger, at odds with the calming blues and greens, as if peace reigns over conflict.

Love over hate.

The painting stokes my rage higher.

Adam has it backward. He sees hope where there is none. Tonight, I'll show him how wrong he is. I'll show the optimist that darkness always wins.

My fingers curl tighter around the stun gun. I creep forward, easing each foot down on the floor, wary of squeaky boards. I am just a few feet away when Adam freezes. His head cocks. Did he hear my breathing, or did his survival instinct sense my presence?

My muscles tense. He turns. I lunge. And for the second time that night, I'm surprised by my quarry's speedy response. He's quicker than I expected. With Farah, I realized my error. She's one of the fittest, strongest people I know. Hauling yourself up vertical walls will do that. But this artist . . . He doesn't do anything. He should be a slug.

His eyes register confusion, but he doesn't dawdle on it. He draws a foot back and raises his hands in front of his body, palms facing me, in a classic defensive posture. I thrust the stun gun at him again. I don't need a body strike for the first zap. A hand will do just fine to slow him down for a second, better-placed jolt.

He jumps backward and bats my hand away. Size-wise, we are well matched, about the same height and weight. I stay fit, while he paints all day. Overpowering him shouldn't be that hard. It's hard to swallow, but the artist seems to have some natural skill.

Continuing the physical conflict tempts me. I like a challenge, and I'd like to claim a true combat victory. But I don't have the time.

Maintaining eye contact, Adam stoops and picks up a hammer.

Well, that settles it. I'm not interested in a fair fight *that* fair.

I step backward, draw the pistol from my pocket, and aim it at his chest. "Drop the hammer. I don't want to shoot you, but I will."

He hesitates, clearly weighing his odds. We both know that once I disarm him, it's game over.

"I won't miss," I say.

His gaze drops to the gun as he considers his surrender. Will I have to shoot him? I raise the gun higher and extend my arm. Barely six feet separates us. I'm no crack marksman, but I'm a decent shot. I'll hit him.

As if he comes to the same conclusion, he bends his knees and carefully sets the hammer on the floor.

"Turn around and put your hands on your head."

He nods, but before he turns, I catch a gleam of defiance in his eyes. "What do you want?" he asks, the first words he's spoken during our confrontation.

I consider the plastic ties in my pocket. The sleeves of his worn T-shirt ride up his arms as he laces his fingers behind his head, revealing larger biceps than a simple painter should have. It would take two hands to bind his wrists. I'd have to put the gun down. He intends to try and break free when I'm within range, which is why he's placed the hammer so carefully at his feet, to keep it within easy reach.

Can't have that.

With the pistol aimed at his back, I use my left hand to retrieve the stun gun from my pocket. I shove it at him, pressing the button and delivering a hefty jolt of current to his back. He goes stiff, and his body quakes. Angry at his defiance, I hold it longer than usual, and he goes down hard. His body strikes the table, and his brushes and other painting paraphernalia go flying.

Only when he's on the ground twitching, his nervous system short-circuiting, his muscles unresponsive, do I put away the pistol. I make sure the zip ties are nice and snug on his wrists and ankles. I'm not taking any chances with him.

He's done.

While I wait for him to regain a little control, I carry a kitchen chair into the studio. Then I force him to sit up. With two hands under his arms, I drag him onto the chair. He's heavy and complete deadweight. I'm sweating by the time he's seated. I cut the ties on his ankles and bind them to the chair legs. Then I do the same to his wrists, fastening each to a chair arm. For good measure, I use another tie to fasten one of the belt loops on the back of his jeans to a slat on the back of the chair. I bring another chair into the room and position it so that it faces him about ten feet away.

They can watch each other suffer. I stand back and survey my work. The scene feels Shakespearean. Two lovers doomed by their passion, locked in a tragic fate, a tale of deceit and betrayal. Goose bumps lift on my sweaty arms.

When I'm satisfied, I give Adam another quick jolt to make sure he won't recover while I'm getting ready. He slumps. The plastic ties are the only things keeping him upright. He's limp when I leave him. Time to set the rest of the stage for tonight's performance. A thrill rides my spine. This kill will be different. I'll have an audience, and I have a greater purpose. The sheriff's brother is the ultimate target. His death will destroy her. And after Adam and Farah are both dead, I'll get to watch the sheriff follow my carefully constructed trail of evidence to arrive at the wrong conclusion.

It couldn't get any better.

With Adam trussed like a Thanksgiving turkey, I head outside and open the cargo door of the Jeep. First, I pile the hand warmers on the mesh top of the snake's tank, then I carry it into the house. The animal is still angry—and active—so the hand warmers must have worked. I set the aquarium down in the studio. Adam can't move yet, but his eyes go wide as the snake goes through its usual hiss-and-rattle routine. I left the front door open, and the room is chilly.

I return to the Jeep. A frigid gust of wind rips across the open meadow. Tall weeds and grass bend to its strength. Farah isn't wearing a coat, and she's shivering. I show her the gun. "Follow my instructions or you die right now."

She doesn't respond, but her eyes shine with tears. I cut the binds to her ankles. She immediately stretches her legs. No doubt she's cramped up after being in the same awkward position for at least an hour. I help her out of the cargo bay. I hope the bitch can walk. I don't feel like carrying her. She's thin, but muscular and surprisingly heavy. Getting her into the Jeep at my house was a task.

"Sit up," I command.

She tries, but she's weak, either from muscle stiffness or the head wound. I grab her ankles, haul her toward me, and swing her legs over the side. I pocket the fabric I used to cushion her binds. Taking her by the arm, I heave her out of the vehicle. She sways. I give her a minute. Thankfully, there isn't a soul anywhere nearby. I'm excited to get started, but there's no immediate rush.

The anticipation will build my enjoyment.

Her eyes scan the meadow. She's thinking about running.

"Don't do it." I open my jacket and point to the pistol, then lift the stun gun from my pocket.

Clearly remembering her experience, she recoils and shakes her head.

"That's right." I half drag her toward the door. "If I can't stun you, I'll shoot you. You can't outrun a bullet. You wouldn't get twenty feet away."

Even if she managed to escape, where would she go? She has a head wound and isn't wearing a coat.

I tug her inside and close the door behind us. We move through the living area and into the studio. Her head snaps up as she sees Adam tied to the chair. She trips. My jerk to her arm to keep her upright isn't gentle.

"Sit," I command.

She obeys, crying and whimpering behind the gag. I tie her to the chair as securely as I did Adam but taking care to pad the binds so they won't leave marks.

"What the hell?" Adam mumbles. He shakes his head, as if clearing it.

I ignore him, speaking to Farah. "You're going to watch your lover die."

"We're not lovers," Adam croaks, his voice faint.

I point the gun at him. "Shut up! Shut up! Shut up!"

Self-control begins to fade, disappearing like taillights in the darkness. I want to pull the trigger so badly, but I resist. A few deep breaths restore my composure. They're both restrained. I shove the gun into my waistband.

I pick up the artist's worktable and use it to lay out my duct tape and plastic wrap. The pistol is digging into my waist. I set it on the table within easy reach. Then I pick up the duct tape and slap a piece over the artist's mouth. Satisfaction blooms.

The stage is set.

I'm free to carry out my grand finale.

CHAPTER THIRTY-SIX

Clammy sweat slicked Bree's palms as Matt slowed the SUV near her brother's driveway. She wiped her hands on her thighs. Fear surged like ice water through her veins. Adam's house sat on the other side of a football field of empty meadow. She studied the structure, then fished her binoculars out of the glove box. "The light is on in his studio."

"There are two vehicles parked out front. Can you ID them?"

She lifted the binoculars and adjusted the focus. "Adam's Bronco and a slick-looking compact SUV, which is probably the Porsche Cayenne he just bought."

"No other vehicle?"

"Not in sight." She shifted her attention to the studio window. "I can see Adam's painting, but I don't see Adam." She lowered the binoculars.

Matt tapped his fingers on the steering wheel. "Do we drive up to the house or leave the vehicle here?"

"Rhys had a head start," Bree said. "He could be inside right now." *Murdering my brother.*

A slideshow of Spencer's and Julius's bodies ran through Bree's head. Sickness rose in the back of her throat. "If Rhys is in there, he can see us if we park here. There's nothing to block his view."

Matt shifted into drive, clicked off the headlights, and turned onto the narrow dirt lane that led to Adam's converted barn. Halfway up the driveway, he eased the vehicle to a stop. They were out of direct view of the studio window but not close enough that Rhys would hear their approach.

She turned off the interior dome light. She glanced at Matt. "Ready?"

He adjusted his earpiece. "Let's go."

She reported their location and status to dispatch. Backup was still a full ten minutes away. They couldn't wait. A person could suffocate in six.

Matt tugged on a black knit cap and leather gloves. Bree did the same, then slid out into the darkness. They eased their doors closed. The wind ripped across the meadow, cold enough to make her eyes water and her teeth ache. Matt carried the AR-15 across his chest. Bree held her Glock as they ran across fifty yards of frozen earth. They slowed at the head of the driveway. Bree veered left. She jogged to the corner of the house, stopped, peered into the side yard, and saw Rhys's Jeep. Fear weighted her heart. They'd been right. He was inside.

With Adam.

She drew her head back and whispered in her earpiece, "There's Rhys's Jeep. Looks empty."

The wind muffled Matt's response, but it sounded like, "Fuck."

Was her brother still alive? Bree fell back on one of her greatest strengths. She compartmentalized. She locked her terror for her brother into the back of her mind and focused on saving him.

Weapons raised, she and Matt rounded the corner and circled the Jeep. The barn blocked the wind. Bree shined her flashlight inside.

Empty. Matt pulled a folding knife from his pants pocket. He opened the blade and slashed all four of the Jeep's tires.

Then they continued around the next corner to the back of the barn. The wind hit her full in the face, but she barely felt the cold. Windows were at head height. Crouching, they approached each one and peered over the sill. The first two looked into the living quarters, which were dark. Adam's studio had big windows on the back and side of the building.

Bree approached the studio windows, all her senses tuned. She crouched beneath the sill, her back to the wood siding, shoulder to shoulder with Matt. They exchanged a glance. Light glowed through the window, and she could see Matt's face clearly. His eyes were as grim as she felt. They nodded, afraid to even whisper for fear of alerting Rhys.

Sticking their heads into a potential line of fire wasn't the brightest move. If he shot them, there would be no one to rescue Adam. Bree pulled out her cell phone. Shielding the screen to contain the light, she opened the camera. Switching the perspective to selfie mode, she raised it until the top inch—the camera lens—was just above the sill. She and Matt could both see into the room. She rotated the phone until three people came into view.

Bile rose into her throat at the sight. Adam and Farah faced each other, tied to chairs. Blood dripped from a nasty gash on Farah's head into her eyes. She saw no visible wounds on her brother. He looked disoriented.

But he was alive.

Rhys stood on the other side of Adam, a box of plastic wrap in his hands. He was going to kill Adam the same way he'd murdered Spencer and Julius.

Like hell.

Anger surged, hot and heady, through her. She wanted to put a bullet or ten in him right then and there, but she wouldn't have a clean shot. Adam was between the window and Rhys. She turned the phone to scan the rest of the room. A pistol lay on Adam's worktable.

She lowered the phone and turned to Matt. They both knew Adam didn't have much time.

Bree had a key, but Rhys would surely hear her enter through the front door. They could break the window and charge in. Could they get inside before Rhys grabbed his gun? Not likely. Better to sneak up on him. Bree could go in the front door, while Matt covered her from here. He could enter through the window if necessary. His long gun was a more accurate weapon in case they needed to risk a shot at Rhys.

She jerked her head and they retreated to the opposite corner of the barn, where she laid out her plan in a low voice. He didn't like her idea because he always wanted to be the first one through the door, but he didn't argue. They needed a clean shot at Rhys without Adam being in the middle.

She held up two fingers. "Give me two minutes."

"I won't let him kill Adam," Matt whispered back.

The cold stabbed her lungs as she raced back to the front of the house. On the way, she used her radio and earpiece to inform dispatch—and the deputies on the way—that they were going in. Then she dug into her pocket for Adam's key. Her fingers were numb with cold, and she fumbled, almost dropping it. She removed her gloves and tried again. Moving slowly, she inserted the key and turned it. The click of the dead bolt sounded as loud as a gunshot. She could only hope the wind covered the noise.

Her heart jackhammered. Her pulse began to echo in her ears. To prevent adrenaline-induced tunnel vision, she inhaled deeply and held her breath for a minute, forcing her heart rate to slow. She returned her keys to her pocket and drew her gun. Then she turned the knob, eased the door open, and stepped into the darkness.

Chapter Thirty-Seven

Matt checked his watch and counted down the final seconds. He used his phone to watch Rhys. On the screen, he could see Rhys digging at the roll of plastic wrap with his thumb. He lifted the edge, then unwound about a foot of wrap and approached Adam.

He pictured Bree going in the front door of the barn. Would Rhys hear her?

Adam pulled his head back and strained against his binds. The chair rocked as he thrashed. Before Matt could react, Rhys pulled out a stun gun and gave Adam a jolt. Adam seized up as the current rushed through his body, disabling him. A sick sensation filled Matt. Then anger flooded in.

Fuck this.

He shoved his phone into his pocket, stood, and turned, his rifle pressed into his shoulder. Rhys's back was facing him, but Matt still didn't have a clear shot at him.

As Rhys extended the sheet of plastic, Matt turned the rifle and used the butt to smash the window. Glass shattered. Broken pieces rained into Adam's studio.

Farah screamed, the high-pitched wail muffled by the gag.

Still behind Adam, Rhys whirled, dropping the plastic wrap and snatching his pistol from the table.

Without a clear shot, Matt couldn't take out Rhys through the window. There was no way around it. He had to go in—and he had to do it fast, or he'd be a target.

He swept the rifle stock across the bottom of the window frame, clearing the largest shards. He grabbed the sill with gloved hands, pulling himself over. His chest and belly slid across the window, protected from the sharp points of glass by his vest. He ignored a quick slash of pain across his thigh. A gunshot ripped through the studio. A bullet struck the windowsill a few inches from Matt's head. Then he was through the opening and dropping to the floor. He landed on a carpet of glass shards and other objects that littered the floor. A tube of paint sat next to his face. A stick under his elbow felt like a paintbrush. Another shot rang out. The bullet struck the wall, sending bits of wallboard flying. He rolled, coming to a stop on his belly, with the rifle aimed at Rhys. He switched on the flashlight mounted on the long gun.

Rhys was behind Adam, stooping to better use him as a shield. Rhys shifted his aim from Matt to press the muzzle against Adam's temple. "I'll shoot him."

"You won't get away." Matt held the rifle steady, scanning Rhys from his feet to his head, looking for any target, but Rhys was smart enough to keep his entire body behind Adam's.

"*You* are not in control!" Rhys shouted. "*I* am in charge. *I* say what happens."

A figure moved behind Rhys. Bree appeared, her gun aimed at Rhys. Farah was in the way. Bree stepped around the restrained woman, putting herself in position for a shot. Something snapped under her boot. Rhys spun and ducked just as Bree fired. Her shot hit the wall where his head had been a fraction of a second before. He dived for the floor.

Matt's heart jackhammered as he squeezed off a shot. Bree fired again as well. Rhys grunted. She must have hit him.

"Fuck you!" Rhys yelled as he fired at Matt, then turned and shot in Bree's direction. He was moving, not aiming, and both shots went wide. Bullets pinged off the walls.

Matt lined up his rifle again. Rhys was working hard to keep either Adam or Farah in front of him, but Bree was moving, trying to get clear. Rhys kept rolling. He was headed for the broken window, toward the fastest escape. He lurched to his feet. Then his shoes slipped on broken glass and debris. His arms pinwheeled as he careened across the floor—right into the snake tank.

The tank toppled. The snake's heavy body thudded on the glass. The lid popped off. Both man and snake came flying at Matt. He scuttled backward like a panicked crab to get out of the way. He lost sight of the snake. Matt heard Bree fire again. The shot echoed in the small space. Rhys scrambled away. He cursed. Had Bree hit him with a second bullet?

Where was the snake? Matt felt the sting in his calf.

Fuck.

Snakebite.

CHAPTER THIRTY-EIGHT

Bree extended her gun, sweeping her aim across the debris on the floor. Where the fuck was the snake? Something moved through a shiny patch of glass. A long green-brown body slithered faster than anything without legs should be able to move. Bree pulled the trigger three times in rapid succession. The snake's body jerked as the bullets hit it. She didn't shift her aim until she was sure it was dead.

Lungs heaving, Bree pivoted back to the men just in time to see Rhys go out the broken window.

"Did you kill it?" Matt was dragging himself toward Adam.

"Oh, yes," Bree said.

He nodded. His pant leg was rolled up to his knee. A single puncture wound marred his calf.

"It bit you?" A wave of cold terror swept through Bree. She used her radio to call for an ambulance. "Officer down. Rattlesnake bite." She released the button on the mic. "Any other injuries?"

"No." But he was pale and shivering. Blood stained the thigh of his khaki pants. He pulled out his knife and freed Adam's hands. Adam ripped off the duct tape and took the knife from Matt.

She searched her memory for the information the animal control officer had given her back in Julius's house. "Lie still so the venom doesn't spread. Bites aren't usually fatal if you get prompt medical care. You'll be OK." But the area around the bite was already beginning to redden and swell.

Was she trying to convince him or herself?

"Sheriff?" dispatch said on the radio. "Where's the rattlesnake?"

"Dead." Bree glanced back at it. "In pieces, actually."

"Please text a photo of the snake's head and body to Dr. Young at the ER." The dispatcher gave her a number.

"I'll do it." Matt pulled out his phone.

Bree pointed at him. "You don't move." She ran to the snake, took a photo, and sent it to the ER doc.

Cold air poured through the broken window. Farah moaned, likely in shock.

"Can you see to Farah?" she called to Adam.

"I'm on it." Adam freed his legs, then reached behind him and severed a plastic tie holding his jeans to the chair. Adam went to Farah. He was shaky but moving with determination as he freed her. She fell sideways to the floor, sobbing.

Bree's phone went off. The ER doc. She answered, and he didn't bother with niceties. "That's a Mojave rattler. Very toxic venom. Get him here ASAP. Don't wait for the ambulance. We'll have the antivenin ready when he gets here."

"We'll be there in twenty." Bree went to Matt. The redness and swelling were spreading up his leg. She swallowed the panic rising in her throat. "We're going to the ER."

Sirens approached.

She levered her shoulder under his. "Adam. Little help."

Adam took Matt's other side. Together they heaved him to his feet.

"I can walk," Matt protested, but he was limping as they helped him out the front door.

"You must move as little as possible. Every beat of your heart pumps that venom through your body. This isn't something you can power through." The ER doctor's tone rang in Bree's ears. *Very toxic venom.* "Please," she begged, desperate. She could not lose him. "Be still."

Two patrol cruisers sped up the driveway. Juarez and Todd leaped out of their vehicles.

Bree wanted to stay with Matt, but her duty was to prevent more people from dying and to protect her family from potential retaliation. There was only one way to do that: find Rhys Blake.

"I will. I'll be fine." But Matt was shaking. Actually shaking. Seeing his huge, muscular body visibly weakened shocked her. She felt the stirrings of panic behind her breastbone. Her lungs and throat constricted.

She swallowed a lump of cold terror the size of a baseball. Then she made one of the hardest decisions of her life. She had to do her job and trust the ER staff to do theirs. She put one hand on Matt's chest, rose onto her toes, and kissed him on the mouth. "I have to go. Please cooperate. I need you to be OK. I love you."

Matt kissed her back. "I love you back. I know you want to catch him, but don't risk your own life. Promise you won't take any unnecessary risks. I need you to be OK too."

"Deal." She dropped her hand and pointed to Juarez. "Get him to the ER. Fast."

"Yes, ma'am." Juarez opened the rear door of the vehicle. Once Matt was inside, Juarez jumped behind the wheel and sped off, lights and sirens wailing.

Bree turned to Adam.

Her brother waved her away. "I'll wait for the ambulance with Farah. Go get that bastard. This is what you do."

Bree turned to Todd. "You're with me."

"Yes, ma'am." Todd opened the trunk of his cruiser and retrieved his own rifle. He grabbed a hat and gloves. "Let's go."

Forcing her worry for Matt into the background, she led Todd around to the studio window. While he examined the weedy grass with his flashlight, Bree called dispatch and requested assistance from other agencies. Then she joined Todd with the search of the ground. A spot of blood shone in the light. She moved the beam and found another, then another. She followed the bloodspots around the barn to the Jeep.

In front of the vehicle, Bree found four droplets in one place. She imagined Rhys standing still, absorbing the fact that his Jeep was useless and deciding which way to run.

"Do you know how badly he's wounded?" Todd asked.

"I think I shot him, but I don't know where he took the bullet. He's definitely bleeding, but nothing's gushing." Bree could have winged him, or he could be bleeding internally. "He was wearing a hat, coat, and boots. He won't immediately succumb to hypothermia."

Light pointed toward the ground, Todd stopped. "Here's a few footprints. Well spaced and even. He's moving OK."

Bree moved along a parallel track to the prints. "Adrenaline could keep him going for a while."

The wind kicked up again. Tall weeds in the meadow bowed as it swept across the open land. Todd began scanning the ground with his light. Bree did the same.

"I found more drops of blood. He's definitely headed this way." Todd pointed across the meadow, away from the main road. All she could see in that direction was fields and darkness. They had no choice but to use their flashlights, even though the lights made them targets. Bree updated dispatch. "Pursuing on foot in an easterly direction. Fugitive is wounded and armed." She gave a basic description of Rhys's clothing and hoped state police or other local police departments could cut off his escape.

They moved at a brisk pace, stopping every few minutes to examine the ground. Both Bree and Todd found the occasional footprint or spot of blood. The cold air stung her cheeks, but her muscles stayed warm as they jogged across the rutted, uneven field. Bree tripped over a lump of dead vegetation. Landing on her knee, she felt the zing of her kneecap as it struck a rock. They crossed a ditch with a thin stream of ice in the bottom.

She guessed they'd traveled about a mile and a half when Todd stopped and pointed to the ground. Five footprints led toward a patch of woods about fifty yards away.

"The footprints are uneven and closer together," Todd said. "He's struggling now."

"Running out of adrenaline." Bree spotted a small puddle of blood. "And he's bleeding more heavily."

Todd walked farther, crouched. "It looks like he stumbled, went down on one knee, bled some more." He straightened and nodded toward the trees in the distance. "He's headed for those trees."

Bree followed the projected trajectory with her gaze. "I don't know how many bullets he has left, but if I were him, that's where I'd hide and set up an ambush."

She and Todd fanned out about a dozen feet apart so they would be two separate targets and walked toward the woods.

CHAPTER THIRTY-NINE

The darkness closes over me as I stumble into a small patch of trees. My foot catches on a root, and I fall to my knees. I'm already in so much pain, I barely feel the impact of my knees on the ground. Winded and lightheaded, I crawl behind a fallen tree. Pressing my back to the rotting bark, I breathe. They won't be able to see me here.

I can't believe she fucking shot me. Twice.

Agony radiates through the whole left side of my body from two bullet wounds. I can't see them under my jacket, and I'm not taking it off to get a better look. Not in this cold. The one in my upper arm isn't bleeding much, but my arm is useless. My fingers won't work at all. My whole arm is on fire. But it's the wound in my side that worries me the most. It's bleeding enough to have soaked through my shirt, sweater, and jacket. I can feel blood running down my side. I need to find a place to bandage it before I bleed to death, but I'm in the middle of the fucking countryside. There's nowhere to wash and dress a wound. I search my pockets for something to bind it, but there's nothing.

My heart races, but the beats feel ineffective, as if I just don't have enough blood left to keep my body going. I can't believe I lost that much blood so quickly, though running didn't help. My lungs ache, starved for oxygen. In the darkness, the trees seem to blur. The air heaves in and out of my chest. It's so cold out; it feels like I'm inhaling needles.

The farther I run, the more heavily I bleed. But I have to keep moving. If I stop here, I'll die here.

I push to my feet. The darkness spins around me. Swaying, I reach out for a tree trunk to steady myself and wait for the dizziness to pass. A light shines in the near distance. For an instant, hope deadens some of my pain. I stagger toward the light. Pain radiates through my side and arm. Every step produces excruciating, blinding agony.

That fucking sheriff ruined everything. Fifteen minutes more. That's all I'd needed. I would have killed them both and successfully exited the scene. I'm going to kill that bitch sheriff if it's the last thing I do.

Nausea rises in my throat. I lean over and vomit into the dirt. I wipe my mouth with the sleeve of my good arm. I try to listen for the sound of footsteps, but I can barely hear over the sound of my own wheezing. But I know she'll follow me. She isn't the type to give up.

I emerge from the trees into another small field, bisected by a road. A two-story farmhouse faces me from the opposite side. The light shines from the front porch. I stumble across fifty feet of frozen ground. After crossing the road, I stagger up the driveway and onto the front porch. I use the butt of the pistol to break the small square of glass next to the dead bolt. Reaching through, I unlock the door and push it open. Inside, I fall to my knees in what I think is a foyer.

A scrape on the hardwood catches my attention. I lift my head. A young woman of about twenty-five stands in a doorway. She wears baggy sweats and those big sheepskin boots. A hostage would improve my situation immensely.

I lift the gun. "Don't move or I'll shoot."

CHAPTER FORTY

Bree led the way through the trees. Each shadow was a potential ambush location. She rounded a tree trunk and pointed her AR-15 into the darkness. Nothing. They crept through the trees without being accosted and paused at the edge of an open space. Just beyond, she saw a road and a house. A light shone from the front porch.

Todd crouched at her side.

"Think he went in there?" she asked softly.

"Yes," Todd whispered back.

"Do you know where we are?"

Todd squinted at the mailbox, then opened the map app on his phone. "The house number is 401. This should be Route 77."

Bree touched her mic and updated dispatch. Rhys was wounded and cold. His recent trail indicated he was less steady and still losing blood. He wouldn't be able to keep running for long. Bree scanned the property. A barn sat behind the farmhouse.

Dispatch spoke in her earpiece. "The homeowner at your location just called 911 to report a home invasion by a wounded man."

"Is the homeowner in the home?" Bree asked.

"Yes," dispatch said. "She locked herself in an upstairs bedroom with her baby."

Hostages.

Bree quelled a quick surge of panic. She and Todd were the only things standing in the way of Rhys harming a mother and baby.

"What's the ETA of the closest backup?" Bree asked.

"State police are eight minutes away."

Too long.

Todd adjusted the grip on his AR-15. "Let's get him."

If Rhys was inside, he'd be watching for pursuit. When he saw them approach, what would he do? Make a stand and shoot at them, or slip out the back door in another escape attempt? Set the house on fire as a diversion to occupy Bree and Todd while he escaped? Bree couldn't wait. Rhys was capable of anything. There were no lines he wouldn't cross, and she wouldn't sacrifice a woman and her baby.

"I'll go in the front. You circle around back in case he tries to escape." Bree waited until her chief deputy rounded the corner of the house. Then she lifted her AR-15 and approached the front walk, trying to stay behind the few shrubs on the exterior landscaping.

Foliage was not adequate cover. Bullets traveled through walls. A few leaves wouldn't be much of an issue. Bree popped her head over the shrub and saw a shadow through the tiny panes of glass next to the front door.

Was that Rhys?

Where were the mother and child?

CHAPTER FORTY-ONE

I'm weaker than I thought. The handgun feels like it weighs twenty pounds. Before I can point the gun at the young woman, she turns and flees. I hear her feet thunder up a flight of steps. A door slams.

She's no doubt locked herself in a room upstairs. She should have run out the back door. Dumb bitch.

If I had acted faster, I could have made her stay with me. But quick movement doesn't seem to be an option. I crawl on my hands and knees through the doorway into an old farm-style kitchen. The stairs lead up from the back of the kitchen. I contemplate them but decide I don't have the strength to follow her.

I sit on the floor, my back against the butcher-block island. The drawer next to me contains dish towels. I grab one and unzip my jacket. A long furrow the width of my finger extends just below my rib cage. The bullet clearly didn't hit any vital organs, but it made a mess as it plowed through the fleshy part of my side. I should survive if I can stop the bleeding. I grab two folded dish towels and look for something to tie them around my waist. I pull myself to my feet. Leaning on the countertop, I search drawers. Ironically, the only thing I find that will work is plastic wrap. Pressing the folded towels against the wound, I bind it tightly with the wrap. That should help. At least it's warm inside the house. But how long can I stay? The woman probably has a cell phone. She'll call the police. They'll know where I am.

The idea of running out into the cold again exhausts me. My head swims from pain and blood loss. But I need to keep moving, keep running. They won't be far behind me.

The warmth and bandage revive me. I find a glass in a cabinet and fill it at the tap. My throat and mouth are parched, and the liquid feels luxurious as I swallow. I find a bottle of pain reliever and take four tablets. As I regroup, my head clears a little. The woman must have a vehicle. I spot a key rack next to the back door and shuffle over. Two labeled key chains read SHED and TRUCK.

Truck? I look out the back window. About seventy-five feet away, a pickup sits next to a small barn. Hot tears fill my eyes. I can get away.

A heavy barn coat hangs on a peg by the door. I take off my wet jacket and slide into the dry one. The heavy canvas will block the wind. After pocketing the bottle of pain reliever, I turn off the kitchen lights. I spot a stainless-steel bottle in a drying rack. I fill it at the tap to take with me. Food. I need food. I root through the pantry and find a box of protein bars. I shove a handful into another pocket. I tuck my gun into my waistband and scan the fields behind the house.

A figure creeps toward me. The sheriff? I hope so. I want to shoot her more than almost anything. I pull out the pistol and aim through the broken glass pane. But the figure blurs. I squeeze my eyelids shut and open them again. The figure is closer, only about thirty feet away now. I can't see the face, but the figure moves like a man. It's not her. Disappointment rises, bitter in my mouth. The sheriff probably brought the big investigator. They likely split up, one to approach the front of the house, the other to cover the back and cut off my escape.

Divide and conquer and all that shit.

Where is the sheriff? She's the one I want.

I hear the scuff of a shoe on the front porch and turn toward it. Through the kitchen doorway, I see a shadow through the narrow panes of glass next to the door. She looks bulky because of her body armor, but I know it's the sheriff by her size.

I draw aim on her head. The vest won't stop me from putting a bullet through her skull. My hand shakes. I'm going to miss at that distance. I move closer and use the back of a chair to steady my arm. Then I sight on the sheriff and pull the trigger.

CHAPTER FORTY-TWO

A shot rang out, the bullet shattering the glass next to the door. Bree dived sideways. After landing in the grass, she rolled to her stomach and belly-crawled up the front lawn until she was behind a railroad tie the homeowner had used in the landscape architecture.

"Give it up, Rhys!" she shouted. "There are guns behind you too. You can't get away."

"Fuck you!" Rhys shouted back. "I'll kill the woman here. You know I will."

She didn't doubt it. Probably the only thing Bree could say for certain about him was that he was willing to do the most horrendous things imaginable. He only cared about himself.

"You'll still die," Bree yelled.

"You care about this woman. You can't deny it," Rhys called.

He wasn't close to the woman, Bree realized. He didn't even know about the baby. If he did, he would be using the child as leverage.

Bree inched closer. "Put down the gun, Rhys!"

No answer.

"Sheriff?" Todd's voice sounded in her ear. "I heard a shot."

"He missed." Despite the cold, sweat dripped down Bree's chest and back. She inched her way up the lawn but didn't see Rhys. She tapped the mic attached to her earpiece. "Todd, what do you see?"

He responded, "Nothing. Back of the house is dead still."

Where is Rhys?

Bree popped up her head but saw nothing. He'd been near the front door just a minute ago. She couldn't take the chance he would hurt the mother and baby. Crouching, she jumped back onto the porch. Staying low, she tiptoed silently up the wooden steps. She went to a front window, but the blinds were drawn. She couldn't see inside.

She checked with Todd again. "Anything?"

"No, ma'am."

Bree rose and peered through the side window next to the front door. "I don't see him. He might be headed your way. We're going in."

"Ready," Todd said.

"On three." She pressed her back to the doorframe and counted. Her heart set a dizzying pace as she said *three*, kicked open the door, and leveled her gun into the house. She heard Todd break in the back door and yell, "Sheriff's department!"

Bree crept down the hall but saw no one. She noticed a spot of blood on the floor. Then another. She followed them to the steps. A trail of dark smears led up the treads. Rhys had crawled up the stairs.

Todd appeared in the darkness. Bree pointed at the stairs. He nodded and fell in behind her. She started up, staying low, beneath where Rhys might expect her head to be. Three steps from the top, Bree stopped and peered over the edge of the landing.

"I'll kill her." Rhys stood behind a young woman holding a sleeping baby, a little boy in blue footed pajamas with trains printed on them. He pointed his handgun at the woman's back. Unsteady, he swayed. "Put down the gun."

"What do you want, Rhys?" Bree prayed he didn't fall over and accidentally discharge his weapon. Or shoot the woman and child on his way down out of pure spite.

The woman's eyes were wide as she rocked the baby in her arms.

Rhys wasn't restraining her. "I'm going to leave here in her truck, and she's coming with me."

"OK." But Bree didn't put down her weapon. "Just don't hurt her."

"Back up. Slowly." Rhys stumbled forward. He shoved the gun into the woman's back. "You, move."

The woman shuffled forward. Behind her, Rhys tripped. The young woman spun away. Bree hurled herself at Rhys's leg. He went down hard. The gun hit the floor and slid away.

Todd rushed past Bree, putting his body between Rhys and the young mother.

Bree kept her gun trained on Rhys, but he wasn't moving. She kicked away his pistol. Then she pushed him onto his side with her boot, cuffed his hands behind his back, and patted down his pockets. She found keys, a wallet, and extra ammunition.

Todd's shadow appeared beside her. "Is he alive?"

Still catching her breath, Bree pressed two fingers to Rhys's neck but felt no pulse. "No." She removed the handcuffs, rolled him onto his back, and began CPR. "Call an ambulance."

Todd didn't look concerned with Rhys's survival. Honestly, Bree couldn't find enough empathy to care if he lived or died either. He'd tortured and killed two men in horrific ways with zero remorse. He'd tried to do the same to her brother. The image of Adam tied to that chair would haunt her forever. Did Rhys deserve to live?

She had a job to do, and it didn't include passing judgment. There was a whole legal system to determine his fate. Right now, her responsibility was to put aside her personal feelings and provide first aid to the man in her custody.

"See how badly he's injured." She pressed her palms into his chest.

Todd lifted the hem of Rhys's shirt to reveal the makeshift plas-tic-wrapped bandage. He peeled up the edge and lifted the dish towel. "Here's where most of the blood is coming from."

Bree peered at the long furrow. "The wound itself doesn't look too bad. Bled a lot, but I don't see how it could have hit a critical organ."

Todd replaced the bandage, keeping the wrap tight enough to put pressure on the wound.

"There's blood on his sleeve too." Todd used his folding knife to cut off the sleeve of the canvas coat Rhys wore. "Shit."

Bree counted compressions. "What?"

"Look." Todd pointed to Rhys's arm. Instead of a bullet hole, graze, or laceration, he'd found two deep punctures, swollen skin, and a red-dish-brown discoloration that streaked across his shoulder toward his heart. "That's not a bullet wound. That's a snakebite."

Rhys's face, already the color of skim milk, turned to the palest shade of gray.

Bree replayed the chaos in Adam's place. "Rhys must have been bitten when he fell into the tank."

Todd touched Rhys's neck. "Still no pulse."

"I know." But Bree continued with CPR.

Todd watched for a minute, then sighed. "Let me have a turn. You can't keep this up."

Administering CPR to a serial killer was exhausting, physically and emotionally. Bree's arms ached after just a few minutes. She moved aside, and Todd picked up where she left off.

A moment later, Bree pressed her fingertips to Rhys's neck and felt a very faint, irregular pulse. His chest rose and fell with a painful rattle.

"He's back," she said.

Todd sat back and wiped his brow with a sleeve.

The baby fussed. The woman bounced and jiggled him, then kissed him on the temple. Watching them, Bree allowed a small surge of relief to wash over her. Mother and child were fine. Propping the baby on one hip, the woman fetched an afghan from the next room. She handed it to Bree. "He'll be in shock."

They exchanged a look, two people wanting to do the right thing but not knowing exactly what that was. The woman stepped back, distancing herself from Rhys.

The state police and ambulance arrived a few minutes later. Attendants wheeled in a gurney and loaded Rhys onto it. The EMT didn't bother with an assessment. "We need to get him to the ER ASAP."

Bree snapped handcuffs to one of Rhys's wrists and attached the other end to the rail. "I need to go with him." Rhys didn't look capable of harming anyone, but Bree had made the decision to try and save him. He was her responsibility. She would take no risks. She turned to Todd. "Coordinate with the troopers."

"Yes, ma'am." He nodded.

Since Bree was involved in tonight's shooting, the state police would take charge of the investigation, which was just fine with her.

They followed the gurney outside. The attendants slid it into the back of the ambulance.

"This guy is the one who killed those two guys?" one of the state troopers asked.

"We believe so," Bree answered. She climbed into the back of the ambulance, trying to stay out of the EMT's way as he set up an IV. "Did you come from the hospital?"

"Yes." He hung a bag of fluids.

Bree unzipped her jacket. Dried sweat under her body armor had left her clammy and gross. Matt hadn't responded to her text. "Did you see Matt Flynn in the ER?"

"No, sorry." He shook his head.

Bree texted Matt: R u OK? When he didn't respond, worry for him returned. She tried Juarez, but he didn't respond either. She sat back, with nothing to do but wait.

Outside the ambulance, a trooper said, "He looks dead already."

"He ain't going to make it," the other agreed. "I don't know why she tried so hard to save a killer."

She heard Todd speak as the driver closed the rear doors. "It has nothing to do with who he is, and everything to do with who *she* is."

CHAPTER
FORTY-THREE

Deputy Juarez walked around the curtain in Matt's ER bay. "Sheriff Taggert is OK, and so is her brother."

If Matt hadn't been lying down, relief would have made him light-headed. Of course, he was already dizzy from the snake venom and cocktail of drugs he'd been given. But still . . .

Bree's alive.

The deputy waved. "I thought you'd want to know, considering you and the sheriff . . ." He trailed off, as if unsure whether he'd overstepped.

Matt didn't make him finish his sentence. "Thanks."

Juarez cleared his throat. "Not that any of us care. We support the sheriff a hundred percent. She's the real deal."

"She is," Matt agreed. "And I'm glad you have her back."

"We do. Totally." Juarez nodded hard. "You OK?"

"I've never been so happy to feel like roadkill." Matt's head swam. He was still amazed how much that damned snakebite had hurt.

Juarez agreed with one word: "Dude." He added, "They're bringing in the suspect by ambulance."

"Gunshot?" Matt asked.

"That, and a snakebite."

"Really?" Matt leaned back on the gurney. An IV line dangled from one arm. Next to the IV pole full of hanging bags—he'd lost track of the meds they were giving him—a heart monitor blipped along in a reassuring rhythm.

Juarez shrugged. "That's what I heard."

By the time Juarez had gotten him to the hospital—twenty minutes after he'd been bitten—Matt's vision had been blurry and his speech slurred. With terrible fascination, he'd been able to watch the red line of venom spread up his leg. A ladder of permanent marker lines and their corresponding times climbed his leg where the nurses had kept track of the venom's progression, which had slowed thanks to multiple doses of antivenin.

A commotion sounded in the hallway, with doors swishing, monitors beeping, footsteps pounding, people yelling. Someone was coding.

"Maybe that's him. I'll go find out what's what." Juarez left the room.

Twenty minutes later, a knock sounded on the doorway. The curtain shifted, and Bree limped through the opening. Her hair was tumbling out of its pins. Blood and a little dirt streaked her face. She'd never looked better. She approached the bed.

Matt grabbed for her hand, just wanting—needing—the physical connection. "Your blood or his?"

"Pretty sure it's all his." Bree leaned over and planted a soft kiss on his mouth.

He wanted to kiss her a hundred more times. He wanted a week with her and no distractions. He made do with squeezing her fingers. "Good. What about Adam? Farah?"

"Adam is OK. Farah is being evaluated for a concussion."

"Todd?"

"He's fine. Still at the final scene," Bree said. "I just spoke with him and told him to go home as soon as he can. He did good."

"Did Rhys make it?"

"Don't know." Bree looked troubled. "His chances didn't look good, but I did everything I could to save him."

"I know you did. I might not have tried so hard."

Her head tilted. "Yes, you would have. This job often requires us to do things we don't want to do."

"Can't argue with that."

The doctor stopped in the doorway. "Sheriff. There you are." He stepped into the room, looking grim. His surgical mask hung around his neck. "Your prisoner didn't make it."

Bree nodded.

"There wasn't much we could do," the doctor continued. "The snake nailed the brachial artery with both fangs. Between the location of the bite and his sustained physical exertion, the venom fast-tracked through his body. I suspect the snake bit him first and unloaded most of its venom." He turned to Matt. "You were lucky. Your bite was limited to the muscle, where it took longer for the venom to spread. You minimized movement, only one fang punctured your skin, and you got here fast."

"Small favors." Matt couldn't imagine twice as much venom entering his body.

"I didn't know they could bite more than once," Bree said.

"Not only can they bite multiple times, they can control how much venom they release." The doctor checked Matt's heart monitor.

"That's creepy," Bree said.

The doctor removed his wire-framed glasses and wiped them on the hem of his scrub shirt. "I did my residency in Arizona. The Mojave rattlesnake is very deadly. It can have one type of venom, which is a neurotoxin, or another, which is hemorrhagic, *or* a combination of both." He set his glasses on his face. "We can be thankful they don't live in this area. Do you know where the snake came from?"

"A private collection," Bree said.

The doctor shook his head. "People are stupid."

Understatement of the century.

Bree shifted her weight and winced.

The doctor squinted at her. "Why are you limping?"

She held up a hand. "Just banged my knee. I'm sure it's fine."

The doctor propped a fist on his hip. "I think I should be the judge of that."

Bree shook her head. "I'll ice it tonight."

He frowned. "If you change your mind, let us know." He pointed to Matt. "We're finding a bed for you. You're staying the night, at minimum." After a quick check of Matt's wound, the doctor left.

"I'm feeling incredibly lucky." Matt tugged Bree closer.

She perched a hip on the edge of the gurney. "Me too."

"I wish I could go home with you."

"Same, but let's not take any chances."

"Definitely not. For once, I'm fine with staying there. That was not an experience I want to repeat. It was damned freaky." He rubbed her hand with his thumb. "What are you doing now?"

Her smile was exhausted. "I should go to the station. I have reports to write, and a statement to give the state police detective." She touched her empty holster. "He already collected my weapon."

The state detective would run ballistics tests on her handgun and then return it.

She swiped at her hair. "But I'm not doing any of those things. I'm going home. Adam is there. The work can wait."

"You're learning."

"Imagine that." She kissed him again, longer and sweeter. "I'll see you tomorrow."

"I can't wait."

CHAPTER FORTY-FOUR

Bree woke to Ladybug's hot breath wafting onto her face. The dog's nose was approximately a half inch from Bree's. Next to her, Vader uncurled his body—he'd stuck close all night—gave the dog a disdainful glare, moved a few feet away, and curled up again.

She rubbed the dog's ears. "How's Adam?" she asked Ladybug.

The dog jumped off the bed and waited for Bree.

"OK. I'm getting up." She glanced at the clock. It was after ten o'clock, but then she hadn't gone to bed until five a.m. She stepped out of bed and limped into the hallway. Ladybug raced down the stairs, slipped on the hardwood, and nearly slid into the opposite wall.

Adam's voice carried up the steps. "Easy, girl!"

Bree exhaled at the sound of her brother's voice. She was exhausted, and her knee had swelled a little overnight. She hadn't put ice on it when she'd gotten home. She'd checked on Adam, who'd been asleep on the couch, taken a quick shower, and collapsed into bed face-first.

Walking gingerly, she went downstairs and entered the kitchen. Adam sat at the table, eating a plate of pancakes. Dana faced the stove. She waved a spatula at Bree. "Did you get some sleep?"

"I did." Bree limped to the table.

Dana flipped a flapjack and pointed at Bree. "Sit."

Bree did as she was told. She scanned her brother. "How are you?"

"Nothing but a few bumps and bruises." Adam squeezed her hand. "I'm fine, thanks to you. You saved my life."

Physically, he was all right. But Bree knew the night would take an emotional toll. "You should talk to someone about what happened."

He cocked his head. "I'll think about it."

"It can sneak up on you."

"I believe you," he said. "I promise to see someone if I need to, if you promise the same."

"OK," Bree agreed.

Dana brought a mug of cappuccino dusted with cocoa powder. Bree leaned back in the chair and drank deeply. Usually, she took her time, inhaling the aroma, savoring the taste. Today, she downed the first cup like a frat boy with a beer bong.

Dana took the cup. "I'll refill that." A minute later, she set a plate of pancakes in front of Bree, then brought her a second cappuccino.

"Thank you. This will definitely get me moving."

"You should stay off that leg," Dana warned.

Bree added maple syrup to her pancakes. Today, she needed all the sugar and caffeine she could get. "I'll do my best."

Dana brought her an ice pack. Bree propped her foot on a chair and set the ice on her knee while she worked on her breakfast.

"Have you been out to the barn?" Bree asked.

Adam shook his head. "I'm not allowed. Kayla gave me strict orders to wait for her." He grinned. "She is not good at keeping a secret."

Bree smiled. "But you'll act surprised?"

"Of course." Adam crossed a finger over his heart. "Do you know when my house will be accessible?"

Bree shook her head. "I'm meeting with the state police detectives today. I'll find out."

"Thanks." Adam set down his fork. "The guy—Blake? He died?"

"Yes," Bree answered.

"You shot him?" Adam pushed his plate away. The sleeve of his sweatshirt rode up, exposing ligature marks around his wrists.

Anger bubbled up inside Bree at what Rhys had done to her brother. She'd tried to save Rhys's life, but his death wasn't going to keep her up at night. The violence inflicted upon Adam might, though. "Yes, but that's not what killed him."

"What did?"

"Karma." Sometimes, Bree loved that bitch.

An hour later, Bree limped into the station.

Marge met her at her office door with a cup of coffee. "The investigator from BCI—Phillip Ash—is here. As you instructed, I put him in the conference room."

The New York State Police Bureau of Criminal Investigation conducted its own investigations but also assisted local and county law enforcement with major cases. Bree could not investigate her own shooting of Rhys, and with Adam as one of the kidnapping victims, she needed to recuse herself from the case.

"Thanks, Marge." Bree had worked with Ash on a previous case. Their relationship had started off rocky. He'd been an ass. In his defense, he'd thought she was corrupt at the time. Since then, they'd come to an agreement of sorts.

Bree carried her coffee into the conference room. Ash sat at the table, reviewing case reports. He'd made himself comfortable. His suit jacket hung over the back of a chair, and his shirtsleeves were rolled up to expose muscular forearms. Beefy and bald, he reminded her of Popeye.

He stood as she entered. "Sheriff."

She nodded and shook his hand.

He frowned at her leg. "Are you injured?"

"Nothing serious." She eased into a chair. "Where do we stand?"

"Reports are still coming in, but there haven't been any bombshells. The most information came from Rhys Blake's computer. He outlined everything. He was obsessed with Farah Rock and her rejection of him. He stalked and killed Spencer LaForge and Julius Northcott because they dated her. He planned their deaths in great detail. Your brother's kidnapping was less structured. It seems he was unraveling at that point."

"Is there anything in his past that indicated this could happen?" Bree wondered what had set him off.

Ash nodded. "I spoke with his brother this morning. He said women never liked Rhys, and that had always been a sore spot."

Bree pictured Rhys. "He was average looking, but there wasn't any obvious reason for females to reject him."

"Maybe they could sense he was a potential psychopath," Ash suggested, his voice heavy with sarcasm.

"It's possible," Bree acknowledged. Survival instincts were stronger than most people suspected.

"Our profiler believes Farah's rejection flipped a switch in his brain. Not only did Farah reject him, but she talked about her subsequent dates, rubbing them in his face, until he wanted to kill them and her. He started with detailed plans. But once he started killing, he went off the rails and became impulsive, adding the snake, leaving the note for you, going after your brother. None of that was in his original plan." He paused. "His perceptions and reality became farther and farther apart."

"That makes sense in a weird way." Bree sipped her coffee.

"He planted Farah's hairs, the chalk dust, and the receipt at the Northcott crime scene. His intention was to implicate her for the murders of LaForge, Northcott, and your brother. He was then going to fake her suicide."

"I don't see how he hoped to make us think that, especially not with her head wound and all the evidence we found at his house."

Ash shrugged. "He was definitely less logical at that point. He never thought you'd suspect him or search his house."

"When will my brother's house be released?" Bree asked.

"By tomorrow. We boarded up the broken window." Ash hesitated. "I hate to bring it up, but there's a bullet hole in his canvas. I did a little research. I know what that painting is probably worth."

"Not more than his life," Bree said. "I'll tell him."

Painting was Adam's outlet. He couldn't wait to get back to work. How would he take it?

She extended a hand. "I'll have the case files packed up for you. Hopefully, we won't be needing your assistance for a while."

"Maybe if you don't shoot anyone else." Ash's tone was a little sarcastic but also not. He held her hand a second longer than necessary.

Still an ass.

Bree didn't blink. She maintained direct eye contact. "If only the bad guys would stop committing crimes."

"From your lips." He snorted. "I'll need a formal interview and statement."

"And I'll be happy to give one, but not today."

"The faster—"

"Not today," Bree said. They both knew the investigation was a mop-up. The suspect was dead. There would be no charges, no trial to prepare for.

Ash's nod was unhappy but resigned. "Your chief deputy?"

"Is off today." Bree had instructed Todd to stay home, hang out with Cady, and play with his dog. There would be time to cross t's and dot i's tomorrow.

CHAPTER FORTY-FIVE

The cold spell broke on Sunday, granting upstate New York a rare nice December day. Bree stood in her kitchen, marveling at the crowd she'd managed to gather for Adam's birthday brunch. A year ago, she wouldn't have been able to scrape together a carload of people, let alone a houseful. Matt's father helped Dana in the kitchen. His mother, Anna, sipped a mimosa and watched the kids and dogs play in the backyard. Actually, Goldie and Ladybug played. Brody supervised while Cady and Todd looked on. Adam and Matt's brother, Nolan, were having a serious conversation in the corner of the kitchen. Adam stood, crossed the kitchen, and refilled his plate.

Nearly empty plates of food lined the counters. Bree eyed another scone but decided she needed to ration her intake. There were still a couple of weeks before Christmas, and Dana showed no signs of slowing her baking frenzy. Before being banished to the yard, Ladybug had claimed an unattended omelet. Vader had been caught licking the butter. The cat showed no remorse. In other words, everything was normal.

Adam stood and crossed the kitchen to put his plate in the sink.

"How bad is the bullet hole in your canvas?" Bree asked him. "Can you fix it?"

He contemplated an elephant ear and picked one. "I've decided to leave it there and work around it." He took a bite. "The painting tells a story."

Hyped up on sugar, Kayla stormed through the kitchen door, her cheeks pink. She took Adam by the hand and dragged him from the house. "It's time to get your present, Uncle Adam."

Everyone grabbed jackets and followed them outside.

Matt pressed his arm to hers. "Our families get along well."

Bree leaned her head on his shoulder. "It's nice."

Luke led the Standardbred from the barn.

"He doesn't have a name yet," Kayla said to Adam. "But I have a whole list of ideas."

Adam walked to his horse and placed a hand on his nose. "He's perfect." The Standardbred bobbed his head.

"He's a good boy," Luke said. "We should go for a ride later."

Adam stroked his horse. "Definitely. I can't wait."

"Isn't he a beauty!" Matt's mother clapped her hands. "Matt, where's your horse?"

The sound of a hoof striking wood punctuated her question.

"I'd better get him before he kicks down the door." Matt disappeared into the barn, returning a few minutes later with the Percheron. Bree was happy to see the horse walking with no limp. His leg was healing nicely.

"He's just like Beast!" Kayla said, excited. "But Matt hasn't named him yet." Her voice rang with impatience.

"I should name him FOMO. He has serious fear of missing out. He has to be in the middle of everything." Matt leaned closer to Kayla. "But you know what? Beast does fit him best."

"Really?" Kayla jumped up and down.

"Really." Matt picked her up and swung her onto the giant horse's back. Beast stood politely, not batting an eye as Todd's dog raced under his belly.

Todd caught and leashed Goldie. "Girl, he's nice, but that's not OK." The oblivious young dog wagged.

Kayla bent forward and hugged the massive neck. "He's a very good boy."

"Oh my goodness," Matt's dad said. "I've never seen a horse that big up close. Can we pet him?"

"He's very gentle, and he can't get enough attention." Matt stood back as the family crowded around the two horses, fussing and stroking, making sure both received equal attention.

"I love that you rescued them." Cady straightened the Standardbred's forelock. She touched a mark on his shoulder where years of wearing a harness had rubbed off the hair. "It's beautiful when animals in need find a safe place to land."

"Uncle Adam, you have to pick a name." Kayla put out her arms, and Matt lifted her off Beast's back.

Adam crossed his arms and propped his chin on one hand. "You said you had ideas?"

"I do! I do!" Kayla nearly squealed. "I have a list."

Adam grinned. "What's your front-runner?"

"Bullseye, because he's brown and sweet and loyal," Kayla said.

"I like it," Adam said. "Bullseye it is."

"Yay!" Kayla hugged Bullseye.

Bree touched Adam's arm. "I thought you'd pick an artsy name."

He shook his head. "It's more important to Kayla. The horse doesn't care."

Todd and Cady approached Bree.

"We have to go," Todd said.

"Already?" Bree asked.

"I have a window to replace at Julius's elderly neighbor's house," Todd said. "Cady's going to help me."

Cady adjusted her ponytail. "I love a chance to swing a hammer."

Bree smiled. "Thanks for coming."

They said more goodbyes and left, hand in hand.

Bree looked out over the pasture, where Cowboy, Pumpkin, and Riot grazed, to the two new additions to the family. She caught Matt's eye. They were building something here, and he was clearly a large part of it. She couldn't even think about the snakebite without choking up.

"Today was a good day," he said. "And we all needed it."

The family time, the togetherness, the connection and love between all of them, helped refill the places in Bree's heart that their last case had left hollow. They recharged her.

"We did," she agreed. She lowered her voice. "I love to see the kids so happy. But I'm still worried about Christmas. It's going to be hard."

"I've been thinking about that." Matt gazed over the crowd. "What would you say to taking them on a trip? They might want to be home, near their mother, for Christmas morning, but I thought we could leave the day after, give them a new experience."

"A trip?" Bree let the suggestion roll around in her head. "I like the idea, but I thought you wanted a more private getaway."

"It wasn't fair of me to ask you to leave them with the holidays and the anniversary of their mother's death coming up. They're going to need lots of support to get through the next month. The only question I should have asked is, How can I help?"

"Have I told you I love you today?"

"Yes."

"Well, I'm telling you again." Bree's eyes misted. Again. *So annoying.* "But where should we go?"

"Disney World," he suggested.

"That is the absolute last suggestion I expected to come out of your mouth."

He shrugged. "The trip is for the kids. Besides, I can now name all the princesses."

Bree laughed. "I think Luke and Kayla would enjoy that." She wrapped her arm around his waist. "But we have five horses. Taking a vacation isn't as simple as—"

"Adam will take care of the horses."

"You already asked?"

"Yep."

"What about hotel and airfare? Last-minute travel right after Christmas has to be crazy."

"It's all arranged. I have a travel agent who's put a suite and plane tickets on hold until tomorrow. Frankly, we could all use a vacation to the happiest place on earth. All you have to do is say yes."

Bree turned and threw her arms around his neck. "Yes."

He pulled her close, hugged her hard. "We'll get away on our own one day, when the kids are in a better place. There's no rush. I'm not going anywhere."

ACKNOWLEDGMENTS

Special thanks to the writer friends who help me every day: Rayna Vause, Kendra Elliot, Leanne Sparks, Toni Anderson, Amy Gamet, and Loreth Anne White. Cheers, ladies! As always, credit goes to my agent, Jill Marsal, for her continued unwavering support and solid career advice. I'm also grateful for the entire team at Montlake, especially my acquiring editor, Anh Schluep, and my developmental editor, Charlotte Herscher. As far as teams go, I am lucky to have the best.

ABOUT THE AUTHOR

Photo © 2016 Jared Gruenwald Photography

Melinda Leigh is the #1 Amazon Charts and #1 *Wall Street Journal* bestselling author of *She Can Run*, an International Thriller Award nominee for Best First Novel, *She Can Tell, She Can Scream, She Can Hide*, and *She Can Kill* in the She Can series; *Midnight Exposure, Midnight Sacrifice, Midnight Betrayal*, and *Midnight Obsession* in the Midnight Novels; *Hour of Need, Minutes to Kill*, and *Seconds to Live* in the Scarlet Falls series; *Say You're Sorry, Her Last Goodbye, Bones Don't Lie, What I've Done, Secrets Never Die*, and *Save Your Breath* in the Morgan Dane series; and *Cross Her Heart, See Her Die, Drown Her Sorrows, Right Behind Her*, and *Dead Against Her* in the Bree Taggert series. Melinda's garnered numerous writing awards, including two RITA nominations; holds a second-degree black belt in Kenpo karate and has taught women's self-defense; and lives in a messy house with her family and a small herd of rescue pets. For more information, visit www.melindaleigh.com.